JUNIE B.
DOUBLE EDITION!

Laugh out loud with Junie B. Jones!

JUNIE B. DOUBLE EDITION!

BARBARA PARK

Junie B., First Grader (at last!)

and

Junie B., First Grader Toothless Wonder

illustrated by
DENISE BRUNKUS

A STEPPING STONE BOOK™

Random House 🏠 New York

Junie B., First Grader (at last!)
Copyright © 2001 by Barbara Park.
Illustrations copyright © 2001 by Denise Brunkus.
Junie B., First Grader: Toothless Wonder
Copyright © 2002 by Barbara Park.
Illustrations copyright © 2002 by Denise Brunkus.

Published in the United States by Random House Children's Books,
a division of Random House, Inc., New York.

Random House and colophon are registered trademarks and A Stepping Stone Book and colophon are trademarks of Random House, Inc. Junie B., First Grader® stylized design is a registered trademark of Barbara Park, used under license.

The titles in this work were originally published separately by Random House Children's Books, a division of Random House, Inc., in 2001 and 2002.

Visit us on the Web!
www.randomhouse.com/junieb
www.randomhouse.com/kids

Educators and librarians, for a variety of teaching tools, visit us at
www.randomhouse.com/teachers

Library of Congress Cataloging-in-Publication Data for
Junie B., First Grader (at last!) is available on request.
ISBN 978-0-375-80293-5 (trade) — ISBN 978-0-375-90293-2 (lib. bdg.)

Library of Congress Cataloging-in-Publication Data for
Junie B., First Grader: Toothless Wonder is available on request.
ISBN 978-0-375-80295-9 (trade) — ISBN 978-0-375-90295-6 (lib. bdg.)

Printed in the United States of America   10 9 8 7 6 5 4

First Omnibus Edition

Contents

BARBARA PARK

Junie B., First Grader (at last!)

illustrated by
DENISE BRUNKUS

Contents

1

First-Grade Surprises

Thursday

Dear first-grade journal,

Yesterday was the first day
of school. It is new here.

Today my teacher handed out
these journals. He is making us
write in these dumb things.
Only I don't even know what to
write.

My teacher has muscles and

mustache
a ~~mustash.~~

  His name is Mr. Scary.

  He made that name up, I
believe.

  I am not even scared of him,
hardly.

                From,

        Junie B., First Grader

I put down my pencil. And I looked at
what I wrote.

  I did a sigh.

  "I would like to go home now," I said to
just myself.

  "Shh!" said a girl named May. "I'm still
trying to do my work."

May sits next to me in the back of the room.

I do not actually care for that girl.

Just then, my teacher stood up at his desk. His mustache smiled real friendly.

"Okay, boys and girls. You can stop writing now," he said. "As I told you earlier, we will be working in our journals quite often this year. In fact, it won't be long until your journal starts feeling like an old friend."

I rolled my eyes at the ceiling.

"What kind of an old friend looks like a dumb notebook?" I said.

"Shh!" said May again. "You shouldn't talk while the teacher is talking, Junie Jones!"

I looked at her real annoyed.

"*B.*," I said. "My name is Junie *B.* I

think I have mentioned that to you before, May."

I leaned closer to her face.

"B., B., B., B., B.," I said.

After that, I slumped in my seat. And I put my head on my desk.

I peeked at the other children who sit near me.

Their names are Herb. And Lennie. And José.

I do not know them from a hole in the ground.

I did another sigh.

First grade is not what it's cracked up to be.

My room is named Room One.

I was nervous when I came here yesterday.

That's how come Daddy had to carry me all the way to the room. 'Cause my legs felt like squishy Jell-O.

He put me down outside the door.

"Well, here we are, Junie B.," he said. "*First* grade. At *last*."

My stomach had flutterflies in it.

Also, my arms had prickly goose bumps. And my forehead had drops of sweaty.

"I am a wreck," I said.

Daddy smiled very nice.

"There's nothing to worry about, Junie B. I promise," he said. "You're going to *love* first grade. Just think. There's a whole roomful of brand-new friends just waiting to meet you."

He ruffled my hair. "Are you ready to go in now?" he asked. "Hmm? Are you ready to begin your first-grade adventure?"

I looked at him a real long time.

Then I quick spun around. And I zoomed down the hall as fast as I could!

Daddy zoomed after me!

He caught up with me speedy quick. And he carried me back to my class.

Only this time, he carried me straight into the room!

As soon as he put me down again, I hid behind his legs.

'Cause that place was a zoo, I tell you!

There were people *everywhere*! There were girls and boys. And mothers and daddies. And grandmas and grampas. Plus also, there were drooly babies in strollers.

Then, all of a sudden, my whole mouth came open!

Because good news! I finally saw someone I knew!

I jumped up and down and all around.

"DADDY! DADDY! IT'S LUCILLE!" I hollered. "REMEMBER LUCILLE? LUCILLE WAS MY BESTEST FRIEND FROM KINDERGARTEN LAST YEAR!"

Lucille was standing at a desk next to the window.

I ran to her in a jiffy.

Then I hugged and hugged that girl! And I couldn't even stop!

"LUCILLE! LUCILLE! IT'S ME! IT'S ME! IT'S YOUR BESTEST FRIEND FROM KINDERGARTEN . . . JUNIE B. JONES!"

I tried to pick her up.

"I AM SO GLAD TO SEE YOU, FRIEND!" I shouted real joyful.

Lucille pulled my arms off her.

"Stop it, Junie B.! Stop it!" she said.

"You're wrinkling my new back-to-school dress! This thing cost a fortune."

I stopped hugging her.

Lucille smoothed and fluffed herself.

I smoothed and fluffed her, too.

"There," I said. "Good as new."

After that, I grabbed Lucille's hand. And I started to pull.

"Come on, Lucille. Let's go find two desks together," I said. "I think we should sit near the door. Want to? Huh? If we sit near the door, we can stare at people who walk down the hall."

Lucille yanked her hand away.

"*No*, Junie B. No. I'm going to sit at this desk right here," she said. "I already picked it out with my two new friends, Camille and Chenille."

She pointed at the door.

"See them over there?" she said. "I met them before you came. They are saying good-bye to their mother. Aren't they precious?"

I looked at Camille and Chenille.

And guess what?

My eyes popped right out of my head!

Because wowie wow wow!

Those girls were *twins*, that's why!

I sprang way high in the air.

"TWINS! TWINS! THEY'RE TWINS, LUCILLE! THIS IS OUR LUCKY DAY!"

I pulled on her again.

"Come on, Lucille! Let's go touch them!

Hurry! Hurry! Before a line forms!"

Lucille did not budge a muscle.

"Stop it, Junie B.! Quit pulling on me," she said. "Camille and Chenille don't want to be touched. And besides, *I* am their new best friend. Not *you.*"

I looked surprised at that girl.

"Yes, but I can be their bestest friend along with you. Right, Lucille?" I asked. "All I have to do is meet them, right? And then all of us can be bestest friends together."

Lucille shook her head.

"No, Junie B. I'm sorry. But you and I have already *been* best friends, remember?" she said. "We were best friends for a whole long year. And so now it's time for Camille and Chenille to get a turn."

She did a shrug. "It's only fair of me,"

she said. "And besides, their names *rhyme* with my name. And yours doesn't."

She wrinkled her nose very cute. "*Camille* and *Chenille* and *Lucille*. See? Isn't that darling?"

After that, Lucille gave me a pat.

"Don't be sad, okay?" she said. "You and I can still be friends, Junie B. Just not on a regular basis."

After that, she waved her fingers.

And she said *ta-ta*.

And she skipped to Camille and Chenille.

2

■ ■ ■ ■ ■ ■ ■ ■ ■ ■

More Surprises...
Plus Herb

Mother and Daddy keep trying to cheer me
up about first grade.

Mother says sometimes life has disap-
pointments in it.

Daddy says sometimes you have to roll
with the punches.

I say first grade is a flop.

Last year, I had two bestest friends.

First, I had Lucille.

Plus also, I had that Grace.

Me and that Grace rode the school bus together every single day.

Only too bad for us. Because this year, Grace got put in a different room than me. And that was not even fair.

But hurray, hurray! Me and Grace still decided to ride the bus together! Because that's what friendship is for, I think.

And so last week, both of us sat next to each other . . . just like we always did!

Only, what do you know?

On Monday morning, Grace got on the bus with a *new* girl from her class. And those two plopped down in the seat right in front of me!

I quick jumped up. And I tapped on Grace's head.

"Grace?" I said. "*Excuse* me. Grace? What kind of shenanigans do you call this,

madam? Didn't you see me sitting here?"

Grace waved at me real friendly.

"Yes. Hi, Junie B.," she said. "I'm sorry I can't sit with you today. But I promised Bobbi Jean Piper I would sit with her this morning. Okay?"

I stamped my foot.

"No, Grace. *Not* okay. You can't sit with Bobbi Jean Piper," I said. "You and I have to sit together every single day. 'Cause we sat together every day last year. And this year shalt be no different."

Just then, Mr. Woo, the bus driver, closed the bus door.

He looked in his mirror at me.

"Sit down, please, Junie B.," he said.

Bobbi Jean Piper pointed and grinned.

"You got *yelled* at," she said kind of mean.

I made a scary face at that girl.

"*Grr!*" I said. "*Grr,* Bobbi Jean Piper."

Behind me, I heard a loud laugh.

I quick spun around.

And guess what?

It was Herb who sits in front of me in Room One!

"*Herb!*" I said real surprised. "I didn't even know that you rode this bus!"

Herb kept on laughing.

"You said *grr!*" he laughed. "*Grr!* Ha! That's a good one!"

I wrinkled my eyebrows at that boy.

"Yeah, only here's the problem, Herbert," I said. "*Grr* is not actually a joking matter. Plus, I wasn't even talking to you."

Herb quit laughing.

"I *know* you weren't talking to me," he said. "No one on this bus ever talks to me. That's because last year I went to a different school. So I don't have any bus friends yet."

Just then, the bus stopped at the next corner.

Herb came around the seat and sat next to me.

"Maybe, just for today, I can sit here,"

he said. "Just until you get your bus friend back, I mean."

I tapped on my chin very thinking.

Then, all of a sudden, I raised my voice real loud.

"Why, *sure* you can sit here, Herbert," I said. "You can sit here *forever* if you want to! Because I *used* to have a bus friend named Grace! But today I am dropping her like a hot tomato!"

Bobbi Jean Piper peeked over the seat at me.

"You mean *potato*," she teased.

I sprang up again.

"BOBBI JEAN PIPER WEARS A DIAPER!" I hollered.

Mr. Woo frowned in the mirror.

"Sit *down*, Junie B.!" he grouched.

I sat down.

Then I did a big breath. And I looked at
Herb.

"Today is not off to a good start," I said
kind of quiet.

Herb nodded. "I hear you," he said.

I slumped way down in my seat.

"My bestest friends are dropping like flies," I said.

Herb nodded. "Join the club," he said.

"First grade is a flop," I said.

Herb nodded. "Totally," he said.

I looked out the window.

"*Grr,*" I said.

"*Grr,*" said Herb.

I smiled to just myself.

I think I might like this Herb.

3

██ ██ ██ ██ ██ ██ ██ ██ ██ ██

Stumped

Me and Herb walked to Room One from the bus.

He waved to Mr. Scary.

Then I waved, too.

"I am not even scared of that teacher, hardly," I said to just myself.

We kept on walking to our seats.

May was already sitting at her desk. She was organizing her pencil box.

Lennie was at his desk, too.

Only wait till you hear this.

I didn't even recognize that guy, almost!

Because Lennie had a thrilling new haircut, that's why!

It was pointish and spikish and stiffish and straightish.

That hair can puncture you, I think.

"Whoa!" I said.

"Cool!" said Herb.

"*Gel,*" said Lennie.

"Shh!" said May.

Just then, José came hurrying down the row. He was rushing real fast. 'Cause the bell was almost ready to ring.

"*Hola,* everyone," he said, out of breath. "*Hola, hola.*"

Me and Herb and Lennie looked curious at him.

José grinned.

"Whoops," he said. "*Hola* means *hello* in Spanish. I know two different languages,

and sometimes I forget which one I'm speaking."

"Wow, José!" I said. "You really speak two languages?"

"Cool," said Herb.

"Big deal," said May. "I know Spanish,

too. I can count all the way to three in Spanish. Does anyone want to hear me?"

The rest of us looked at each other.

"Not really," said Herb.

"Not me," said Lennie.

"Me neither," said José.

May didn't pay attention to us. *"Uno, dos, tres,"* she said real loud.

I leaned nearer to her.

"Shh!" I said.

Then everyone laughed and laughed.

But not May.

Pretty soon, the bell rang for school.

Mr. Scary got our morning started.

First, he took attendance of the children. Then we said, *I pledge allegiance to the flag*. Plus also, we listened to boring bulletins from the office.

Finally, Mr. Scary walked to the chalkboard. And he printed a list of words.

"Boys and girls," he said. "This morning, I have a fun assignment for you."

He winked at us and pointed to the list.

"I want you to read these words to yourselves," he said. "Then—without talking to your neighbor—choose any word from the list and draw a picture of it in your journal."

May squealed very thrilled.

"Oh, goody, goody!" she said. "I love this kind of assignment, Mr. Scary. I am perfect at not talking to my neighbor!"

After that, she quick took a pencil out of her box. And she started to draw.

I stared at the words.

Then I tapped on my chin. And I scratched my head.

'Cause I didn't actually *get* this assignment, that's why.

"Hmm," I said. "Hmm. Hmm. Hmm."

I glanced my eyes at Herb and Lennie and José.

All of them were drawing, too.

I looked back at the board again.

Then I stretched my neck as far as it could go. And I squinted my hardest.

But those words had me stumped, I tell you!

Finally, I reached out to Herb real secret. And I tapped on his back.

"Psst. Herb," I whispered. "Quick question. Which word are you drawing?"

May did a loud gasp.

She jumped up from her seat and pointed at me.

"Mr. Scary! Mr. Scary! Junie Jones is talking to her neighbor! See her? She's talking to Herbert. And that is against the rules!"

I turned my head.

"Blabber-lips!" I yelled. "Blabber-lips May."

Mr. Scary looked back at us.

His mustache was not smiling.
I did a gulp.
Then I quick opened my journal.
And I started to draw.

4

■ ■ ■ ■ ■ ■ ■ ■ ■ ■

Clucks

We drew and drew in our journals.

Mr. Scary waited until all of us were done.

Then he walked around the room. And he looked at everyone's pictures.

He gave out shiny gold stars.

First, he gave stars to Camille and Chenille.

"What great-looking dogs you drew, girls," he said. "Look at those floppy ears."

Lucille raised her hand.

"Look at mine, Teacher!" she said. "I

drew a cat with *pointy* ears. See? My rich nanna has an expensive cat just like this. Its fur is a foot thick, almost."

Mr. Scary looked strange at her.

"Really, Lucille? A whole foot of fur?" he said. "My, my."

He gave her a gold star and moved on.

He went to a boy named Roger. Roger was in my same class last year.

"*Excellent* job, Roger," Mr. Scary said. "You drew a man wearing a coat. The words *man* and *coat* were both on the board, weren't they?"

I did a little frown.

'Cause none of these words were actually sounding familiar.

After that, Mr. Scary walked to Sheldon and Shirley.

"Cool bat and ball, Sheldon," he said.

"And, Shirley! You drew a bat and ball, too, didn't you?"

I put my head on my desk.

Something was very wrong here.

Finally, Mr. Scary got to May.

"Oh, May," he said. "What a special clock you drew. The big hand has five fingers. That's very unusual."

"Yes," said May. "I created it myself. Plus, *clock* was the hardest word up there, wasn't it, Mr. Scary? I am the only one who even knew the word *clock*, I bet."

Just then, my stomach felt sickish inside.

I quick closed my journal and stuffed it in my desk.

Mr. Scary saw me.

"Junie B.?" he said. "Don't you want to show me your drawing? Don't you want a gold star for today?"

I shook my head real fast.

"Nope. No, thank you. No, I don't," I said. "Not today. I really, really don't care for a gold star today. But thank you for asking."

Mr. Scary kept on standing there.

"The end," I said.

He did not budge.

"Please move along," I said.

Finally, Mr. Scary bent down next to me.

He lowered his voice so no one could hear.

"I'm sorry, Junie B. But I'd really like to see what you drew," he said. "I need to make sure that you understood the assignment."

Then—before I knew it—he took my journal out of my desk. And he gave it to me to hold.

After that, he walked me into the hall. And he let me show him my drawing in private.

And guess what?

He liked it, I think!

"Oh, wow. Look at *that*, Junie B.," he said. "You drew a wonderful picture of a . . . a . . ."

He kept on looking. "A . . . a . . ."

"A screaming chicken," I said finally.

Mr. Scary did a strange face.

"Yes. *Right*," he said. "It's a . . ."

"Screaming chicken," I said again.

I pointed at the chicken's mouth.

"See how it's screaming, 'CLUCK! CLUCK! CLUCK!'? I used capital letters for the clucks. Capitals are for screaming. Correct?"

"Well, yes. I *suppose* so," said Mr. Scary.

"But—the thing is, Junie B.—the word *cluck* wasn't on the board today."

"I know it," I said. "The word on the board was *clock*. Only I didn't read all the letters right, I guess. 'Cause I accidentally thought it was *cluck*."

I tapped on my chin.

"What I actually wanted to draw was the *but and bull*," I said. "I really liked the sound of that one. But I didn't know how to get started, exactly. So I went ahead with the *cluck* idea."

Mr. Scary looked confused at me.

"The *but and bull*?" he asked.

I smiled kind of embarrassed.

"Yeah . . . well, I read those words wrong, too, I guess," I said. "They turned out to be *bat and ball*."

Mr. Scary frowned.

"Hmm," he said. "What about the other words on the board, Junie B.? Do you remember how you read some of the other ones? How about *dog* and *cat*? Or *coat* and *goat*?"

I thought back. Then I made my voice real quiet.

"*Dug* and *cot* and *coot* and *yoot*," I said.

Mr. Scary nodded his head.

Then he patted my hand very nice.

And he gave me back my journal.

And we walked back into Room One.

5

Bug Bag

Tuesday

Dear first-grade journal,

Mr. Scary just called me in from recess. All the other children are still playing out there.

He said for me to write in my journal for a minute and he will be with me soon.

I keep peeking at him from

behind these pages.

He is printing sentences on the board. It is extra work for me, I think.

I do not actually approve of this.

From,

Junie B., First Grader

Mr. Scary put down his chalk.

"You can stop peeking at me now, Junie B.," he said.

I looked at him real surprised. 'Cause that guy has eyes in the back of his hair, apparently.

He turned around and smiled.

"Do you see these three sentences that

I just wrote up here?" he asked.

"Yes," I said. "I see them."

"Excellent," said Mr. Scary. "Could you stand up and try reading them from back there, please?"

Just then, my heart got pumpy and pounding inside.

'Cause I'm not good at reading from the board, that's why.

I kept on sitting there.

"Please," said Mr. Scary. "Just give it a try, okay?"

Finally, I stood up. And I squinted at the sentences.

I read real slow.

"Bob . . . is . . . a . . . bug . . . bag," I read.

I did a teensy frown at that news.

"Really?" I asked. "Bob is a bug bag?"

Mr. Scary pointed to sentence number two. "Try this one," he said.

I squinted some more.

"I . . . like . . . my . . . hog . . . spit," I read again.

I looked at my teacher very curious.

"These sentences are oddballs, aren't they?" I said.

Mr. Scary pointed at the last one. "Just one more to go," he said.

This time, I stretched my neck. And I strained my eyes.

"Jack . . . is . . . going . . . to . . . to . . ."

I scrunched my eyes even smaller.

". . . to *jail*," I read.

I did a gasp.

"Really? No fooling? Jack who?"

Mr. Scary came back to my seat.

He took my hand and walked me closer to the board.

"Could you try reading them again from here, Junie B.?" he said.

I made my voice real whiny.

"But I don't *want* to read them again, Mr. Scary," I told him. "I already know what they say."

"Just one more time," he said.

And so finally, I did a big breath. And I read the sentences all in a row.

"Bob is a big boy."

"I like my dog, Spot."

"Jack is going to Jill's."

I covered my mouth very surprised.

"Hey! What do you know? He's going

to *Jill's,* Mr. Scary!" I said. "Whew! That's a relief, right?"

Mr. Scary laughed. "Right," he said.

After that, I headed for the door.

"Okey-doke. Well, I guess I'll be getting back to recess now," I said. "See ya."

I waited for him to answer.

He did not say *see ya.*

I turned around.

"See ya?" I said a little bit softer.

But Mr. Scary just shook his head no.

'Cause too bad for me.

He had other plans.

Mr. Scary took my hand.

We walked out of Room One and down the hall.

"You and I are going to visit Mrs. Weller, Junie B.," he said. "You remember

Mrs. Weller from last year, don't you?"

I shook my head no. 'Cause that name did not ring a bell.

"Mostly I would just like to remember recess," I said.

Mr. Scary patted my shoulder.

"Mrs. Weller is a lovely person," he said.

"Recess is a lovely person, too," I said.

"Mrs. Weller is the school nurse," he said.

I quick stopped walking.

Because the school nurse is where you go when you are sick or tired. And I was totally fine.

"But I am in good shape," I said. "See me? I don't even need a Band-Aid."

Mr. Scary smiled.

He pulled me along again.

"Of course you're in good shape, Junie

B.," he said. "But Mrs. Weller does lots of nice things besides giving out Band-Aids."

Just then, we walked into Mrs. Weller's office.

And guess what? I remembered her perfectly well! I just never knew she had a name before!

"Why, Junie B. Jones," she said. "What a nice surprise to see you again."

"It's a surprise to see you, too," I said. "'Cause I'm not even sick or tired. Plus also, I'm supposed to be on the playground right now."

Mrs. Weller laughed out loud. Only I don't actually know why.

After that, she and Mr. Scary whispered real quiet to each other.

Then finally, Mr. Scary patted my shoulder.

"I'm going to leave you with Mrs. Weller for a while, Junie B.," he said. "The two of you are going to play a game with her eye chart. Okay?"

All of a sudden, my stomach felt kind of jumpy.

'Cause playing a game with the nurse did not sound fun.

No, I said inside my head. _Not_ *okay.*

Mr. Scary waved.

"See you," he said.

I watched him go.

I did not say *see you* back.

6

The E Game

I sat in a chair next to Mrs. Weller's desk.

She asked me lots of questions.

First, she asked me how I liked my summer vacation. Then she asked me how I liked first grade. And how I liked Mr. Scary.

That is called stall talk, I believe.

Finally, Mrs. Weller stood up.

"Have you noticed the eye charts I have hanging on my wall, Junie B.?" she asked.

She pointed at them.

"Eye charts are posters that help us test our eyesight," she explained. "I have two different kinds. See? One has alphabet letters on it. And the one right next to it is filled with funny *E*'s. That one is called an E chart."

I looked at that funny thing.

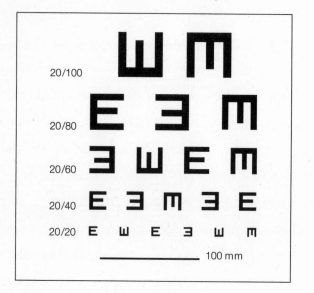

"Whoa," I said. "Those are the craziest *E*'s I ever saw. They are backwards and forwards and upside down."

"You're right," said Mrs. Weller. "The *E*'s are all mixed up, aren't they? And today you and I are going to play a game with those mixed-up *E*'s. It's called the E game."

After that, Mrs. Weller got a little paper cup. And she showed me how to hold it over one of my eyes.

"We're going to be testing each of your eyes separately," she said. "While one eye is hiding under the cup, the other eye will play the game. Okay?"

I shrugged my shoulders. 'Cause what choice did I have?

Mrs. Weller showed me where to stand to play the game. Then she went back to the E chart.

"All right," she said. "Now each time I point to one of the *E*'s, I want you to tell

me the direction it's facing. Are you ready, Junie B.?"

I shrugged again. Then I hid one eye behind the cup. And Mrs. Weller pointed at the first *E*.

I pointed my finger up. "That one is facing up at the ceiling," I told her.

"Good," she said. "Excellent."

I felt a little better inside.

Mrs. Weller pointed to the next *E*.

I turned my finger down at the floor. "That one is facing down," I said.

Mrs. Weller smiled and nodded.

I stood up taller. 'Cause this wasn't as hard as I thought.

After that, the nurse kept on pointing at more *E*'s. And I kept on telling her which way they were facing.

"Right . . . left . . . down . . . left . . . up . . ."

I stopped and grinned. "Hey, what do you know? I'm a breeze at this game. Right, Mrs. Weller? Right? Right?" I said.

Mrs. Weller winked at me.

"We're almost done," she said. "Only a few more *E*'s to go."

She pointed to a new row.

There was a fuzzy smudgie next to her finger.

"Whoops," I said. "What happened there? Did someone spill something on your chart?"

Mrs. Weller did a little frown. She kept pointing at the smudgie.

"Can you tell me anything about this mark at all, Junie B.?" she asked.

"Yes," I said. "It's a smearball."

Mrs. Weller moved her finger over a little bit.

"What about this mark here? Can you tell me anything about this one?"

I stared and stared at that thing.

"Hmm. That one's a toughie," I said.

Finally, Mrs. Weller came over to me.

"That's fine," she said. "You did just fine, Junie B."

After that, we played the same game with my other eye.

And guess what?

I saw three more smudgies and a smeary.

After I was done, I sat down in the chair again.

Mrs. Weller said I need glasses.

I do not like Mrs. Weller.

7

Good Guessing

The nurse called Mother at her work.

She tattletaled about the glasses.

Then Mother tattletaled to Daddy. And those two would not let the matter drop.

They talked about glasses all during dinner that entire night.

I couldn't even digest my food that good. Because they kept talking about those stupid, dumb glasses.

"Sooner or later, almost everyone ends up wearing glasses, Junie B.," said Daddy. "Really. They *do*."

I put my chin in my hands real glum.

"Really. They don't," I grumped.

"Daddy's telling you the truth, Junie B.," said Mother. "And besides, you're going to look absolutely adorable in glasses."

"No, I am absolutely not," I grumped again.

"Sure you are," said Daddy. "And just think how great it will be to see the words on the board."

I covered my ears.

"*Not* great, *not* great, *not* great," I said.

Mother took my hands away.

"Listen to me, honey. *Please*," she said. "Glasses are like magic windows for the eyes. When you put them on . . . poof! . . . the whole world becomes crystal clear."

I did a huffy breath.

"Poof, yourself," I grumped.

After that, Mother picked me up.

And she carried me to my room.

'Cause that was one grump too many.

The next morning, Daddy took me to the eye doctor.

The eye doctor did lots more eye tests with me. They were sort of fun. Only I didn't tell Daddy.

Also, the doctor put drops in my eyes. Drops make your eyeballs get biggish and darkish.

Eyeballs look very attractive that way.

After the eye doctor, I went home till my drops wore off.

Then Daddy drove me to school.

And guess what?

All of the children stared at me when I came in the room.

'Cause I was a *late kid,* that's why.

I walked to my desk kind of shy.

Herb's face smiled when he saw me.

"Junie B. Jones! Where *were* you?" he said. "I saved your seat on the bus. But you never came."

"We were afraid you might be sick," said José.

"Yeah," said Lennie. "You're *not,* are you?"

"I certainly *hope* she's not sick," said May. "You shouldn't come to school sick, Junie Jones. Coming to school sick is how germs get started."

I sucked in my cheeks at that girl.

"I'm not *sick,* May. I'm just *late,* and that's all."

May made a grouchy face.

"Well, being *late* isn't good, either," she

said. "Being late gets you a black mark on your permanent record."

I covered up my ears at her.

"Blah, blah, blah, May," I said.

Herb and Lennie and José laughed out loud.

Those guys are starting to enjoy me, I think.

Pretty soon, I took out my workbook. And I tried to do my math.

Only too bad for me. 'Cause I kept on worrying about my new glasses.

What if I look dumb and silly in those things? I thought. *What if Room One laughs their head off at me? What if I look like a goonie bird and no one wants to be my friend?*

The worrying would not go out of my head.

Maybe I needed to talk to someone about this, possibly.

Finally, I reached out and I tapped on Herb.

"Psst. Herbert," I whispered real soft. "I have something I need to tell you. Only I am really afraid to say it. 'Cause what if you laugh at me? Only you probably won't. But I still don't think I should take the chance. And so please do not ask me more about this. And I mean it."

After that, I waited and waited.

But Herb did not ask me.

I tapped on him again.

"Okay. Fine. I'll give you a hint," I said. "But first you're going to have to turn around and sneak a peek at me."

Herb turned around and sneaked a peek.

I quick made round circles with my

fingers. And I held them in front of my eyes.

"Okay, what am I doing here, Herb?" I whispered again. "Huh? What does this look like to you? I'm making round circles in front of my eyes, see? What do you think they are?"

May leaned over to my desk.

"Shush!" she said. "Stop bothering Herb, Junie Jones! If you don't shush right now, I'm going to tell the teacher."

Suddenly, I jumped right up from my chair.

'Cause I *had* it with that girl, that's why!

"NO! *YOU* SHUSH, YOU SHUSHY-HEAD MAY!" I said. "I AM NOT EVEN BOTHERING HERBERT! I AM GIVING HIM A HINT ABOUT MY NEW

GLASSES! AND THAT IS NONE OF
YOUR BEESWAX, SISTER!"

May's face looked shocked at me.

Her mouth came all the way open.

"You're getting *glasses*?" she said real
loud.

"You're getting *glasses*?" said Herb.

"You're getting *glasses*?" said all of
Room One.

The children stared and stared.

My head felt hottish and sweatish.

I sat back down in my chair.

Then I looked at Herb kind of sickish.

And I whispered the words *good guess*.

8

Showing-and-Telling

Friday

Dear first-grade journal,

Today I brought my new glasses to school.

They are hiding in my sweater pocket. 'Cause I don't want to put them on, that's why.

My ~~stomick~~ stomach is in a knotball.

Also, there is tension in my head.

We are having Show-and-Tell
soon.
   I wish this day was over.
              From,
       Junie B., First Grader

Mr. Scary clapped his hands.

"Okay, boys and girls. Please put your journals away now. I'll give you more time later if you need it. But right now, we have to get started with Show-and-Tell. Who would like to go first this morning?"

May sprang out of her chair.

"I would! I would!" she called out.

Then she quick grabbed a brown envelope out of her backpack. And she ran to the front of the room.

"It's my report card from kindergarten, everyone!" she said real thrilled. "I brought my report card to share with you!"

May waved it all around in the air.

"Look! Look! Can everyone see this? I got all E pluses! E is for *Excellent*! See? There's an E plus next to every single subject!"

She held the report card in front of her. "Okay. Now I will read you each subject one by one," she said.

After that, she took a deep breath. And she started to read.

"Number one: I followed directions.

"Number two: I used my time wisely.

"Number three: I observed school rules.

"Number four: I cleaned up my work area.

"Number five: I—"

Mr. Scary stood up.

"Thank you, May," he said. "That is very interesting. But I'm afraid that we're going to have to move along now and—"

May raised her voice.

"NUMBER FIVE: I WAS COURTEOUS AND RESPECTFUL.

"NUMBER SIX: I USED MATERIALS WISELY!

"NUMBER SEVEN: I—"

Just then, Mr. Scary took May's arm. And he led her back to her seat.

Lennie raised his hand to go next.

He passed around his new styling gel. Plus also, he let us touch his hair.

After that, Sheldon showed us how long he could stand on one foot.

And José sang a song about frogs.

And Shirley showed us her turkey

sandwich. She showed us the bread and the mayonnaise and the tomato.

Finally, Mr. Scary stood up again.

"All rightie, Shirley. Excellent sandwich," he said. "But I really think it should go back in its bag now."

Shirley sat down.

Mr. Scary looked around the room.

"Okay. Who wants to go next?" he said.

My stomach flipped and flopped.

'Cause a nervous idea popped into my head, that's why.

I looked down at my glasses in my sweater pocket.

Then I swallowed very hard. And I quick raised my hand in the air.

"Me!" I blurted out. "I do!"

Mr. Scary smiled. "Great, Junie B.," he said. "Did you bring something to share?"

I quick pulled my hand down again.

"No," I said. "I just changed my mind."

My heart was thumping and pumping.

I peeked at my glasses one more time.

Then all of a sudden, my legs stood up. And they rushed me to the front of the room!

My knees were wobbly and shaking.

I bent over and did deep breaths.

Mr. Scary came over to me.

"Are you okay, Junie B.?" he asked. "Would you like to sit down and wait to do this another day?"

"No," I said. "I want to get this over with."

Then, fast as anything, I reached into my pocket. And I pulled out my new glasses.

May started to laugh.

It was loudish and meanish.

"LOOK! IT'S HER *GLASSES*!" she yelled. "SHE BROUGHT HER GLASSES FOR SHOW-AND-TELL! AND HA! THEY'RE *PURPLE*!"

Tears came into my eyes.

I quick covered my face with my hands. I wanted to sit down real bad. But my legs would not even move.

I stood there very frozen.

And then—all of a sudden—I heard a noise!

It was the sound of running feet, I think!

I looked up.

My new friend Herb was hurrying to the front of the room!

And guess what?

He took the glasses right out of my hand. And he put them on his own face!

"Cool!" he said. "Purple glasses!"

He looked all around.

"Wow," he said. "My eyes could *never* see out of these, Junie B. Your eyes must be really special."

He looked admiring of me.

"How do your eyes even do that, huh? Do you have X-ray vision or something?" he asked.

I shrugged my shoulders kind of shy.

"I don't actually know, Herbert," I said. *"Possibly."*

Herb gave the glasses back to me.

"Here," he said. "Put them on and read something."

I rocked back and forth on my feet.

"Well, okay, Herb. If you insist," I said.

After that, I put on my glasses. And I walked all the way to the back of the room.

I read the announcement off the board.

"Friday, September 23," I read. "Today, get ready for Show-and-Tell."

I smiled real proud.

"The end," I said.

After that, I went back to my desk.

Herb hurried over to me.

He gave me a high five.

And guess what else?

Lennie and José gave me high fives, too!

Mr. Scary did a thumbs-up. *"Excellent glasses, Junie B. Jones,"* he said.

"Sí," said José. *"Excelente!"*

"Yes," called Lucille. "I like those glasses, too, Junie B. 'Cause purple is a popular fashion color this fall."

My heart felt cheery at that news.

I looked at May very smuggy.

"Well, yay for purple," I said.

After Show-and-Tell was over, Mr. Scary gave us more time for our journals.

I picked up my pencil real happy. And I added two more lines.

P.S. Hey! What do you know?
I think I might like first grade!

I looked around the room and grinned.

Everything was crystal clear.

BARBARA PARK

Junie B., First Grader
Toothless Wonder

illustrated by
DENISE BRUNKUS

Contents

1

Prizes

Friday

Dear first-grade journal,

Today we are having a
speaker
~~speeker~~ in Room One. She is
going to tell us all about
recycling
~~restkaling~~. Recycling is when
you wash your trash, I believe.

Mr. Scary said to write in
our journals till the speaker
gets here. Only I don't even

feel like writing today. Because
I have a loose tooth, that's why.
And that thing is driving me
crazy.

Also, every time I write in
this journal I have to look up
words in the dumb ~~dikshunary~~ dictionary.
Except sometimes Mr. Scary
spells the words on the board
for us. And then I have to
cross out my mistakes. Plus
also, I erase holes in my
paper.

Spelling is not a ~~brees~~ breeze, I tell
you.

That is all I feel like writing

today. I am done with this thing. And I mean it.

                From,

                    Junie B., First Grader

I put down my pencil. And I opened my mouth. Then I reached in my finger and I wiggled my tooth.

That thing has been loose for a very long time. Only no matter how hard I wiggle it, it still won't come out.

I pulled on it a teensy bit.

"Ow, that hurt! You dumb bunny tooth!" I said.

May turned her head and looked at me.

May sits next to me in Room One.

She is not a pleasure.

"You shouldn't say *dumb bunny*, Junie

Jones," she said. "*Dumb bunny* is not a nice word."

I raised my eyebrows at her.

"Oh, really?" I said. "Well, thank you for telling me that, dumb bunny May."

Just then, May's face got puffy and red.

"DON'T SAY THAT WORD, I TOLD YOU!" she hollered.

My teacher stood up at his desk.

"Problem back there, girls?" he said.

"Yes, Mr. Scary!" said May. "There's *always* a problem back here. And her name is Junie Jones!"

I stamped my foot.

"*B.*, May!" I said. "B., B., B., B., B.! You're always forgetting my B.!"

Mr. Scary closed his eyes. "*Please*, girls. Can't we just have one morning without any spats?"

I looked surprised at that man.

"But I didn't even *spat,* Mr. Scary," I said. "My mother doesn't let me spat. Not even on the sidewalk."

After that, I went up to his desk. And I smiled very cute.

"I have a loose tooth," I said. "Would you like to see it, Mr. Scary? Huh? Would you?"

I opened my mouth and wiggled it for him.

"See it? See how loose it is? It is a loosey goosey, isn't it?" I said.

He smiled. "Wow. It really *is* loose, Junie B.," he said. "And it's a *top* tooth, too. Losing a top tooth is the best."

I looked puzzled.

"It is? How come it's the best, Mr. Scary?" I asked. "Is a top tooth funner than a bottom tooth, do you mean? Because last year I lost a bottom tooth. And I didn't actually get a kick out of it."

My teacher did a chuckle. "Ah . . . but when you lose a *top* tooth, your smile looks really cute, Junie B.," he said. "And when your new tooth comes in, you'll start looking like a *big* kid."

I did a gasp at that news.

"A big kid?" I said. "Really? I'm going to look like a big kid?"

Mr. Scary nodded. "Sure you are," he said. "Here. I'll show you what I mean."

He looked around the room. "Class? Does anyone in here have their big top teeth yet? If so, please raise your hand," he said.

All of the children looked and looked at each other.

But no one raised their hand.

Mr. Scary was surprised.

"Really?" he said. "No kidding? No one in our class has lost a top front tooth, huh?"

He turned around and shook my hand.

"Well, congratulations, Junie B. Jones," he said. "It looks like you're going to be the first person in Room One with a big top tooth!"

I felt very thrilled. "Thank you!" I said.

Then I skipped back to my seat. And I sat down real proud.

May did a huffy breath at me.

"Big deal. What's so special about losing a top tooth?" she said. "Everyone in our whole room is going to lose their top teeth, Junie Jones. It's not like you're the only one, you know."

I did a huffy breath right back at her.

"Yes, May. I know I'm not the *only* one," I said. "But I am the *first* one. And the *first* one is the winner. So there. Ha ha on you."

May crossed her arms. "Well, if you're the winner, then where's your prize? Huh, Junie Jones? I don't see a prize. Do you?"

I tapped my fingers kind of stumped. Then I hurried back to my teacher's desk again. And I patted him on the shoulder.

"Okay, here's the thing," I said. "The children are wondering where's my prize for being the tooth winner. And so how would you like to handle this situation?"

Mr. Scary did not answer right away.

Finally, he shrugged. "Well, the truth is, there *aren't* any prizes," he said. "I wasn't exactly running a contest, you know."

"Yes, I know," I said. "But I bet you could still come up with a little something to make me happy."

I pointed at his desk drawer.

"I bet there's something in there, probably," I said. "Teachers always have good stuff in their desk drawers, right? And so why don't we take a little look-see?"

Mr. Scary ran his fingers through his hair.

Then at last, he opened his drawer.

"Whoa! Is that a stapler I see there?" I said. "A stapler would be good, don't you think? I could really pound that thing, I bet. And so if you'll just hand it over, I will be on my way."

Mr. Scary shook his head. "No, Junie B.," he said. "No stapler."

I looked some more.

"Hey! Hold the phone!" I said. "Is that Tums I'm looking at?"

I leaned closer.

"Yes! Yes! It *is* Tums, Mr. Scary! You've got Tums just like my grampa Miller! And so I bet you suffer from gas and bloating. Am I correct?"

Mr. Scary quick closed the drawer.

Then he went to the supply closet and he got out a piece of shiny silver paper. And he scribbled a star.

He cut it out and pinned it on my shirt.

"There," he said. "That's your prize for your tooth, okay? You get to wear a shiny star for being the winner. Now please go back to your seat."

I looked down at my star.

"Yeah, only I don't actually think this is your best work," I said kind of quiet.

Mr. Scary pointed to my desk. He was not having a good morning, I think.

I went back and sat down.

May sneaked a peek at my star.

I tried to act proud of it.

"Well, well, well. What do you know . . . a *prize*," I said.

May did a mad breath and quick turned away.

I looked down at my star again.

This time it looked prettier, I think.

2

Uncle Lou

The speaker came at ten o'clock.

Her name was Miss Chris.

Miss Chris told us all about recycling.

Also, she showed us a movie.

It was called *Dan, Dan the Soda Can.*

It was very thrilling, I tell you. 'Cause Dan, Dan the Soda Can lived in a soda machine at a gas station. Then one day, a lady bought him to drink. Only too bad for Dan, Dan. 'Cause after the lady drank his soda, she threw him right out her car window. And Dan, Dan got his can all dented.

But hurray, hurray! A cop saw the lady littering. And he gave her a big fat ticket!

Then a can man took Dan, Dan to a recycling center. And the man got cash money. Plus Dan, Dan got fixed up good as new. And bingo! He turned into Dan, Dan the *Orange Juice* Can!

It was a miracle, I tell you!

Room One clapped and clapped at that happy ending.

Then Miss Chris passed around stickers of Dan, Dan the Soda Can for us to stick to our shirts. And the stickers said RECYCLING MAKES CENTS. Ha! Get it?

Cents sounds like *sense*! And that is a good one, I think!

After that, all of us went to lunch and recess. And we were still in happy moods.

On the playground, José and Lennie and Shirley asked to see my loose tooth. Then pretty soon, the other children wanted to see it, too.

And so finally, I stood them all in a row. And I let them look real close.

After they looked, I walked down the row. And I showed them how far I could bend it.

Herb clapped and clapped.

José and Lennie whistled.

Sheldon tried to pick me up.

That is not a normal reaction, I think.

"You're going to look cool when it finally comes out, Junie B.," said Herb.

"Sí," said José. "You're going to look *really* cool. Like a hockey player, I bet."

"Yeah," said Lennie. "Hockey players almost never have any teeth."

"Neither do kick-boxers," said Shirley. "Maybe you'll look like a kick-boxer, Junie B."

Just then, Sheldon did a sigh. "I just hope you don't look like my toothless uncle Lou," he said. "My toothless uncle Lou never brushed or flossed. And then all his teeth fell out."

I made a sick face.

Sheldon shrugged. "Well, it's not like he's *totally* toothless," he said. "He still has one bottom tooth left. It's kind of yellow. But it still can bite an apple."

After that, Sheldon walked away.

I watched him go.

Then I sat down in the grass.

And I tried and tried not to think of toothless Uncle Lou.

After school, me and Herb rode the bus home together.

We sit with each other every single day. Except not on Saturdays or Sundays or weekends.

Me and Herb talk about lots of stuff on the bus. Only today I didn't feel like talking, hardly. 'Cause I was still upset about looking like Uncle you-know-who.

I slumped down in my seat very glum.

"What if I look like a weirdo?" I said. "Huh, Herb? What if I look like toothless Uncle Lou?"

Herbert patted me. "Don't worry. You won't . . . probably."

I kept on worrying.

"Yeah, only today is Friday, Herb," I said. "And so by Monday my tooth will already be out, I bet. And so what if I come to school looking like toothless Uncle Lou? And then all of Room One starts making fun of me? And they form a circle around me, and they laugh and skip and throw fruit?"

Then, all of a sudden, I did a gasp. 'Cause an even *worser* problem popped in my head.

I grabbed Herb's shirt.

"Oh, no, Herb! Oh, no!" I said. "What if I don't even *look* like myself on Monday! Not even a tiny bit, I mean! And then I get on this bus. And you don't even recognize me. And so you pass right by my seat. And then I have to sit by myself.

All alone . . . and toothless."

Herb looked down at his shirt.

He said to please take my hands off of him.

He smoothed himself out.

"Maybe you should look on the bright side, Junie B.," he said. "Even if all of that bad stuff happens—which it won't, probably—you'll still end up with a bunch of money from the tooth fairy. Right? And that's good, isn't it?"

As soon as he said that, chill bumps came on my skin. And my stomach got flutterflies in it.

I quick looked out the window so Herb couldn't see my face.

'Cause guess what?

The tooth fairy is a whole other can of worms.

3

Ow!

I walked home from my bus stop very slow.

Walking is good for thinking, I think.

Talking is good for thinking, too.

"I just wish I wasn't the *first* one, that's all," I said out loud to myself. "I wish the other children in Room One were losing their teeth, too. Then all of us would look toothless together. And no one would throw fruit."

I did a big breath at me.

"Yeah, only that is the dumbest thing I ever heard of," I said. "'Cause you can't make other children have loose teeth, Junie B."

I rolled my eyes.

"Yeah, only I already *know* that, Junie B.," I said. "But I really don't want to be first. And so why can't my tooth just stay in my mouth a little longer? That's what I would like to know."

I crossed my arms at myself.

"'Cause you keep *wiggling* it, that's why," I said. "Maybe if you didn't wiggle it, it would get tight again. Did you ever think of that? Huh? Did you?"

I walked and walked some more.

Then, all of a sudden, I did a gasp.

'Cause I *did* think of that! Ha!

I ran to my house speedy quick.

My grampa Frank Miller was baby-sitting my fussy brother named Ollie.

"Grampa Miller! I know what to do about my tooth! I know what to do about my tooth!" I hollered real happy.

Grampa Miller was bouncing Ollie on his lap.

Ollie was wearing his drool bib. Also, he was slobbering and chewing on his arm.

Ollie will not be popular in school, probably.

Mother says he is drooly and fussy because he will be getting teeth soon.

She is kidding herself, I think.

Just then, Ollie started to cry.

Grampa Miller looked weary of that boy.

I took Ollie away from him.

"Don't worry, Grampa. I know how to calm this baby down," I said.

After that, I patted Ollie's back very nice.

Then I hummed real soft in his ear.

And I put him in the hall closet.

Grampa quick got him out of there.

He put Ollie in his playpen. And he gave him animal crackers.

Animal crackers are crackers that make babies stop crying.

Also, I enjoy an occasional cracker myself.

After Ollie stopped fussing, Grampa Miller came back in the kitchen. And he put me on his lap.

"Okay, little girl. I'm ready to listen to your news now," he said. "What were you saying about your tooth? Did it get any looser at school today?"

I clapped my hands together.

"That's what I was going to tell you about, Grampa!" I said. "'Cause at school I found out that I am the first person in Room One to lose a top front tooth. And so at first I felt proud about that news. Only then I got nervous. On account of who wants to look like toothless Uncle Lou, that's why. And so then I had a long talk with myself. And hurray, hurray! I decided not to lose my tooth after all!"

My grampa raised his eyebrows at me.

"Really?" he said. "You're not going to lose your tooth, huh? Do you really think you can do that, honey?"

"Yes!" I said. "I know I can do it, Grampa. 'Cause all I have to do is not wiggle it anymore. And then it will get real tight in my mouth again! I am *sure* of it! I'm positive."

I reached in my mouth and touched my tooth very light with my finger.

"Yup!" I said. "I can feel it! It's tighter already!"

I opened my mouth and pointed. "See it, Grampa? See how tight it's getting?"

Grampa Miller squinted his eyes. "Gee, honey, I don't know," he said. "It still looks pretty loose to me."

Then—without even asking—he reached in my mouth. And he started to *wiggle* it.

"No!" I yelled. "No! No! No!"

I snapped my mouth shut.

"OW!" said my grampa.

He quick pulled out his finger.

"OW!" I said right back.

'Cause I felt a pinch, that's why!

I poked all around with my tongue.

Something did not feel right in there.

My heart started to pound very fast.

I held my breath.

Then I opened my mouth kind of sickish.

And I spit my tooth right into my hand.

4

Freako

I ran and ran all over the house.

"OH, NO!" I shouted. "OH, NO! OH, NO! MY GRAMPA FRANK MILLER KNOCKED MY TOOTH OUT! MY GRAMPA FRANK MILLER KNOCKED MY TOOTH OUT!"

Grampa ran after me.

"No, I didn't. Of *course* I didn't, Junie B.," he said. "Your tooth came out when you bit down on my finger."

I kept running and shouting.

"I LOOK LIKE UNCLE LOU! I LOOK

LIKE UNCLE LOU! HELP! HELP! HELP!
I LOOK LIKE UNCLE LOU!"

I zoomed to the front door and opened
it wide.

"911! 911! MY TOOTH'S KNOCKED
OUT! MY TOOTH'S KNOCKED OUT!"

Grampa quick picked me up and carried
me back inside.

Then he took me to the bathroom. And he gave me a paper cup with water.

"Rinse and spit," he said.

I did what he said.

Only that's when the worstest thing of all happened.

'Cause my spit water turned *pink*!

I did a gasp at that sight.

"BLOOD! BLOOD! THERE'S BLOOD IN MY SPIT!" I hollered some more.

Grampa Miller covered his ears. "*Please, Junie B. Just stop the screeching.*"

After that, he took an aspirin. Plus also, he ate two Tums.

I kept on rinsing and spitting.

Then finally, my spit water turned regular.

"Whew," I said. "That was a close one. I was almost out of blood."

Grampa bent down next to me and smiled. "Well, let's have a look," he said.

I opened my mouth for him.

He looked in and did a chuckle.

Then he lifted me up to the mirror so I could see, too.

I quick closed my mouth again. 'Cause I was nervous to see myself, of course.

My tongue felt my tooth hole. It felt very roomy in there.

"Well?" said Grampa Miller. "Aren't you going to look, honey? It looks cute, Junie B. It really does."

My heart pounded and pounded.

Then—fast as a wink—I opened my lips. And I did a little peek at my mouth.

I quick closed my eyes again.

'Cause what do you know?

A freako.

"Put me down, Grampa," I said. "Put me down right now. I don't want to look at myself again. I don't, I don't, I don't."

Grampa Miller put me down.

Just then, my nose started to sniffle very much. And my eyes got tears in them.

"I *hate* me," I said. "I hate the way I look."

Grampa blew my nose on toilet paper.

"I'm never going to look at myself again," I said. "Not ever, ever, *never*! And I *mean* it."

Grampa bent down next to me again.

"I want you to listen to me, little girl," he said. "I would never lie to you, Junie B. You look every bit as cute without your tooth as you did with it."

He gave me a hug. "Your new smile is wonderful," he said. "You didn't even give it a chance, honey. You really need to look at it again. Honest you do."

He ruffled my hair. "Do it for me, okay? Just give yourself one more chance."

I rocked back and forth on my feet very slow. 'Cause I needed to think this over, that's why.

Finally, I did a big breath. "Oh, okay, Grampa," I said. "If you really want to lift me up there again, I guess I will let you. But I'm only doing this to be nice."

Grampa Miller patted my head. "You're very kind," he said.

After that, he lifted me back up to the mirror.

Very slow, I opened my mouth again. And I peeked at my new tooth hole.

"Try smiling," said my grampa. "You'll love your new smile. I know you will."

I did a nervous breath. Then I smiled at myself kind of shy.

"See?" said Grampa Miller. "See how cute it looks?"

I didn't answer him. Instead, I made another face at myself. And then another one. And another one.

Pretty soon, I tried every face in the book.

Finally, Grampa winked at me.

"So what do you think, little girl?" he said. "Hmm? How do you think you look?"

I smiled kind of shy again.

"I think I look fascinating, Frank," I said.

Grampa Miller put me back on the floor. Then he went to the kitchen. And he got a stool. And he brought it back to the bathroom.

He helped me up to the top step.

I stared at myself till Mother came home.

5

The Fairy

That night we had festivities.

Festivities is when my grampa and grandma come over. And all of us eat cake.

Grandma Helen Miller made the cake herself. She put a big smiley face on the top. Only that is not all. 'Cause the smiley face had a tooth missing! Just like me!

I laughed and laughed at that silly thing. Then I reached in my pocket. And I got my tooth. And I passed it all around the table.

"Oh, that's a *beaut*, Junie B.," said Grandma Miller.

"I know it, Grandma. I know it is a beaut," I said real proud. "I can't wait to take it to school for Show-and-Tell. The children are going to love this thing."

Daddy looked strange at me.

"Oh, gee . . . I don't know, honey," he said. "I'm not really sure you should take your tooth to school."

Mother shook her head.

"No, Junie B. That's *definitely* not a good idea," she said. "And besides, you won't even have your tooth on Monday, remember? You have to leave it for the tooth fairy tonight."

Just then, my skin got chill bumps again. And the flutterflies came back in my stomach.

'Cause I know stuff about the fairy, that's why.

My voice felt kind of shaky.

"Yeah, only what if I don't want to leave my tooth for the fairy, Mother?" I said. "What if I just want to take it to Show-and-Tell, and that's all?"

Mother shook her head again. "No, Junie B. No Show-and-Tell," she said. "Taking a tooth to Show-and-Tell is just . . . well, it's just—"

"Disgusting," said Daddy.

"Yes," said Mother. "Disgusting."

I whined at those two. "No, it isn't," I said. "Lots of kids bring teeth to school. 'Cause one time Roger brought a shark's tooth. And he even let me and Herb put it right in our mouths. And then we looked like sharks, too."

I thought some more.

"Plus another time, Shirley brought her

grandmother's dentures. And lots of us put those in our mouths, too."

Grandma Miller did a little gag. Only I don't actually know why.

My grampa patted her hand. "Just be glad she doesn't want to take the spit cup," he whispered.

Just then, my whole face lighted up. 'Cause I have ears like a hawk, of course!

"The spit cup! The spit cup! I will take the spit cup!" I hollered.

I jumped down from my chair. And I zoomed to the bathroom.

Then I got the spit cup out of the trash. And I dusted it off real good.

"Good news, people!" I shouted real loud. "There's still some blood around the edges!"

I quick ran back to show them.

Grandma Miller closed her eyes at that sight.

Then Mother put her head on the table and hid her face in her arms.

The festivities were over, I believe.

After Grandma and Grampa Miller left, Mother took me into the bathroom. And we brushed my teeth real careful.

Then I took my loose tooth out of my pocket. And I brushed that guy, too.

I held it up to the light. "Look," I said. "Look how shiny I made it. I really wish I could take this tooth to school, Mother. I really, really wish that with all my might."

Mother gave me a hug. "I know you do, Junie B.," she said. "But it's still going to be fun to put it under your pillow tonight, isn't it?"

She smiled. "I remember when I was a little girl. I couldn't *wait* to wake up in the morning and find out how much money the tooth fairy had left me."

My skin got prickly at that name again.

Also, sweaty came on my head.

I thought and thought about what to do.

Then finally, I stood on my tiptoes. And I whispered in Mother's ear.

"Yeah, only I know stuff about the fairy, Mother," I said. "I know the *truth*."

Mother looked shocked at me.

"The truth?" she said. "You know the truth?"

"Yes," I whispered again. "I know the *exact* truth, Mother. 'Cause last year Paulie Allen Puffer told me the whole entire story."

I took another big breath. Then I cupped

121

my hands around her ear. And I talked even quieter.

"The fairy isn't *real*," I said. "The tooth fairy is just *pretend*."

Mother's eyes got big and wide at me.

"No!" she said.

"*Yes*," I whispered back. "Paulie Allen learned it from his big brother. The tooth fairy isn't a fairy at all. She's actually a teensy little tooth witch."

Mother's mouth came all the way open. "A tooth *witch*?"

"Shh!" I said. "We have to talk soft, Mother. If the tooth witch hears anyone telling her secret, she flies into their room at night. And she pinches their cheeks."

Mother covered her face with her hands. She was in shock, I believe.

"Paulie Allen's brother even *saw* the tooth witch," I said. "'Cause one night he put a tooth under his pillow. And then he stayed awake all night. And he saw the tooth witch fly into his room on a teensy little toothbrush."

"Oh, my," said Mother.

"I know it is *oh, my*," I said. "And that is not even the worstest part. 'Cause the witch walked right under his pillow. And she carried out his tooth. And then she chomped a big bite out of it. Just like it was a little tooth apple."

Mother made a noise behind her hands.

I patted her very nice. "I know how you feel," I said. "This is very hard to hear."

Finally, Mother took her hands away.

"But it doesn't really make sense, Junie B.," she said. "I mean, why would a mean little witch leave *money* under the pillow? A witch would never do something that nice, would she?"

I rolled my eyes way up to the ceiling. 'Cause sometimes I have to explain *everything* to that woman.

"Of *course* she would, Mother. Don't you get it? The witch leaves money so that children think she's really a fairy. 'Cause if children don't think there's a fairy, they won't leave their teeth. Right? And if they don't leave their teeth, the witch won't get any tooth apples."

Mother closed her eyes very tight.

Then, all of a sudden, she opened up the bathroom door.

And she ran right out of the room.

She was taking it harder than I thought.

6

■ ■ ■ ■ ■ ■ ■ ■ ■ ■

Full of Soup

That night, Daddy tucked me into bed.

He said that Paulie Allen Puffer's brother is full of soup.

"There's no such thing as a tooth witch, Junie B.," he said. "I promise you there isn't. Paulie Allen Puffer's brother just made that up to scare Paulie Allen. And then Paulie Allen said it to scare you, too."

I shook my head. "No, Daddy. No. It's not made up. I know it isn't. 'Cause the tooth witch makes *sense*, that's why," I said. "She makes *way* more sense than a fairy."

Daddy raised his eyebrows.

"Why?" he asked. "Why does a witch make more sense than a fairy?"

"*Because,*" I said. "Because the tooth witch likes to *chomp* the teeth. But the tooth fairy doesn't do anything with the teeth at all, right? And so why would she even pay money for them?"

Daddy did a little frown.

"Well, I don't know, exactly," he said. "But I'm sure that she must do *something* with the teeth, Junie B. There are other things to do with teeth besides just chomping them, you know."

"Like what?" I asked.

Daddy put his head in his hands. Then he thought and thought and thought.

After he got done thinking, he went to get Mother.

She came into my room carrying fussy Ollie.

She handed him to Daddy and sat down on my bed.

"Daddy said you have another problem about the tooth fairy," she said.

I nodded.

"Yes," I said. "'Cause if there's really a fairy, then she has to have a reason to want the teeth. Right, Mother? She wouldn't just

throw them in the garbage. 'Cause that doesn't make any sense. Plus also, it would hurt my feelings."

Mother hugged me.

"No, Junie B. Of *course* she doesn't throw them in the garbage," she said. "I'm sure the fairy does something very special with the teeth."

"Like what?" I said.

Mother ran her tired fingers through her

hair. She stood up and walked back and forth on my rug.

Then, all of a sudden, her face got brighter.

"*I* know. I bet the fairy uses the teeth to make *jewelry*," she said.

At first, Daddy and I didn't say any words. We just stared and stared at that woman.

"Jewelry?" I said finally.

Mother smiled. "Yes, of *course*," she said. "She probably uses the teeth to make little tooth necklaces and bracelets and cute little toe rings. How does that sound?"

I made a sick face.

"It sounds repulsive," said Daddy.

Mother stopped smiling.

She quick took Ollie back from Daddy. And she hurried out of my room.

After she left, Daddy finished tucking me in bed.

"I'm sorry about that, Junie B.," he said. "I'm afraid Ollie has your mother worn to a frazzle these days. But I'm sure she's not right about that jewelry thing."

He did a little shiver.

"No. Certainly she's not," he said.

Then—before I could ask any more questions about the fairy—he kissed me good night. And he rushed out of my room as fast as Mother.

That night, I did not put my tooth under my pillow.

Also, I did not put it under there the night after that. Or the night after that.

Because what do you know . . .

The fairy still did not make sense.

7

A Stumper

The next morning was school.

I put my spit cup into my backpack. And I took it to my bus stop. 'Cause Mother said I couldn't take my tooth. But the spit cup was Grampa's idea.

I saved Herb a seat. Then I bounced up and down real excited. 'Cause I couldn't wait for him to see me, of course!

Finally, we got to his bus stop.

I waved to him from the window.

Then, ha! I leaned my face real close to the glass. And I smiled my biggest smile!

Herb's eyeballs popped out of his head!

He ran on the bus zippedy quick.

"It came out, Herb! It came out!" I said. "My tooth came out on Friday! And it's been out ever since!"

I smiled for him again.

"See me, Herb? See how I look? I look fascinating, right? I don't look like Uncle Lou, hardly."

Herb's eyeballs kept popping out at me.

"Whoa!" he said. "Wow!"

I laughed at that nice comment.

I smiled and pointed.

"See my tooth hole, Herb? Huh? I look cute, right? I don't even look like Uncle Lou! Correct?"

Herb said *Wow* again.

After that, I quick got my backpack. And I unzipped the zipper.

"Yeah, only wait till you see *this*, Herbert!" I said. "I brought something special for you to see!"

After that, I pulled out the cup. And I put it right on his lap.

"Ta-daaa! It's my *spit* cup, Herb! I used this cup to rinse my actual spit!"

I showed him the edges. "See the pink color right there? That pink is from the bleeding."

Herbert's face did not look delighted.

"Okay. Thank you," he said. "Please get it off of me now."

I got it off.

"But I thought you would like this," I said very disappointed.

Herb patted me. "Live and learn," he said.

Pretty soon, his face got normal again.

"So how much money did you get from the fairy, Junie B.?" he asked. "Did you get a lot of cash?"

My stomach did a flip-flop at that question.

'Cause I didn't want to discuss that matter, of course.

I squirmed in my seat kind of worried. Then I looked out the window. And I didn't talk.

Herb tapped on me.

"What's wrong, Junie B.?" he said. "How come you're not answering me? The fairy did come, right? She didn't forget you, did she?"

I looked all around. Then I scooted next to him very close. And I quieted my voice to a whisper.

"Yeah, only I can't even discuss that matter, Herb," I said. "'Cause I know stuff about that fairy."

"Stuff? What kind of stuff?" he asked.

I whispered even softer.

"Sorry," I said. "But I have to keep it a secret. And so please don't ask me any more questions. And I mean it."

After that, I pretended to lock my lips. And I threw away the key.

I saw that on TV once.

Herb looked annoyed at me.

I unlocked my lips again.

"Don't be mad at me," I said. "I can't help what I know, Herb. And anyway, all you have to do is think about it. 'Cause the fairy doesn't make sense."

Herb scratched his head. "What do you mean she doesn't make sense? Why doesn't she?"

I crossed my arms.

"Because what does the fairy do with the teeth, Herbert? Huh? Did you ever ask yourself that problem? Why would a fairy pay money for teeth when she doesn't even use them? It sounds kind of fishy, don't you think?"

Herb just stared at me.

"Well?" I said. "Do you know the answer, Herb? A fairy wouldn't just throw the teeth in the garbage, would she? 'Cause that doesn't even add up. Only nobody knows *what* she does with them, apparently. Not even you, I bet."

Herb wrinkled his eyebrows.

"I never thought about it," he said.

He tapped on his chin. "What does the fairy do with the teeth? Hmm . . . that's a stumper, all right."

After that, he slid way down in his seat. And he thought and thought some more.

I thought some more, too.

We rode to school real quiet.

8

Smiling

When we finally got to school, I started feeling shaky inside.

'Cause I didn't want to get laughed at, remember? Plus I was still concerned about the fruit throwing.

I closed my mouth real tight. And I walked back to my desk.

Lennie smiled and waved at me.

I waved back. Then, very slow, I did a shy smile.

That's when Lennie jumped up from his desk. And he did a loud whoop!

"Cool!" he said. "You look cool, Junie B.!"

José heard Lennie and came to see. Then he grinned and grinned at my brand-new smile. And he gave me a happy high five.

And that is not even the *best* part!

Because Mr. Scary saw what was going on. And he came all the way to my desk to see my tooth. And he gave me a smiley-face sticker!

After that, he clapped his hands together. And he made a 'nouncement to Room One.

He told them I lost my tooth. And he asked me to stand up and show them my special new smile.

I swallowed real nervous.

Then I stood up kind of jittery. And I opened my lips a teensy bit so the children could see my tooth hole.

And what do you know?

Room One was happy for me!

All of them smiled real nice.

Except, not May, of course.

May just rolled her eyeballs.

"I think you look weird, Junie Jones," she said. "I think your smile looks silly."

I sat down. "No, May. *This* is a silly smile," I said.

Then I put my fingers in the sides of my mouth. And I stretched my smile across my face. And I wiggled my tongue at her very fast.

Lennie and José laughed and laughed.

And guess what? At lunchtime, I made my smile even funnier. 'Cause Lennie gave me a raisin. And I put it right in my tooth hole! And it stuck there very hilarious!

Shirley laughed her head off at that joke.

I am beginning to enjoy that girl.

"So how much did the tooth fairy leave you?" she asked. "Did you get a bundle?"

"Yeah," said Lennie. "I was wondering that, too."

I started feeling squirmy again. I looked at Herb kind of worried.

He tried to explain the matter to them.

"Well, uh . . . Junie B. didn't exactly leave her tooth for the fairy yet," he said.

All of the children looked at me. "Why?" they said. "Why didn't you leave it, Junie B.?"

I squirmed some more. Then finally, I took a deep breath.

"I've got *issues* with that fairy, that's why," I said kind of quiet.

"Issues?" asked Lennie. "Like what kind of issues?"

I swallowed real hard. "Issues like . . . well, you know . . . like what does she do with the teeth, for instance," I said.

For a minute, nobody said anything.

Then May made the cuckoo sign at me.

"What does the fairy do with the teeth?" she said. "What kind of dumb issue is that?"

I flashed my angry eyes at that girl.

"Well, if it's so dumb, then you must know the answer. Right, May?" I said. "And so what *does* the fairy do with the teeth? Huh? She doesn't pay money just to throw them away, does she?"

After that, I waited and waited for her to answer.

The other children waited, too.

But May didn't say anything.

"Well?" I said.

"Well?" said Shirley.

"Well?" said José.

Finally, May's face turned red. And she went to get a drink of water.

After that, the whole lunch table started talking about the fairy. Only no one knew what she did with the teeth.

We wondered and wondered.

Then, all of a sudden, Lucille stood up.

And she fluffed her fluffy dress.

"Well, guess what? I don't really *care* what the tooth fairy does with the teeth. All I care about is how much money she leaves."

She looked at Room One. "You're nothing without money, people. Remember that," she said.

I tapped my fingers on the table kind of annoyed.

"Yeah, only that doesn't even answer my question, Lucille. 'Cause I still don't know what she does with the teeth."

Lucille put her hands on her hips.

"Well, maybe she just *collects* them," she said. "Did you ever think of that? Huh? Collecting stuff is a hobby, you know. My richie nana collects tons of junk. And she pays good money for it, too."

I tapped my fingers some more.

Then I put my chin in my hands. And I thought about Lucille's nana.

Finally, I started to smile a little bit. 'Cause maybe Lucille's idea might make some sense, possibly.

Pretty soon, Herb smiled a little bit, too.

"A *tooth* collection, huh?" he said. "Hmm. Maybe that's the answer, Junie B. Yeah, that just might be it. The fairy might collect teeth as a hobby or something."

"Sure," said Lennie. "There's nothing wrong with collecting stuff. Like, I collect baseball cards. But I don't really *do* anything with them."

"Sí, and I collect matchbox cars," said José. "What's wrong with that?"

Just then, Sheldon sprang up from the table.

"Yes! And I collect vacuum-cleaner bags! And the doctor says that's perfectly normal!"

After that, Sheldon laughed. And he pretended to vacuum his pants.

All of us moved away from him.

Then the bell rang and everyone went outside for recess.

That afternoon, I wrote in my journal.

Dear first-grade journal,

Me and Herb talked some more on the playground. We decided that the tooth fairy has a tooth colekshun [collection], probably. And that is not even werd [weird], possibly.

Also I promised Herb I would put my tooth under my pillow tonight.

I hope we are right about this woman.

> From,
>
> Junie B., First Grader

P.S. I wish me all the best.

9

Miracles!

That night, Mother put me in bed.

Daddy was in baby Ollie's room. He was trying to rock that cranky boy to sleep.

We heard Ollie fussing.

"I bet you're glad I'm not that bad. Right, Mother?" I said. "That baby is a pain in our necks. Right?"

Mother laughed. "Oh, believe me, Junie B., you were no peach when you were teething, either," she said.

She tickled me a little bit. "Speaking of teeth . . . tonight's the big night, right?"

she said. "Tonight's the night you're finally leaving your tooth for the fairy."

I covered my face with my sheet.

"Don't remind me," I said.

Mother laughed again. "Don't be silly. This is going to be fun."

She handed me my tooth to put under my pillow.

I handed it right back to her.

"You do it, Mother. You put it under my pillow, okay?" I said. "And put it close to the edge, please. 'Cause I don't want the fairy tramping around down there."

Mother put it close to the edge. She let me check it.

After that, she leaned down. And she gave me a big hug.

"I'm very proud of you, Junie B.," she said. "I'm proud that you got over all that silly nonsense Paulie Allen Puffer told you."

"Thank you," I said. "I am proud of me, too."

After that, Mother kissed me good night. And she turned out my light.

I quick turned it on again.

"Yeah, only I think I will sleep with the light on tonight," I said. "You know . . . just in case I have to come running out of my room in the middle of the night because there's a witch in here."

Mother did a sigh.

"Whatever," she said.

After that, she gave me another hug. And she closed my door.

I jumped up and opened it again.

"Yeah, only I think I will sleep with the door opened tonight," I said. "You know . . . just in case I start screaming my head off in the middle of the night because there's a witch in here."

Mother said, *"I give up."*

I give up means the same as *whatever,* I believe.

After that, she kissed me one more time.

And she left my room.

The next morning, I woke up very relieved.

Because guess what?

I made it through the night! That's what!

I hugged myself real happy.

Then, all of a sudden, I remembered about the fairy. And my heart started to pound and pound. 'Cause maybe there was money under my pillow right that very minute!

I took a big breath.

Then, very careful, I reached under

there. And I felt all around.

And bingo!

My fingers touched something!

I grabbed ahold of it and pulled it out.

Then I sat up straight in bed.

And I laughed and laughed.

'Cause good news! Ha!

CASH!

I zoomed to the kitchen and skipped around the table.

"CASH! CASH! I GOT CASH!" I hollered real thrilled.

"WHO WANTS TO SEE IT? HUH? WHO WANTS TO SEE MY CASH? PLEASE RAISE YOUR HANDS!"

I looked all around the kitchen.

Then I stopped skipping.

Because no one was actually in there.

I zoomed back down the hall.

"MOTHER! DADDY! WHERE ARE YOU? WHERE ARE YOU? THE FAIRY LEFT ME MONEY!"

Mother stuck her head out of Ollie's room. "We're in here, honey!" she called.

I skipped into Ollie's room and showed them my money.

"Look, people! I got cash! I got cash!" I said. "Only I don't know how much it adds up to. But it is a bundle, I bet!"

Daddy's eyes got big and wide at my money.

"Whoa! The tooth fairy must have been feeling very generous last night," he said.

"I know it," I said. "I love that fairy, Daddy. She left me money. And she didn't even pinch my cheeks!"

Ollie was sitting in his crib. He smiled out the bars at me.

I looked surprised at him.

"What's wrong with Ollie, Mother?" I asked. "Why is he smiling? Is he sick or something?"

Mother laughed. "No, silly," she said. "When I came in this morning, he was playing in his crib . . . happy as can be."

I scratched my head. "Really? Ollie's *happy*?" I said. "That's odd."

Daddy picked him up.

"Well, actually Ollie had a little surprise for us this morning, too," he said.

He sat down with Ollie on the floor. Then, very gentle, he took my finger. And he rubbed it against Ollie's gums.

"Hey!" I said. "It's *ridgedy*!"

Daddy grinned. "It sure is," he said. "That's Ollie's first tooth, Junie B."

My whole mouth came open at that good news!

"A *tooth*?" I said. "Ollie got a tooth?"

I felt the ridges some more.

"Wowie wow wow! Last night was a good tooth night for *both* of us!" I said.

"Yes, it was," said Daddy. "What a neat coincidence, huh? Ollie got his first tooth

on the very same night that the fairy came to get yours."

Mother ruffled my hair. "It's almost like Ollie was waiting for the tooth fairy to come, too, Junie B. Just like you."

I smiled at the thought of that.

Then, all of a sudden, I stood real still.

And goose bumps came on my arms.

"Wait a minute," I said real soft. "*What* did you just say, Mother?"

Mother looked at me kind of strange. "I said it's almost like Ollie was waiting for the tooth fairy to come, too."

Just then, I did a loud gasp.

"That's *it*!" I said. "That's *it*! That's *it*!"

I springed way high in the air. Then I twirled all around. And I hugged Mother real tight.

"Ollie *did* wait for the fairy!" I said. "He waited for the fairy, just like me!"

Mother and Daddy raised their eyebrows very curious.

I skipped all around them in a circle.

"Don't you *get* it?" I said. "The fairy *recycled*! She *recycled* my baby tooth! And she gave it to Ollie!"

My feet started to dance.

"It's perfect!" I said. "It's just like Dan, Dan the Soda Can! The fairy took my tooth! And she made it all shiny and new! And then she gave it to my very own baby brother!"

I quick bent down and felt Ollie's gum again.

"Yes-sir-ee-bob! That's my tooth, all right! I'd know that tooth anywhere!" I said.

Daddy scratched his head.

"Well, I'll be," he said.

Mother laughed. "What a great idea."

"It *is*, Mother!" I said. "It *is* a great idea! Plus also, it is a big relief. 'Cause the tooth fairy doesn't just throw teeth in the garbage. Now I know that for *sure*."

I looked at my money again.

"It's just like Miss Chris told us!" I said real squealy. "Recycling makes *cents*! Get it, Mother? Get it, Daddy? *Cents* sounds like *sense*! Ha! That's a good one, right?"

After that, I zoomed to my room to get dressed for school.

"I CAN'T WAIT TO TELL THE CHILDREN!" I hollered. "ROOM ONE IS GOING TO LOVE THIS NEWS!"

I put on my favorite pants and sweater.

Then I quick ran back to Ollie. And I felt his tooth some more.

He smiled at me again.

I smiled back at him.

'Cause what do you know?

I think I might like that boy after all!

Laugh yourself silly

vith Junie B.!

BARBARA PARK is one of today's funniest authors. Her Junie B. Jones books are consistently on the *New York Times* and *USA Today* bestseller lists. Her middle-grade novels, which include *Skinnybones, The Kid in the Red Jacket, Mick Harte Was Here,* and *The Graduation of Jake Moon,* have won over forty children's book awards. Barbara holds a B.S. in education. She has two grown sons, two small grandsons, and a medium-sized dog. She lives with her husband, Richard, in Arizona.

DENISE BRUNKUS'S entertaining illustrations have appeared in over fifty books. She lives in Massachusetts with her husband and daughter.

Also by
Kathleen Benner Duble

❖

Hearts of Iron

The Sacrifice

❖

Margaret K. McElderry Books

QUEST

Kathleen Benner Duble

Margaret K. McElderry Books
NEW YORK   LONDON   TORONTO   SYDNEY

Margaret K. McElderry Books

An imprint of Simon & Schuster Children's Publishing Division

1230 Avenue of the Americas, New York, New York 10020

Book design by Mike Rosamilia

The text for this book is set in Bembo.

Manufactured in the United States of America

10 9 8 7 6 5 4 3 2 1

Library of Congress Cataloging-in-Publication Data

Duble, Kathleen Benner.

Quest / by Kathleen Benner Duble.—1st ed.

p. cm.

Summary: Relates events of explorer Henry Hudson's final voyage in 1602 from four points of view, those of his seventeen-year-old son aboard ship, a younger son left in London, a crewmember, and a young English woman acting as a spy in Holland in hopes of restoring honor to her family's name.

ISBN-13: 978-1-4169-3386-1 (hardcover)

ISBN-10: 1-4169-3386-7 (hardcover)

1. Hudson, Henry, d. 1611—Juvenile fiction. [1. Hudson, Henry, d. 1611—Fiction. 2. Explorers—Fiction. 3. Espionage—Fiction. 4. Seafaring life—Fiction. 5. America—Discovery and exploration—Fiction. 6. Great Britain—History—Early Stuarts, 1603-1649—Fiction. 7. Netherlands—History—17th century—Fiction.] I. Title.

PZ7.D8496Que 2008

[Fic]—dc22

2006102712

For Deven Gregory Romain:

Go forth, young man! Explore new lands!
And know that I will always be there for you,
should you need me in your questing!

Acknowledgments

Writing a book is a journey in and of itself. On my quest to discover Henry Hudson, I was not alone. My thanks go out to the following:

To my daughters, Tobey and Liza: You were great sports, listening patiently (or perhaps half-sleepily) to my attempt to educate you as we waited for the bus. Those tedious lessons inspired these pages. I love you both with all my heart.

To my husband, Chris: I knew that memorization technique you kept trying to teach me would come in useful somehow. If ever I can no longer write, at least I will be able to spy. I love you with all my heart too.

To my production editor, Jen Strada, and my copy editor, Valerie Shea: You both have consistently sought out the best in what I have written, tweaking my stories with great skill and knowledge before they head out into uncharted waters. Many, many thanks!

To the sales force at Simon & Schuster: While you are the great unknown, as I have not met you face-to-face, I have seen the results of your valiant efforts. You are indeed a force to be reckoned with! I am eternally grateful for all your hard work.

And finally, to my editor, Lisa Cheng, thanks for coming aboard and steering me safely and effectively through the production process. I am looking forward to many more voyages with you!

MEMBERS OF THE CREW
OF THE *DISCOVERY*—1610

Henry Hudson, Master
John Hudson, Age 17
Silvanus Bond
Michael Bute
Robert Bylot
Francis Clements
Sidrack Faner
Henry Greene
Robert Juet, Mate
Henry King
Arnold Lodlo
Bennet Mathew

Adam Moore
Adrian Motte
Adrian Motter
Michael Pierce
Abacuk Prickett
Philip Staffe, Carpenter
Nicholas Syms
John Thomas
John Williams
Edward Wilson, Surgeon
William Wilson
Thomas Wydhouse

JOHN HUDSON

At last, we are off! Lord, it is good to have the feel of a
ship beneath my feet again. It has been too long!
I have climbed the mast, swinging myself into the
air. Twenty feet below, things wheeled and rolled beneath
me. I felt my stomach heave. What a glorious feeling!

Father yelled for me to come down before I killed
myself. But as usual, I have ignored him. I love these
heights. I love the feeling of the boat, rolling side to side
with the wind. I love the feeling that I *may* fall to my
death. For how can one ever really enjoy life if you are
not always living constantly at its edge? That's the place I
most want to be.

Already I am thinking on what we may see this trip.
How my heart goes out to all those poor boys left behind
in London: farmers who must rise each day to milk the
same infernal beast, butchers who spend their days bloody
with dead carcasses, blacksmiths who must pound over and
over the same shape into their iron. Other than being a

prince, there is nothing I would rather be than an explorer. It is a grand life. One never knows what to expect—white bears with huge fangs, fish as big as my own vessel, savages that cannot speak my tongue. These are the wonders I have seen on my last voyages, and God willing, there will be more this time around.

Before we left today, I was forced to attend church with the rest of the crew and their families at St. Ethelburga's. (Father feels God should be on our side before we leave the harbor, but I would say the crew below me is more godless than God-fearing.) My mother sat near me, expecting as always for me to provide a good long snore in the midst of that blasted priest's long-winded prayers. Truly, the man must take lessons on how to bore a person to death. But today, I did not sink into a stupor. No, today, I spent the hour recalling each and every minute of last night.

This is the first time I can ever remember that I have actually been a *little* sad on leaving London. I know it is all due to Isabella. I have wooed many a girl before, but never one quite like her. Mostly, I find girls mere distractions, but there is something wonderfully wild about Isabella. And so today, I am praying that she will be waiting for me at the end of this voyage. Who could have ever guessed that I may be longing more for the kiss of a girl than the good company of my mates after those many long months at sea?

Lord, I hope it is a cheerful crew this time around, for a serious lot can make a voyage dreadful dull. Already I have been aboard ship, making mischief. I have hidden a cask or two of ale from the cook. He will roar when he thinks we are short, and give it good to Henry King, who is responsible for loading provisions. Oh, how it will delight me to watch them argue—with Henry insisting he brought the required number of casks aboard and Cook insisting that he did not. I hope the others will join in the fun when I let them in on the secret.

Below me, I can see Nicholas Syms trying to go about his work. His face seems a bit green—not used to the seas, from the looks of it. I wonder who he truly is. I have sailed with the crafty Nicholas before, and the man below me is not he. It will be good sport spending this journey on a mission of discovery. His story must be interesting to have to pretend to be another. Of course, Father will never notice. He hardly pays the crew any mind, so intent is he on the voyage itself.

Aha, I can see the spires of Westminster Abbey far in the distance. The shore is rolling away from us quickly, and the smell of salt is strong in the air. The seagulls circle our boat, sending out their insistent cries. The wind is in my face. And I am satisfied by my kiss from Isabella last night. A drink of ale tonight, a good night's sleep in my hammock rocked by the waves, and the look on impostor Nicholas's face when he finds I have sewn all his shirtsleeves and necks together. Lord, what more could a seventeen-year-old boy like me want?

RICHARD HUDSON

ow much longer, Richard wondered, *will Mama stand there, just staring like that?* It wasn't that he minded seeing Papa and Johnny off when they left. In fact, he liked it well enough, imagining himself one day, heading out to sea with them, a sword at his side, ready to brave fierce warriors or dangerous animals. But when the boat was lost to the horizon, it was rather boring standing there. How could she not notice that there was nothing left to see but smelly men unloading stinky fish from the dirty brown waters of the river?

"Mama, I'm hungry," Richard said, tugging on his mother's skirts, hoping he could pull her thoughts from the sad ones that always made her cry when Papa and Johnny left.

Mama wrapped her shawl tight about her. "I hope it's not a bad omen," she whispered, her eyes still on the white-capped waters, "leaving on such a raw and cold April day as this."

"What's an omen?" Richard asked, stifling a yawn.

"A sign," his mother murmured.

Richard rolled his eyes. "You always look for signs in everything," he complained.

His mother took his hand and squeezed it. "Let's get you home, little one," she said softly.

"Finally," Richard muttered. His mother laughed.

They hurried down the darkening street. And Richard hoped his mother's laughter was also an omen, one that indicated she would be in good spirits now, though he suspected this was just wishful thinking.

Later, Richard lay in bed, trying to sleep. He could hear his mother rocking back and forth in her chair by the fire. And he could still smell supper in the air—chicken stew, his favorite. He had had bread pudding for dessert and could taste it stuck between his teeth if he sucked hard enough. All in all, it had been a pretty good day, really.

But now he couldn't sleep, and he didn't know why. It wasn't as if he missed Johnny's big body in the bed next to him. Johnny always stole the quilts late at night so Richard woke shivering. Often he had to kick Johnny, since his brother did not waken easily after spending months sleeping on a boat with a lot of loudly snoring men. Richard would poke him until he woke yelling and then grab the covers back, usually taking a smack from his brother for his efforts—a truly disagreeable experience.

And he certainly didn't miss the way Johnny tricked him into doing chores for him or made fun of the fact that Richard was only eight and couldn't tie a proper knot. Richard much preferred the company of his older brother,

Oliver, even though he was married and didn't live with them anymore. Oliver was fun and funny. Johnny was just annoying.

And yet, Richard had to admit, turning over again and again, he did miss Johnny and Papa when they first left for a voyage. He missed Papa's pipe and the sight of smoke curling about the room, even though he hated the smell of tobacco. He missed Papa's charts, scattered all over the room, and the way he lost himself in his thoughts so much that sometimes he hardly even knew Richard was there, even when Richard sat right down beside him and poked his finger in Papa's ear.

He missed Johnny's stupid fits of laughter when he came home late after a night at the pub, tripping over Richard's shoes and falling into the bed and waking Richard the whole way up. He missed Johnny's whacking him with his wet shirt on a hot day, usually giving him a welt the size of a loaf of Baker Bowdoin's bread. He missed Johnny putting syrup in his shoes so that his feet stuck to the bottom even months after Mama cleaned them out.

He didn't know why he missed these things, but miss them he did. It was a very puzzling problem.

"Can't sleep, Richard?" Mama asked, coming to the door. In her hands were some socks she had been darning. With three men in the household, Mama was always darning socks—at least that's what she said.

Richard shook his head irritably. "It's too quiet."

Mama smiled. "You'll get used to it."

"I miss Johnny," Richard cried, embarrassed and mad at himself for admitting it.

"You said you hated him last night when he stole a

sugar sweet from you and dropped it in your chamber pot," Mama reminded him.

"That was last night," Richard said petulantly. "Now it's too quiet. Don't laugh at me."

His mother came and sat on the edge of his bed. She bent over and brushed the hair from his eyes. Her finger-nails were long, and he loved the feel of them in his hair. Richard sighed. "Tell me how you met Papa."

His mother laughed. "Oh, Richard. I tell you that story every time your papa leaves."

"I want to hear it again," Richard protested.

His mother sighed. "All right."

She looked out the window at the dark, stormy sky. Rain pelted the tiny, diamond-shaped panes of glass. Richard snuggled down under his quilt and listened to Mama's soothing voice.

"I was sixteen," Mama began, "and had run off to escape the bickering of my seven brothers and sisters. I wandered down to the wharf, to watch the boats going out to sea. And your father was sitting there, a tall boy with strong arms and legs, throwing rocks out into the harbor."

"And he was alone, wasn't he?" asked Richard.

Mama smiled. "Aye, your father loved sitting there by himself, looking out at the water."

"And you spoke to him, though you knew you might be whipped. Girls aren't allowed to talk to boys alone," Richard told her.

"Aye," his mother said. "That's exactly what I did. I sat down next to your father and let my legs dangle out over the water. And I said hello to him. My heart was beating so fast at my bravery that my face was as red as an apple."

Richard laughed at his mother thinking that talking to
Papa had been courageous. It was a silly idea.

"And then Papa turned and looked at you, and you felt
a shiver down your back," Richard said.

"I did." Mama admitted. "And I asked him what he was
doing. 'Planning,' he said, and I thought he was mad, for I
couldn't *imagine* someone just sitting and planning."

"You never do that," Richard pointed out.

"No." Mama agreed. "I am more like the sea that trips
from shore to shore, I suppose. I live moment to moment."

"Like Johnny," Richard said.

"Aye, like Johnny." Mama sighed. "It isn't always the
best way to live your life, Richard."

"So," Richard said, bringing her back to the story so
she wouldn't lecture him again, as she had in the past when
she reached this part, "you said . . ."

"I said, 'And what have you planned?' and he said . . . ,"
Mama paused.

"To become an explorer of uncharted waters. To sail. To
find new routes, treasures, and riches!" Richard shouted out.

"Right," said Mama, "and I said, 'Can I join you?' teasing him as I did my brothers when they came up with their
own wild schemes."

"But Papa does not joke," Richard went on. "And he
told you yes, and he meant it."

"Aye," Mama agreed, "though I hadn't meant marrying
him when I asked if I could join him. But when your
grandparents found out about my meetings with your
father, for I went and met him often after that, marriage is
what I got. The moment was upon me before I gave it a
thought."

"But not Papa," said Richard. "*He* had thought about it."

Mama laughed. "Aye, he did not protest at all when my parents insisted we marry. And on that day, when he bent to kiss me, I was sure I saw in his eyes a certainty that he had planned for that very day since the first time we met on the wharf."

"As he plans all his trips," said Richard.

Mama smiled. "Aye, as well as he plans all his trips."

"And you were not sad or sorry about what you had done," Richard continued. "For this one time, you were glad that you had acted without thinking."

Mama nodded. "Aye, Richard. For once, I was not sorry I was so impulsive." She bent over and kissed his forehead. "Now it is time for sleep."

"What's impulsive?" Richard asked, wanting to keep her there. He was not yet ready to close his eyes, and he was tired of lying in bed, staring at the ceiling.

"Impulsive means doing something without thinking it through," Mama told him. "Now good night, little one."

She stood and walked to the doorway.

"I know how to play Hazard!" Richard announced, desperately searching for something to interest her and then realizing that *he* had been impulsive as soon as the words came out of his mouth. Johnny had told him never to tell his mother of their games of dice. Would he be in trouble?

"Richard," Mama said, turning around, her eyes wide with shock, "that's gaming, and you know it."

"Johnny said *you* played when you were young," Richard protested. "He said *you* snuck off to play when *you* shouldn't have."

"And where did your brother get that information?" asked Mama.

Richard shrugged. His brother always seemed to know more than he did, and he had given up trying to figure out how.

"I've got the dice." Richard held them up, seeing his mother hesitate.

"And where, might I ask, did you get those?" Mama said, trying to look stern, but Richard could see the light in her eyes.

"I'll bet you sixpence I can beat you," Richard said.

"Who taught you dice?" Mama asked, coming back into the room. "And where did you come up with sixpence?"

"Johnny taught me," Richard said matter-of-factly. "Then I beat him good at his own game. Oh, he was mad."

Mama laughed. "I'll bet he was. John doesn't much like being bested by anyone."

Richard shook the dice. "Johnny says you were quite good in your younger years."

"In my younger years?" said Mama indignantly. "Hand me the dice, Richard. I'll show you a thing or two your brother hasn't even dreamt of."

Richard crowed with delight. His mother would stay!

ISABELLA DIGGES

April 17, 1610

I stood at the dock earlier today with my father and watched them leave the harbor. They sailed away from London and up the Thames, moving quickly as the wind was strong. John waved to me until I could see him no longer. My heart skipped a beat as he swung about the mast, that dark hair of his blown about by the wind, his smile eager, wide, and open. My thoughts are in a tangle about him, a jumble that I hope my father is not able to discern, and one I must work hard to quell. I know that my falling for the Hudson boy is not in our plans.

Lucky for me, my father's thoughts seem to be on the outcome of the voyage only. As the ship disappeared from view, he worried that Captain Hudson and his crew would do as they had on their previous voyage and go off on some lark of their own instead of following the instructions that had been given them by those who had financed the trip.

We have so much more to lose than the other investors should this venture not be successful. They are not as near ruin as we are, nor in as high a disfavor as we have become with our good king these past two weeks. I blame my father wholeheartedly for the predicament he has put us in. It galls me still to remember his whispered confidence to that sniveling mess of a physician. He should have known the man would repeat his words and relay to the king the fact that my father had called Queen Anne a "cheap foreigner." Now we must keep our heads low and our words quiet just to avoid finding ourselves exiled to some godforsaken part of the country.

My father is bent on having revenge. Me, I wish only to reinstate our place at court. If it weren't for my father's indiscreet words, I would be there now, dressing finely and dancing until dawn with wealthy and dashing young men who could help me forget the brown eyes and smooth cheek of John Hudson, who is below me in station and therefore not suitable for anything but a quickly forgotten romance.

And if that is not enough, still the creditors plague us. Lord, we need John's father to find the route to Asia, if for no other reason than to at last restore us to the rightful level of wealth we deserve. In finding the route, our boat and our captain will ensure the supremacy of England, for the country that controls the route to the East, controls all. As my father insists, this shall surely help us find favor once again in the king's eyes. And in this matter, I am in agreement with him.

We have risked everything that this might succeed—the little money we have left, our reputation, and even my own safety. For now, I sit, bundled in worn robes of fur, a carriage pulling me fast over rough roads toward the Netherlands, ostensibly to play nursemaid and companion to Von Dectmer's sickly fourteen-year-old daughter, but in truth, I have been sent to spy.

I admit this does make me queasy at times, and yet I know myself to be a quick and clever girl. If, as I hope, I am able to learn the secrets of England's greatest competitor—the Dutch

East Indies Trading Company—then even should Hudson
fail, our place at court could be restored. For all my father's
shortcomings, he has taught me well in this: One must always
have an alternate plan should the first not succeed.

I was reluctant to go initially, but when my father began to
speak to me about how to obtain the secret information we need,
my mind became intrigued. And I agreed to the schooling at last
and to working for him. I am not stupid, and I quickly surmised
how I might help improve both our situations.

I am beautiful. I do not give myself airs. I simply know it to
be true. I take after my mother, a great beauty herself with her
green eyes and dark lashes. I have her looks and her cunning,
and I know this will serve me well when I arrive. No one shall
suspect me for a spy. For using my charms to obtain what I
want is a trait with which I am quite familiar.

And though I am grateful to my mother for having passed
on to me her comeliness, then again, if it hadn't been for her,
we would not be in the tight financial circumstances in which we
find ourselves. For in addition to beauty, my mother had a quick
hand with my father's purse and a sharp tongue that made
living with her difficult. I know this to be an unacceptable
sentiment for a daughter, but it was no great loss when the
plague took her. My mother was a witch.

Still, at times I miss her company, for she taught me well
how to use my charms. She would have been a great tutor for
this mission my father and I have undertaken.

And yet, my father is not without his own clever ideas. In
spite of his ill-advised words to the king's physician, he has been
using his head since he faltered. Yesterday, he conceived of a third
plan to save us and our estate. Should I fail to uncover the
knowledge that the Dutch East Indies Company retains, should
Captain Hudson fail in his venture, my father has set his sights
on currying favor with a certain duchess. She is only recently

*widowed and is well-endowed monetarily, from what I hear.
This, too, could be our saving grace.*

*So I will brush my hair and pinch my cheeks for color as
we approach the Von Dectmers' household, praying that there
is a man willing to trade a kiss for the secret Dutch maps he
conceals from all others. I will close my eyes and imagine
Captain Hudson returning with riches and the route east,
willing my mind to see only the father and not the son. And
I will dream of a wedding—that of my father to the wealthy
duchess—and the day when her money will be at our disposal.
None of this is beyond the realm of possibility, and so for once,
I might just sleep a little more soundly than I have for a
fortnight since my father's indiscretion. One can always hope.*

SETH SYMS

❧ ❧

April 27, 1610
Dear Mama:

Yer probably wondering right about now where I might have gotten off to. I know ye've been used to me disappearing a day or two, but nothing like I've been gone this time out.

Well, Mama, don't faint. I'm on a boat to find Asia! But Mama, if I'd known what "going to sea" would mean, I'd never have gone.

Now ye know I ain't what ye'd call religious or anything, but that first night on this here boat, I actually prayed—and mighty hard, too—that we'd have to turn back for London. I prayed for some problem 'cause Mama, this boat don't do nothing but roll and roll and roll. Me stomach ached, and I retched something fierce all those first few days, even though there was little left to cough up after the first hours of heaving.

As it is, I am fixing on beating cousin Nicholas to a pulp on me return! Nicholas hadn't mentioned the sickness, only the feeling of freedom and adventure, when

he convinced me to take his place on board the *Discovery*.
But who can feel freedom and adventure when ye ain't
even able to climb from yer bunk, but must cower and
crawl to puke yer guts out in some bucket already filled
to overflowing with other men's puke?

And if that weren't enough to set yer stomach on edge,
the rocking and rolling of that boat and no land in sight,
the smells of unwashed bodies and unclean clothes, of
seawater and salt, of mutton cooking over a fire, those
would surely send any healthy man to the bucket too.

And yet, believe it or not, there are those who seemed
unbothered by it all. The youngest one, John Hudson, son
of the captain, he's been out and about, even with the
storms we hit the second and third days. He was able to run
from one end to the other, to swing from the lines, to fall
asleep like a dead man in his hammock only to rise and run
again the next day. He was like some monkey with no end
of energy. His stomach must be made of iron.

Not me. Ye know I was never strong like that. Ye
always kept me well out of harm's way. Never have I liked
hardships or discomforts. But I had no choice in this
matter. Leaving London is what I had to do and fast. Ain't
much room in a town where lover and husband are on
different sides of seeing the same issue.

Still, cousin Nicholas's solution wasn't all he cracked it
up to be. And by the second night with all that storming
about, and the seawater seeping in with each big wave and
roll the boat took, I was sure me cousin was sitting pretty
now in some smoke-filled pub in London, women on both
knees, laughing at me in this most awful of places.

Still, Mama, much as it must come as a shock that I'm

gone on a sailing ship, I know ye'll be happy knowing
I am alive at all, especially seeing how Elizabeth's husband
meant to challenge me to a duel. Ain't no way I was
sticking around to see that one through! Heard her
husband's a pretty good swordsman, and I ain't never even
picked up a sword. It weren't the odds I liked. So I went
searching for some way to leave the country without
anyone taking much notice. Just wish now it hadn't been
Nicholas that I had run into that day, looking for some
way out. He up and says to me, "I got just the thing for ye,
Seth. I got meself a place on Henry Hudson's boat. It's to
set sail this afternoon, but to save yer skin, I'll give up me
place to ye. Ye just show yerself up at the dock at two
o'clock and say yer me. They won't take no notice that
yer not. Yer on and good as gone."

"What kind o' work I gotta do on this boat?" I'd thought
to ask. Ye know I ain't big on work.

"Whatever's called for," Nicholas had answered smoothly.
"Ain't nothing much. Tying lines, patching sails. It's the
adventure and freedom that's the wonder of the sailing
world. All the places and things ye'll see. That's why ye go."

I see now why some schooling might be a good thing. I
never thought to ask Nicholas how long it'd be before I saw
the shores of good old England again. Didn't think to ask
until we'd set sail, and me stomach took to rising up to me
mouth. And when I did think to ask, I picked the wrong
guy to consult—Robert Juet, the mate. Now I'd been told
he'd traveled with Captain Hudson before, old as he was.
But that man has got a mean streak to him. I ask him just
how long we were sailing for, and he answers with a snarl.

"A few months, or however long it takes. So ye'd best be

about getting yerself feeling used to this boat, sailor. Ye keep up this weak stomach of yers for a month or two, ye'll be dead before we ever see the spires of Westminster Abbey again." Then he'd turned on his heel and was gone.

If I'd thought me stomach was weak, me heart grew weaker still at those words—a few months! I was to be on this horrible ship for a few months? I sank back in me bunk, too sick for words.

Mama, I know you won't be getting these here letters, not until I return. But I'll write them anyway 'cause I feel so bad about leaving you for so long without a word. And I swear here and now, when I get back, I will search out Nicholas first thing. I will not rest until I've found him. That scoundrel cousin of mine is going to regret having put me on this stinking boat!

Yer loving son, Seth

JOHN HUDSON

But of course, I am in trouble with Father again! I know my pranks on board drive him crazy. But they do lighten the mood a bit. It is dreadful dull to do nothing but tar the leaks or shorten the lines or stand watch all day. I want things to happen, and my impatience eats away at me. Besides, a man would go mad if this was all he did for the day. Someone must look to morale, and I have always considered myself just the boy to do it.

Yes, I admit I did push Michael Pierce overboard on our second day out when he was relieving himself. There he was, thrashing about with his breeches down about his knees. Oh, we did laugh ourselves silly over that!

But we had to turn the boat around just to pick old Michael up, sputtering and coughing as he was. And Father gave me a good dressing-down right then and there, reminding me that we could have lost Michael, and that he needs each and every one of his crew members if we are to reach the East.

I did remind *him* then that the investors had told us

only to find the passage and had insisted that we not follow it, even should we find it. At my comment, my father snorted. "As if, John," he said to me, "I should turn back if we find the way. Do they truly think I would do this? They would be mad to think I wouldn't follow it to the end."

I hate how Father is so obsessed with the East. In being so crazy with this quest, he misses out on the fun of life at sea in general. I will admit, though, the idea of the East often fills my head. And it is these lapses in concentration that got me in trouble today. I was doing my chores, as I was assigned, but my mind was darting around like the strange birds we sighted on our second voyage, going hither and thither.

I got to thinking first of Issa. The memory of her face alone can take up many hours of boredom when the sea is calm and there is nothing but your other ugly crew members going about their work to think on.

Then I began to remember our past voyages, for we are not far from Iceland now. I have often wondered, when we have landed there in the past, how those people can live in such a climate. We have only just sighted the shores of this island, and already the weather grows raw. It would be hard to be enthusiastic about much in this cold. Daily, my fingers are numb, and there is ice on the decks.

Both Arnold Lodlo and Michael Bute have already slipped and were almost sent overboard. But for the swift action of myself (I caught Michael's shirt by the tip of my sword, as I had been busy practicing my brandishing) and others (having grabbed Arnold by the seat of his pants), they would be an addition to the cold, gray ocean surrounding us—for no man would last long in these frigid waters.

And to think it is only May! If I had had the misfortune to be born in this part of the world, I might never have gotten out of bed. Of course, that led me back to thinking on Issa and how I wouldn't mind at all being wrapped up in a blanket with her, our lips together.

And with all this thinking and rambling about in my mind, I spilled some oil on the deck. I meant to come back and wipe it up. Truly, I did. But then I got to thinking on Isabella, and I forgot. And it was Juet who later stepped upon the spill, and, like some greased pig, he went flying. Oh, we all did laugh heartily, until he stood up, all red-faced and glaring. That shut us up quick, along with the fact that Father took it upon himself to appear at just that moment. Why is it he is always around when something I do goes wrong? Most times, he shuts himself up in his cabin, poring over his maps. And yet he manages to always make an appearance just when I am shown in the worst light.

And so Father was angry again and has saddled me with the logs. I know they are important to keep, but truly, they are dreadful dull to do—writing, writing, writing. Abovedecks, I can hear the laughter of the others. And here I am, in Father's cabin, his eye watchful on me as I scribble with my quill. If I stop for even a second, Father's head comes up from his maps. So sometimes, I just let my mind wander, never once stopping the movement of the quill even though I am not actually writing anything. Instead I think on the East.

If we do find the passage, and Father disobeys his orders and follows, I wonder what it will be like. I have heard tales of elephants and camels and have seen drawings of them. I have been told it is actually possible to ride these beasts. The men are laying odds as to who shall be brave enough to try. I am winning the pool and am quite proud of it. Why should I not ride one of them? Adventure is what I came for in the first place. I try to imagine myself on such a strange animal. I have heard the camel can spit quite far, but no one can outspit me. I could always beat my brother Oliver in this endeavor. I won our contests every time. I should like to try my hand at outspitting a camel—after riding him first, of course.

I have just heard a call of "Land!" Thank God! We must have arrived at Iceland. Though this country is cold even in May, it is still green and hopefully will improve the morale of Father and the crew. If not, it will be up to me to find some prank or other to lighten the mood.

Ah, why think on that now? A good joke is something that will make fine sport for my mind to think on later—after I have downed a pint or two of ale, taken a swift stroll around the port, and left these dreary logs far, far behind!

RICHARD HUDSON

Richard ran swiftly among the stalls of the marketplace, his friends close on his heels. He'd have to
find a place to hide and quick. He crouched
down between buckets filled with flowers, the smell of roses
overpowering him. He put a finger to his nose and willed
himself not to sneeze. Between the wheels of the flower cart,
he could see Jackie Tanner's dirty bare feet passing him by.
Richard grinned. If even Jack could not find him, then
Richard was truly the best hider in all of England!

"Eh!" came a voice. "What do ye think yer doing there?"

A hand grabbed him by the collar and pulled him up.
An old woman dangled him a few feet in the air. Her eyes
were bloodshot, and she had a large wart on her nose.
Richard twisted and turned, trying to set himself free
from her grasp.

"This ain't a place for playing, ye young scoundrel. And
yer bending the petals of me flowers, ye are!" the woman
screamed.

Just beyond him, Richard could see his playmates laughing and pointing at him.

"Richard!"

Drat! His mother was here too and had spotted him. Already, she was picking her way among the marketplace vendors, the two wooden pails on her arm banging against each other. Richard could see his mother's hair hanging wet against her forehead. She looked hot and cross. He was probably going to be in big trouble for this.

"This yer brat?" the flower vendor asked.

"Yes," Mama said, sighing. "I'll take him now."

The old woman let Richard go, dropping him to the ground so he fell to his knees. "Kids," she grumbled. "They're out of control these days, ye ask me."

"No one did," muttered Richard.

"Richard!" Mama scolded.

In the distance, Richard watched his playmates take off running in the other direction. He stood and kicked at the dirt. His few hours of freedom were over quicker than he had expected.

"What are you doing here, young man? You were supposed to be home chopping wood for the fire," Mama admonished him, taking him by the arm and pulling him along after her.

"And look at you," she added, stopping. "You're all muddy. It's been dry as a bone around here these past few days. Where have you been?"

Richard stared at the ground, hoping that if he just stayed silent, maybe his mother would forget this last question.

"Richard!" his mother said sharply. "I asked you something."

He was in for it now. Mama was in a terribly sour mood. "At the docks to watch for Papa and Johnny," Richard muttered sullenly.

His mother scowled. "You are not allowed near the water, young man. You know that. And as for Papa and Johnny, they have been gone but two months now. You shall have to wait a good deal longer before you see your father's ship sailing up the Thames. Perhaps you need a good whipping to remind you just how dangerous it is at the docks."

"But Willy Barker said that other boats had just arrived from Greenland," Richard protested. "And I wanted to see if they had news of Papa."

Mama raised her head, hope in her eyes. "Had they?" she asked.

Richard felt badly answering her. "No. But Mama, you always say no news is good news."

Mama sighed. "Come along," she said tiredly. "And no more trouble today. It's too hot for it."

Obediently, Richard followed his mother to the vegetable stall. She picked up an onion, sniffed it.

"Really," Mama said irritably, glaring at the vegetable vendor as she chose two onions and dropped them in her bucket, "how long do your men dally on their way from the fields to the city? Do they stop at every tavern they pass to grab a beer and swap stories as these vegetables sit rotting in their wagons in the hot summer sun?"

Richard grimaced. His mother's mood seemed to be worsening.

"Grow yer own then, why don't ye?" the vegetable vendor snapped.

"I just might," said Mama, paying the man and turning to leave.

"No great loss then, madam!" the vendor shouted after her. "Ye never have coin anyway."

Richard waited for his mother to explode, but instead saw her lips press together and tears come to her eyes. He remembered the last voyage of his father's, when his father had stayed out longer than had been expected. Their money had run out, and they had been forced to beg for credit. It had shamed his mother terribly, and she had not forgotten it.

"What's that my mother just handed you, then?" Richard demanded, stepping forward to defend her, his fists tightened into a ball. "How did she pay you for those rotten onions of yours? Coins, I believe."

"Richard!" Mama said. She pulled him away and knelt down next to him. "You shouldn't speak to grownups like that."

"He was insulting you, though," Richard argued.

Mama smiled. "Are you my little defender, then?" she whispered, gathering her son to her and hugging him tightly.

Richard squirmed. It was one thing to have his mother sleep beside him the first night that Johnny and Papa were gone in the privacy of their home, but it was another for her to hug him publicly!

"Word has it Captain Hudson's reached Iceland, madam."

Over his mother's shoulder, Richard saw Mistress Howley, their next-door neighbor, dressed all in black. She always took great delight in saying the nastiest things about the Hudson household. Why Mama bothered being civil to her, Richard would never understand.

"Aye, Mistress Howley," Mama replied, turning and rising. "They have sent word from court that my husband did indeed reach Iceland. It is truly good news."

"Captain Hudson always seems to reach Iceland," Mistress Howley said sharply. "But it would only truly be good news if he found a way to reach Asia. That is the point, is it not?"

The old woman plucked at her black wool dress. *How*, Richard wondered, *can that old lady stand black wool cloth in this heat?* Mistress Howley reeked. And then another thought came to Richard. How did *Master* Howley stand it? Richard giggled, and Mama shot him a look.

"Aye," Mama said, turning back to Mistress Howley. "That is indeed the point. But any news that he is on his way and about to enter new and uncharted territory means that he is on the route we have hoped for."

"Hoped!" Mistress Howley snorted. She coughed and spit into the street. "Let us *hope* that there is more to your husband's adventures this time than in the past. Lord knows we pay dearly for these voyages and *hopes* of his. After three trips, I believe it's time he paid off with something, don't you?"

Mama now gave up all pretense of being polite. "I don't see your husband risking his life, Mistress Howley, to improve the supremacy of England."

"Too smart to even try," Mistress Howley replied tartly, and with a twist of her head, she scurried away.

Richard watched as Mama picked up a rotten tomato and pulled back her hand.

"Mama!" he cried delightedly. "Are you going to throw that at Mistress Howley?"

Mama reddened. Quickly, she set the tomato down.

"Oh, do it, Mama," Richard squealed with delight. "Do it. Do it!"

Mama shook her head. "Violence is not the way to handle disagreements, Richard."

"No," Richard agreed, "but it would be fun."

Mama laughed at that, and Richard grinned up at her. When his mother laughed, she usually forgot to be angry. Maybe now he wouldn't get that whipping for going to the docks.

"What are we having for supper, Mama?" Richard asked, as his mother moved on down the line of stalls.

She stopped in front of the butcher. Flies flew about everywhere, landing on the carcasses that hung above the stall. "Mutton," answered Mama.

Richard grimaced. Rotting fruit and vegetables were one thing, but rancid meat was another.

Richard knew this was one reason everyone wanted Papa to find the fastest way east. The rare Asian spices made meat taste better. A year ago, Papa had brought home just the slightest amount of curry for them to try, and Richard knew at once why the king was so mad to have it. His mouth watered just remembering the deliciousness of that beef with spices.

If Papa did find a route this time, Mama had said they would be richly rewarded. Richard did not care much about wealth, but he did like that curry.

"A side of mutton, please," Mama said, turning to the butcher.

Richard sighed. Perhaps he could find a way to feed his mutton to Mistress Howley's cat without Mama noticing. He hated that cat almost as much as Mistress Howley!

The butcher picked up a small piece. The flies buzzed about his head. "Will this do?"

"No." Mama shook her head. "I'll need a larger piece than that."

"What for?" Richard asked. "I don't even like mutton."

"You may not, but your brother Oliver does," Mama told him. "And he's coming to dinner tonight."

Richard loved when Oliver visited, but then a thought occurred to him. "Are Anne and Alice coming too?"

Mama nodded. "Aye. They'll both be there."

Richard scowled. He liked Oliver's wife well enough. It was Alice who annoyed him.

The butcher held up another, bigger piece of mutton. Mama eyed it carefully. It was only a little brown around the edges. She nodded.

"Don't like your big brother coming for a visit, eh?" the butcher asked as he handed Mama the meat.

"My brother's all right." Richard sighed. "It's Alice. She drools."

Mama laughed. "She's just turned three, Richard. You drooled sometimes when you were that age too."

"I never drooled," Richard stated indignantly.

Mama smiled down at him fondly. "Suit yourself," she said. "But I remember well, young man, what a mess you made."

"I didn't drool," Richard insisted. Why did his mother always say the most embarrassing things right in front of other people?

Mama slid the meat into her wooden bucket and handed the butcher some coins. Then she turned back to Richard.

"Why don't you go on home?" she said, tilting her head toward the setting sun. "I only have strawberries to get. And we'll need chopped wood for the fire tonight."

"It's too hot for a fire," Richard muttered.

"Would you rather not eat, then?" asked Mama.

"Not if it's mutton," Richard said.

Mama laughed. "Well, you may eat with us or you may starve. Your choice. But we are having mutton. And from the looks of what you've gotten yourself into, it may be that you'll need a bath before dinner too."

A bath? Richard moaned. *Could this day get any worse?*

"Oh no, Mama," he protested. "I can wash up good. I will after I finish my chores. I don't need a bath."

"Well, we'll see when I get home," Mama said tiredly. "Lord knows I don't need the added work of heating water for you."

"I'll take a cold one, if I have to," Richard suggested.

"I'll bet you would." Mama sighed. "Right now, a cold one sounds good to me, too."

"Really, Mama?" Richard said, his voice rising with hope.

"No," his mother answered, turning to face him. "I'm only joking, Richard. If you need a bath because you are so dirty from disobeying me, it will be a warm one, young man. Then maybe you will remember not to go near the docks like I've told you."

Richard kicked at the dirt again. "Ahh," he grumbled. "Why are you always so ill-tempered?"

Mama looked at him, shock on her face. "Have I been that sour lately?"

"It's only because it's hot," Richard said quickly, seeing his mother's dismay. "And because you miss Johnny and Papa."

Mama's shoulders sagged. Then she bent toward him. "If you are *good*, young man, and bring in the wood," she whispered in his ear, "I shall let you take a cold bath."

Richard turned, his eyes wide with surprise. "Truly, Mama?"

Mama smiled. "Truly, Richard. Now, off with you, boy," she said, and kissed him on his dirty head.

Without a backward glance, Richard ran toward home as fast as he could to finish his chores. And he tried not to think too much about drooling Alice and the dinner ahead.

ISABELLA DIGGES

June 23, 1610

And so I am now a part of the Von Dectmer household.
The daughter I am to be companion to is a bit of a ninny,
pale and not particularly clever. But of course I have kept these
thoughts to myself and have turned upon her the strength of my
charm and wit, and she now likes me well enough, often sharing
confidences with me. None of these are of great importance, as
most of what she concerns herself with is whether this young
man or that young man has looked her way. All these young
men are Dutch, without a drop of English blood to sustain
them, and as a result, of no consequence to me. And so it is
easy for me to listen and nod and act as if I care about her
romantic inclinations, which of course, I do not. And yet today,
thanks to this little Dutch girl, I believe I have hit upon
information that will be of interest to our king.

This morning there was much commotion in the household,
for a man had arrived to see Von Dectmer. He came into the
drawing room, where I sat sewing with my young charge. He

was of medium age with thinning hair and large brown eyes. Not particularly attractive. Von Dectmer accompanied him, clearing his throat and asking his daughter and me both to leave. But the daughter begged to stay, saying it was too cold in the other rooms, and that the light in this room suited her best. Her father was about to refuse, but I gave him a smile that would have made ice melt and promised that we would be silent if he would allow us to remain.

The father gave me a look and then agreed. His eyes upon me were speculative, and I realized then that his interest in me was growing. With his wife dead, he may have marriage on his mind. I will have to avoid being alone with him in the future in order to discourage such an absurd proposition.

Still, today it was all for the best. Von Dectmer relented, thinking no doubt that his daughter and I, with our feeble female minds, would pose no danger. In point of fact, he was correct about one of us. His daughter cared more about the quality of her needlework for a dowry than about the business her father so studiously undertook. But I? I have never been adept at handling a needle and never intend to be!

Von Dectmer and the unknown man set about discussing their manly topics. I kept quiet, my ears tuned to their conversation. And I gave a small gasp when I finally realized that the man standing in the room was none other than James Dits, an English explorer! I had to swallow my surprised intake of breath, for both men turned at the sound. I quickly stuck my finger in my mouth, as if I had pricked myself. Then I bent my head back down over my needlework, but the needle kept slipping in my fingers, as my hands were sweating at my mistake. Silently, I scolded myself for not being more discreet.

Luckily, they both soon resumed their conversation. Von Dectmer was intent on convincing the explorer to undertake a voyage with the Dutch East Indies Company to find a way east. At last! Information I could send to my father to take to the king. His Majesty would not want any explorer to usurp us in that endeavor—especially one who was English and sailing for others. What a mood he was in over Hudson a few months back—he practically jailed the man for exploring for the Dutch! Not that I blame the king one bit. Why any English explorer would want to do anything for any country but England puzzles me greatly.

When at last they left, Dits promising to give the offer some thought, I pleaded a headache to my young charge and slipped up to my room. There I put quill to paper and, in code, wrote to my father, entrusting to him the information I had just discovered. I dripped wax onto the letter, sealing it with the Digges coat of arms, and then sat back, satisfied, just as a knock sounded at my door.

A letter had arrived for me that very day from my father. I took it, dismissing the servant. The letter set my teeth on edge, for my father did little but complain.

It seems he had gone to court the other day, the first time since his unwisely spoken words. The king passed him but an hour after he had arrived, and though he did bow low to him, as low as was possible for a man to bow, the king looked right through him. I smiled to myself, thinking on how this circumstance was about to change.

He then went on to deny me my request for three new dresses. Thinking on how I was putting myself in danger these days, I could not believe his refusal! How does he expect me to charm the men of this household without the trappings that let men be trapped? Truly, it was absurd, and I vowed to break the seal on my own letter and write a line or two more demanding the dresses. Surely he would not refuse me now that I had delivered what he had been hoping for.

Lastly, my father wrote that he had received letters from

Hudson. The Discovery *had arrived in Greenland. Captain Hudson claimed that all was going well and according to schedule, in spite of the heavy storms and ice. He hoped to remain in Greenland but a fortnight to reprovision, then head out toward Labrador and the Furious Overfall and from there into what he hoped will be the passage east. My father went on to complain about Captain Hudson's request that he visit his wife and assure her of his love and devotion, calling the man mad to think that my father would lower himself to enter that most vile of places where Captain Hudson keeps his abode. Instead, he sent his servant Webster, who complained most bitterly about the task.*

At any other time, I would have laughed to read this, for my father and Webster both give themselves airs and are constantly at odds—a situation that amuses me no end. But today, my thoughts were not on Webster nor on the picture of him braving the muddy streets of London to deliver a message to Henry Hudson's wife.

No, now I could picture only one face—that of a young boy with brown eyes that seemed to look deep into mine before he placed his lips upon mine that day, a boy whose smile was wide when he asked me something I should never have promised. I cursed myself for the relief I felt knowing that that boy had made it safely to Greenland. These thoughts would not do!

Quickly, I broke the seal on the missive to my father, picked up my pen, and responded to his letter, willing the angry words flowing onto the paper in front of me to erase that memory my mind seemed so determined to retain!

SETH SYMS

⁓ ⁓

June 26, 1610
Dearest Mama:

Who could ever have believed that something so simple as air could be so damn cold? While the others around me have suffered through this bitterness before, I ain't prepared, that's for sure. Me shirts are so thin that the cold reaches right through them without any kind of effort on its part. I shiver day and night, even under the woolen blanket I gambled for. Lucky for me, Elizabeth pressed a few gold pieces into me hand before I left her, and lucky that I am a keen card player, otherwise I might wake like the others with a fine coating of frost on me only clothes. Nicholas should die just for that!

And as if this coldness ain't enough, the surroundings make me long even more for them green shores of England. White. 'Tis all you see. White everywhere. I am blessedly sick of white.

When I heard the cry for land two weeks ago, I about jumped up and yelled, "Hallelujah!" At last, off this rocking, stinking boat. Though I ain't puking no more, and I can go about me chores with the best of the other seamen, still I wanted nothing more than solid ground beneath me feet. Dirt. I wanted dirt. I flew to the rail that day, only to see the most plain and empty sight I ever saw. A man couldn't even dream of a land so full of nothing.

Whoever named this strip of snow-covered barren hills "Greenland" must still be laughing his fool head off as he downs another lager. There ain't anything "green" on it. The settlement is nothing but a few ugly run-down old huts. The people who inhabit them are real dreary-looking too.

I had considered hiding out when we reached land this time, but thoughts of deserting turned cold as the air when I saw what I'd be left to endure. This ain't no country. This is a prison. So I ain't returning any time soon, Mama. Not 'cause I truly don't want to, though.

See, there's these rumors around that Captain Hudson means for us to sail on to Asia. So I guess it's better to trust that this ship will find its way to all them riches than to spend me years on this strip of land without trees or shrubs or anything of any kind of value. Still, I worry.

'Cause there's some talk too that there is no way to Asia, and that Captain Hudson ain't nothing but a fool. I don't know who to believe, so I keep me own peace, choosing no side. I have made friends with the son, John. He's a kid, just seventeen, brave but a bit crazy, pulling prank after prank on us every day. His good spirits lighten me mood some, though. He has been teaching me swordplay, being as he is good with one. Maybe now I won't ever have to run to the sea should my adventures in England go all wrong again. Still, I almost lost me stomach yesterday when young John, fooling around as he does, landed his sword just under me arm, an inch from me own heart. He laughed loud at the whiteness of my face. But heck, I weren't used to that kind of fooling.

I like him, though, and mainly feel funny about listening to them others in their criticism of his father, for they do criticize him much. The other day, there was this fight between Greene and the surgeon, Edward Wilson, which Captain Hudson had to settle. Why he sided with Henry Greene during the fight still puzzles the heck out of me. The man's a born troublemaker. Ye know the kind, Mama. Nobody likes him. He's always saying this is bad or that is bad, and his feet stink something awful (and we all stink a bit by now, so that's saying something). But maybe the captain don't know that. I can't figure. It don't matter, anyway. None of the men was happy with the outcome. None of them likes Greene, and it didn't sit well with them that Captain Hudson chose Greene to defend. When the fight had been settled, with none of us really even knowing what it had been about in the first place, and the men broken up to return to their work, I saw Robert Juet whispering to some of the crew. I was in the process of unknotting the lines, and so was able to slip close to the group and listen. Juet was muttering something about the incompetence of Captain Hudson. When he saw me, he got real quiet. Juet doesn't think much of me, I suppose 'cause of the number of times I retched near his hammock without making the bucket at the beginning of the trip. He has little use for me. But then I have little use for him, either.

Philip Staffe, the ship's carpenter, and I have gotten comfortable with each other, if that is what ye can call it

these days on a rotting vessel in freezing waters. He is a
quiet man, not too big on getting angry. Back in London, I
would have teased him for being a man with no spine. But
here, I actually find his quiet, reasonable ways kind of
soothing.

He has taught me to whittle. Wouldn't ye have laughed
yerself silly seeing me pursue something so womanish? But
there is something calming in putting knife to wood. Already,
I have carved a small whale, an animal I ain't never seen until
this voyage, one that still scares the willies out of me. Me
small wooden beast don't even come close to the power I felt
when I saw the real one lift out of the sea. His head that day
was enormous, his tail powerful as it hit the water with a slap,
sending a huge wave toward our boat. I didn't even know it
was possible to feel so small next to a dumb old animal.

Now, Philip has told me that I am a natural at carving.
I think he is just fooling me. Still, I like to hold me small
carving and to remember that day of seeing that beast
rise from those shining waters, its magnificence
something I ain't never gonna forget.

Yesterday, there was a great yell from above. I was below
helping the cook prepare the evening meal, tending to the
fire and peeling a few potatoes that were rotting a bit. I can't
see how we'll have enough food for all the way to Asia.
There ain't so much here for such a long trip. But no matter.
The yell came. Cook and I hurried abovedecks.

We had entered a strait in which there was all this water
pouring from the sea into it. John Hudson was beside me.

"Well, we have reached it," he said. "Onward. Onward."

"Reached what?" I had asked.

"The Furious Overfall," John said. "Looks pretty furious, eh, Nick?"

He laughed, and I laughed at the thick water we was sailing through.

The captain was ecstatic, saying he was sure that this strait was the key to reaching the Orient. I actually felt this little shiver inside of me. At last, perhaps we were really on our way, and the Orient was coming up fast. Me mind filled all up with pictures of hot sands and warm waters. And I was actually thankful to cousin Nicholas for tricking me into going on this expedition.

John, for his part, was all excitement too. He talked at length about how he intended to be the first to ride one of them camels. His enthusiasm was kind of catching. I started thinking I might try my hand at riding one of those beasts. The rest of the crew too seemed more cheery. And Captain Hudson even left his cabin and his charts and his strange-looking navigational tools to stand on the bridge and watch us enter the strait. And he actually smiled as we sailed on.

And so I am breathing easier today, Mama, knowing that we are on course and headed toward warmer waters. And I have spent the last few hours counting up me coins, for I mean to bring you back some exotic object to make up for all the worrying I know you must be going through. In the end, though, Mama, you'll see it was all for naught.

Yer loving son, Seth

JOHN HUDSON

This is the biggest of jokes! Everywhere anyone looks there is only ice and snow. How can this possibly be July fifteenth? The world has gone mad and turned itself over on its head. It is so cold I swear I could be hanging upside down over a fire and not even know it. Ha!

It seems illogical that we are headed east. All sanity tells one that the weather should grow warmer, not colder. We are *all* ready to turn back, myself included. Though I have seen two whales and seven seals, that is the most excitement this trip has afforded. I say we return home, refresh, and try again.

But Father will have none of it. *He* is excited, *actually* excited. He stomps about the ship, yelling orders, rubbing his hands in satisfaction as the rest of us moan and groan and rub our hands together in despair at the cold. It is only because we are in unknown territory that he is like a boy at play. To me, it all looks pretty much the same—white, and icy, and dreadfully dull. Not to Father, though. He spends hours watching the shoreline, measuring depths, taking notes. One could fall fast asleep watching him daily tinkering with all his instruments.

And all this fussing about has made him completely unaware of the growing unhappiness around him. He *is* a smart man—I have known that since I was a lad. He was always showing me maps, plotting out new ways to sail, teaching me the ways of the water. I confess, maps confuse me. I can't tell one direction from another. If I was in charge of this ship, we should be in Africa before I could tell we were lost. (Although at least there the water and the winds would be warm—or so I have heard. Thinking on this now, in all this cold, perhaps I should be in charge of this boat!)

But for all my father's intelligence, as our trips have progressed, I have begun to see his weaknesses emerging. I admit, he does not captain well. He remains so lost in his calculations, his speculations, his charts, his plotting, that he does not pay attention to the morale of the crew. That responsibility has fallen to me.

And while in the past keeping the mood light has been no hard chore, this trip has been different. I can't seem to rouse anyone much. All my efforts seem to come to naught. Today, I might have even made an enemy.

Perhaps it was stupid to do. I don't know. Only time will tell. Stupid or not, it was funny. At least everyone but Juet got a good chuckle out of it. So in the sense of cheering everyone up, it worked. Still, I have a nagging sense that this prank of mine will come back to haunt me.

I couldn't help doing it. Father, in one of his few aware moments, actually heard Juet complaining today. And in response, unspeakably, he brought out his maps to show everyone, trying to "prove" that we were indeed headed toward the East. What he was thinking I'll never know, seeing as how those charts are our most prized possessions—the most coveted of all a captain's items. I asked him if he was crazy but got no response.

It's not as if I am worried about someone memorizing those maps and relaying the information to our competitors. Oliver is always concerned with this. He drives me mad sometimes with his worrying. But we are too long out at sea, and even should Father decide to turn back today, it will be months before we arrive in London. The chance of someone remembering the details on those maps for that long is slim. And yet, they are all the information England has at the moment. And with Father pulling them out for all to see, it only made the men think they could question his authority, his decisions, his right to captain this vessel. And I knew Juet would waste little time in doing just that. And being who I am, boy in charge of crew morale, I decided to end this possibility before it reared its ugly head.

We were eating, later, after Father had shown the charts. No one had said anything yet, but I could sense that Juet was about to insinuate that Father had been wrong in his calculations. Juet, Motter, Syms, Staffe, and I were sitting on a plank across some barrels, our wooden "table" in front of us. I ate a bit of salted cod and then, casually as I could, I said, "I have been told that it is nigh impossible to balance two mugs of ale upon the back of your hands, even if they are lying flat upon the table."

"Ridiculous," sneered Motter. "A fool could do that."

"Do you think?" I asked innocently enough. "What say you, Juet?"

"I agree with Adrian there," Juet said, shrugging. "It would be simple enough."

"Let's have you try it then," I said, and rose quickly to fill two mugs with ale.

Juet willingly laid his hands flat upon the table, and I placed one mug upon the back of each. The mugs, of course, stayed steady.

"There you have it," Juet said.

"So I do," I said, and then I picked up my plate and walked away. It took but a moment before the others caught on and stood too, taking their plates with them.

"Hang it!" Juet yelled. "Hudson, come back here and take these mugs from me!"

The others laughed and just looked at him.

"Motter!" he yelled. "Staffe! Get back here!"

But no one went near him. Instead, we all stood, laughing our fool heads off at him stuck sitting there. I left him like that for a bit. And then I went over and pulled the mugs from the back of his hands. But as I did, I bent down and whispered into his ear. "And so you see who is in charge now, Juet. It's the Hudsons, it is. And don't you forget it." And so I warned him.

He rose and stomped off, and we all shared another hearty laugh at his expense. And tonight, with cards and dice, we are all a merry lot. So it may have been worth the risk I took. Either way, Juet will merit watching.

RICHARD HUDSON

Mama pulled the iron arm from the fire, swinging the kettle with boiling water out from the flames. She stood up, stretching. A strand of hair hung in her face, and she used the back of her hand to sweep it away from her eyes. Richard wished she'd hurry up. He hated washing day.

"Hello, hello," came a voice from outside.

Mama reached out and grabbed a cloak to throw about herself. She had been standing in front of the fire with nothing on but her shift. She tied the cloak around her neck, went to the front door, and opened it just a crack.

Richard jumped down from his chair. Maybe now, Mama would be caught up with whoever had arrived and leave him to put back on the well-worn, grimy clothes he loved so much.

"Not out of bed yet, Mother?" Oliver stood outside, a wide smile lighting his face. In his hands were two grouse. His boots were covered with mud.

"Not out of bed?" Mama said, laughing. "Since when have you known me to stay abed past sunrise?" She opened the door wider to let her older son in.

Richard ran to his brother and jumped into his arms. "Oliver!"

"And what have we here?" said Oliver. "A naked savage?"

"Mama took all my clothes!" Richard grumbled, scratching his behind.

"Washing day, is it?" Oliver set the two grouse down on the floor and turned Richard upside down, making him squeal with delight.

Mama laughed. "And a fine day it is for it," she said, brushing again at that pesky piece of hair that had fallen into her face. "I don't know where it's hotter, inside or out. These clothes ought to dry even before I've done washing them in this August heat. If you want, Oliver, I'll do your clothes now too. That will be less for Anne when she goes to do the yearly wash, which she told me she was to undertake this month also."

"Come on, Oliver," Richard said. "We can sit here naked together."

Oliver shook his head. "It's a lovely invitation, little brother, but I'll not give Mama more work," he said. "Anne can handle washing my clothes."

"Aye," Mama said. "She is a good wife to you, Oliver. I just thought that by doing the task for her, we might hold you prisoner for a while and have a good talk while your clothes were drying."

Oliver's smile faded. "Are you that lonely, Mother? I haven't been around lately, I'm afraid."

"Tsk, tsk," Mama said, clicking her tongue against the roof of her mouth. "I didn't mean to make you feel guilty, Oliver. Richard and I have been getting along just fine. I only meant that I'd enjoy the company while I finished."

"Stay, Oliver," Richard begged. "I'm tired of talking to Mama all the time. She only talks about women's stuff."

Oliver laughed. "Well, we certainly need to remedy that, don't we, little brother? And so it's company you'll have. I'll pluck these two grouse I brought you both while Mama adds my clothes to your pile."

Oliver stepped inside and shut the door.

"Hurray!" shouted Richard.

"I'll get us some beer," Mama said.

"A party," Oliver said, laughing, as he began taking off his clothes.

Mama walked toward the back of the house, in the lee of the roof, where they stored the items they wanted to keep cool. Oliver stripped off everything but his long linen shirt and sat down in a chair, where he began plucking the feathers from the grouse.

"When will you take me hunting with you, Oliver?" Richard asked, leaning against his brother, who smelled of woods and dirt. Richard wished he could smell like that too.

"When you are big enough," replied Oliver.

"I'm big enough now. Look at my muscles," Richard said, making a fist and showing Oliver the strength of his arm.

Oliver reached out a hand and gave it a squeeze. "You're right, Richard. Perhaps you are ready. I will take you with me next time I go."

Richard stared at his older brother. Was Oliver teasing him? Would he really take Richard with him? Richard had been begging forever. Hope rose tight in his chest.

Mama came back into the front room with two mugs.

"What is making you smile so, Mother?" Oliver asked.

"I was remembering seeing you unclothed just now, but a bit smaller," Mama replied. "My, Oliver, when did you get so big and handsome?"

"You see," Richard grumbled, "I told you she just talks women stuff all the time."

Oliver laughed. "She may talk women's stuff, Richard, but she is the loveliest mother on both sides of the Thames."

Richard scowled. Oliver was being silly. His mother was his mother. Mothers weren't lovely. They were just mothers.

Mama picked up Oliver's clothes from the wooden floor and dropped them into the laundry pot. She went to lift the pot from the fire, to pour the boiling water over the clothes. But Oliver was quickly at her side. He lifted the pot for her, pouring the water and then returning the water left to the fire.

"Thank you," Mama said, stirring the clothes in the hot water. She took a bar of lye soap and began to scrub. The water sloshed over the laundry pot, soaking the wooden floorboards. Richard felt content just sitting there with Oliver and Mama working.

"Oliver said he would take me hunting next time he goes," Richard spoke up, wanting to bring the subject back to what was near and dear to his heart and wanting to be sure Oliver had truly meant it.

Mama's head came up. "You are too young yet for that, Richard."

"I am not," Richard protested. "I've been practicing my shot, Mama. I can hit most things dead on from fifty feet away with my bow and arrow."

"Richard's right," Oliver said softly, still plucking the grouse. "He's ready. You can't hold on to him forever, you know, Mother."

Richard loved his older brother! If Johnny were here, he would have agreed with Mama, not because he didn't think Richard could do it, but because he wouldn't have wanted to bother dragging Richard along. Oliver was the best brother ever!

Mama sighed. "You will watch over him, if you take him?"

Oliver nodded. "Aye, Mother. That I promise."

Richard couldn't believe his ears. At last, he was to go hunting. He jumped up and danced about the room. "Can we go tomorrow?" he asked his brother eagerly.

"No, Richard," said Mama. "It will be a while yet. Oliver was obviously out this week."

"When then?" Richard asked impatiently.

Oliver laughed. "In a few weeks, little brother. Thomas and I got quite a bit this time out."

"Ah," Mama said, stopping her scrubbing, "Thomas."

"Mama doesn't like Thomas," Richard told his older brother, trying to mask his disappointment over not going sooner and yet hold on to the glory of knowing that next time, he would accompany him.

Oliver smiled. "I know Mama doesn't like him, Richard. That's because he was always getting me into trouble when I was younger."

"What kind of trouble?" Richard asked. He loved

hearing stories about his brothers when they were his age. Oliver and Johnny had been quite unruly.

"Trouble like the time Thomas made you steal eggs from Farmer Burton's farm," Mama said sharply.

Oliver laughed so hard he sent feathers flying everywhere. "Oh, Mother, I'd forgotten that."

He turned toward his little brother. "Richard, you should have seen Mama standing there that day, whipping up the eggs I had brought home, thinking I had gotten them at the market with the money she'd given me, when I had actually gambled the money away on a game of marbles with Thomas. And Farmer Burton came storming in. And he made Mama so mad, insisting that I had stolen the eggs, that I was a good-for-nothing tramp, that she dumped those eggs right over his head. And while he was standing there, with egg dripping down his face, I told Mama, all red-faced, that Thomas had dared me to steal them and that I *had*. And Father came in and laughed himself silly over the whole affair."

Richard giggled.

Mama laughed too. "It felt good to dump those eggs over that self-righteous old goat!"

"And he did look funny with those eggs dripping in his eyes," Oliver said, his deep, hearty laughter filling the room.

"Mama almost threw a tomato at Mistress Howley a few weeks ago," Richard told Oliver.

"Did you now, Mother?" Oliver asked, grinning.

"I didn't do it," Mama reminded Richard. "I remembered my lesson from Farmer Burton and stopped."

"Well you should have," Richard said to her. "She said mean things about Papa and Johnny. Next time, I'll do it for you."

"You will not, young man," Mama said, pulling out Richard's britches, wringing them out over the pot and laying them on a line by the fire.

"Maybe I'll help you, Richard," Oliver said. "That woman is nasty."

"And she looks like a crow," added Richard.

Mama stood up and made a face. "No more of this nonsense, you two. Oliver, you'll encourage him, and Richard's naughty enough. Besides, how would it look for a successful young mapmaker to the king to be in trouble for throwing tomatoes at the elderly?"

"It would look like I was defending my king's appointed explorer from his most critical of subjects," Oliver said, grinning.

Mama laughed as she lifted Oliver's clothes out and wrung them dry. "A wonderful way to twist words, son, but one I think the king would not find to his liking."

"Do you like clothes when they are newly cleaned, Oliver?" Richard asked, watching his mother.

"No," answered Oliver. "But I believe girls like them better that way."

"Who cares about girls?" Richard grumbled. "I hate clean clothes. They don't fit good. They scratch and won't bend properly. They're much better dirty."

Oliver laughed. "I agree. But unfortunately, Richard, we both live with girls, so we must give ourselves over to their clean habits. At least it's but once a year."

He turned to Mama. "Do you remember the time John got the idea that we should run away rather than have ourselves stripped and cleaned?"

"I remember. Your father searched for hours for you

two," Mama said. "I was sure you had drowned in the Thames. John was forever running down near the river when he wasn't supposed to. Like you, young man," she added, sitting down and giving Richard a stern look.

"What happened, Oliver?" asked Richard, looking up at his brother.

"We had hidden in Steven Barrow's wagon, under the hay," Oliver said. "And we would have escaped if John hadn't gotten the hiccups."

Mama began laughing. "Oh, aye. Steven came here, dragging the two of you by the ears. He had been on his way to Oxford. It would have been many days before we would have seen you again had John not given you away."

Oliver chuckled. "I wouldn't talk to John for weeks after that, I was so mad."

Richard laughed too.

"Aren't memories wonderful things?" Mama said, sighing.

She looked out the tiny diamond-shaped window of the room. "I love memories. I love the memories of you three, here at home, growing up. I love the memories of being with your father."

She grew quiet. "I pray I'll have more memories."

"I miss Johnny and his pranks," Richard put in, suddenly feeling a strange sadness.

"Aye, I miss him too," Oliver said softly. "He was always stopping by early in the evening for a quick pint before he took off for the night."

Mama's eyebrows raised in a question. "You and John have grown quite close now that you're older, Oliver, and John no longer complains about washing. In fact, he'll be begging for a good cleaning when he gets home. You wouldn't know for whom he'd be so anxious, do you?"

Oliver's face reddened a bit. Richard knew, but he was holding his tongue.

"Who is it?" Mama asked. "I can see you both know."

Richard pressed his lips together. Johnny had promised him a farthing if he kept the secret. *He* wasn't going to tell.

"I don't know if he's courting her, Mother," Oliver said. "He hasn't said anything. It may be nothing."

"Who was it, Oliver?" Mama asked again.

"He was only walking her home when I saw them once."

"Home where?" Mama persisted.

"Thorton Hall," Oliver admitted.

"The young Isabella?" Mama exclaimed. "That's absurd. The girl's father would never permit John Hudson, a sailor, to take on his only daughter. He would kill John first." Mama's face creased with worry.

"John can handle himself, Mother," Oliver reassured her. "You mustn't fret."

Richard sighed. He knew that was impossible. Now Mama would be all grumpy with concern. Telling Mama not to worry was like trying to stop rain. And Richard hoped that this stupid girl Johnny had walked home wasn't going to be more trouble than a storm brewing on the horizon. But somehow, he doubted it.

ISABELLA DIGGES

August 12, 1610

   At last! I have discovered it! The map room!

   It was only by accident that I stumbled upon it. I had gone for a long ride early this morning. It was a magnificent day, the sun just rising and clearing out a gray morning mist. My horse was as restless as I felt. I barely needed to touch his flanks, and he was gone. He galloped hard across the flat landscape that surrounds the Von Dectmers' house, and I bent over his mane and let the wind sweep away all the thoughts of John Hudson that have been plaguing my dream-filled sleep of late.

   When I returned, my skin was burnt from the sun, and I felt as if I was glowing as brightly as a star on a clear night. I must have looked glorious, for I felt so.

   I threw the reins to the stable boy and hurried off toward my duties with the Von Dectmer girl. Even this seemed less a burden today, so lovely was I feeling from the freedom of that thrilling ride.

   I came round a corner in the back hallway of the house

and ran straight into a tall, well-built young man about my age coming out of a room. His sudden appearance startled me, and I let out a small shriek of surprise. He jumped too.

I remember putting my hand to my heart to still the faint I felt was about to come over me and saying something like, "I did not see you there."

"Nor I you," he replied softly. His glance swept over me.

I looked beyond him, for I had never before noticed the space from which he was leaving. I knew in a flash that this was the very room I had been searching for.

The young man saw my look. Quickly, he reached behind him and shut the door, locking it firmly and sliding the key into the left pocket of his breeches. He turned back around.

"Emil Von Dectmer," he said, bowing low to me.

I knew then who he was. My young charge's nineteen-year-old brother. The one who had been traveling in Italy.

I told him my name and offered him my hand.

He bent over and turned my hand until it was palm up. Then he lowered his lips and kissed my wrist.

"I am afraid you are still suffering from the shock," he said, looking up at me and smiling, "for your pulse is beating quite rapidly, Miss Digges."

Slowly, I withdrew my hand. The boy was incorrigible. I liked that about him.

He offered me his arm and asked where I was headed to in such a hurry. I told him that I was on my way to be with his sister and that I was her new companion. I slipped my arm into his as I said this.

"Lucky sister," he whispered to me, and I graced him with a small smile.

As we began to walk, he inquired if I was enjoying my time here.

"Oh, yes," I replied, knowing full well what I was about to

imply. "The Von Dectmer household offers many fascinating diversions, and it seems to be growing more interesting every day." I squeezed his arm.

Emil threw back his head and laughed. And I knew I had him.

Before lunch, a courier came with a letter from my father. As I had suspected, the king was in a furor when my father gave him the information on James Dits. He will jail Dits before he lets him sail for the Dutch! Yet my father went on to complain that he was dismissed immediately after delivering the news, without even a word of thanks. I laughed. Those days would be over in a very short time. It would not be long before I would be sending information that would be worth the king's palace itself in gold. We would be welcomed gladly at court once more, and my father could ask the king for an introduction to the wealthy duchess. I hugged myself with delight.

Then I sat upon the settee and once more, in my head, went over the system my father and I have designed to help me memorize and then redraw the maps when I get a look at them. Our system is most ingenious, if I do say so myself. It is really quite clever. We have taken the rooms of our house, and I have memorized the furniture by room, going around piece by piece. Then after setting my eyes upon a map, I relate the lines of it and the markers by associating each object on the map with a piece of furniture within our estate. My father worked tirelessly with me on the system before I left. And he was amazed at how quick to remember and slow to forget I was, even after he showed me map after map of his own and made me memorize and redraw each of them. Truly, he thinks women little more than ornamentation. But in that, I will prove him and all others wrong.

And so I work my mind around our rooms one more time. For one can never be too careful when enacting a plan of this *magnitude, and the more I practice, the more I will ensure my own safety and lessen the chances of being caught for a spy.*

And in an hour or so, I will put on my best dress and go down to dinner with Emil. I will swirl my skirts and flash this boy a look. And when I have him ready to do my bidding, I will suggest we retire to the room he was leaving just this morning so as to have some privacy in this house. I am pleased. This task may not be as unpleasant as I had anticipated. And too, with eyes and a face as handsome as Emil's, perhaps I may no longer need a long gallop across wide meadows to forget Johnny Hudson.

SETH SYMS

❧ ❧

September 15, 1610

Dearest Mama:

And now I have head lice. Lord, I would have been kicked out of every decent house in London if I'd smelled the way I do now and looked the way I imagine I do and had the lice I have. I swear they crawl night and day as if they got nothing else to do. And I guess if yer a lice on a boat a million miles from any dry land, that is all ye got to occupy yerself. But I sure as heck wish they'd get their exercise off of somebody else's head.

I pick at them all day. The boys laugh at me. Say it's not worth the effort. Soon as I get rid of some, others will come. But I just scratch and scratch and feel like poking me head in a kettle of boiling water. Yesterday, John said he'd get dinner for me. And then he handed me a plate full of nits. I jumped up so fast, I upset the entire table. Oh, the crew got a great laugh from that.

Remember me young, Mama? All the other boys loved

the mud and muck—not me. I happened to like being clean, liked the smell of soap on a body. Ye washed me often, more than any other boy around me. But heck, I grew to like it.

Mama, ye would faint if ye saw the state I'm in now. Bet ye wouldn't even let me through the door if I even got meself back to good old England's shores. Ye'd probably make me strip naked out in the street and bring a pot with boiling water out the door for me to soak in before ye'd even start to crying and weeping about how happy ye was to finally set yer old eyes on yer boy again. Ain't I thought on this these past few days and nights of crawling so slow-like through these icy waters?

For that's what we've been in these last days: thick fog, giant walls of ice, and big pieces of the stuff floating all around this here ship. How can I tell ye the fear I felt deep in me gut seeing those great blocks of ice yesterday, blocks that could crush this ship to pieces, and me not being able to see where we was sailing?

I was on watch three times yesterday. Each time was like some kind of nightmare. I stood on the bow, peering out into the fog, straining to be sure that our boat didn't suddenly ram into an iceberg and send us all to a quick and watery death.

The stillness of it all almost drove me mad. Twelve hours ago, I was peering off into the dark, when on me right side, out of nowhere, rose a great wall of ice. I yelled and pointed, me heart in me throat. At the very last minute, the boat turned, and we slid slowly and silently past that great iceberg—with its whiteness and eerie blue color deep inside it. I watched it as we passed, that hard, cold block of ice seeming to make fun out of our smallness.

'Course now, a few hours later, it ain't so bad. We found this little pass, and Captain Hudson sailed our boat right on through it. There was still them big walls of ice on either side, but when we got through that pass, up ahead was open, ice-free sea. Now at last when I stand watch, I ain't got the creeps no more worrying that some big wall of ice is gonna sink us to the bottom of the clear blue. Now, at least it seems we actually might have found a free way to the East. And everyone else is in better spirits too, the mood of the boat going up and down like the waves around us, depending on the conditions.

Philip and me got ourselves a routine now that seems to relieve some of the boredom of this hole. When we aren't on duty, we go back to our whittling together. I made a figure of Elizabeth yesterday. It's nothing much to speak of, but Philip says it's a good first time, and at least it's some girl to feast me eyes on. Philip showed me how to better shape the nose and mouth.

John, when he comes upon us doing our carving, laughs at me, says could I whittle him a pint? I told him he ought to try carving that Issa of his, he thinks on her so much. But he says no, his girl ain't no cold wooden maiden. He says he's got her and all the sights he sees on these adventures right there in that head of his, and he'll share all them sights with her when he returns. I asked him if he'd go to her unbathed, then she could share in the smells of the voyage too. He laughed at me, and I had to laugh back. He's a good sort.

And so I have to admit, Mama, there is something awful beautiful about being out on a boat. There's this kind of awe-inspiring power in the world around you and the movement of yerself over the waters. Tonight, I sit on the deck and listen to the waves slap our bow, this here boat moving forward fast with the wind. And I see them stars above me, so many of them, it about takes your breath away. It ain't so bad, Mama. Not all of it. Nah, not all of it at all.

Yer son, Seth

JOHN HUDSON

E ven I cannot find any humor in the situation we find
ourselves in today. And to think how well the day
started—with a fine wind and a clear October sky.

Two days ago, I had at last convinced Father to turn
back. We have not found the way to the East—at least not
unless the East is cold and frozen, and I have been told this
is not the case. But we have found much territory that is
new and unexplored, and our discovery of it will be
warmly received at home—I am sure of it.

For weeks, I have been telling Father that. And for a
while, he would have none of it, but continued day after
day searching for that passage east like a woman who has
lost a piece of precious jewelry.

We didn't make it. So? We did not make it the last three
journeys either but were welcomed when we returned
with what we had discovered. And, too, I reminded Father,
Mother would at least be happy to see him. At that, he did
soften a bit. I saw the chink, and I worked days to widen
it. Until at last, I put down my foot and told him I would

run him through with my sword if we didn't turn and head back to London.

He laughed. "And are you so good with a sword now, young John?"

"Aye," I said.

Whereupon I drew my sword to show him, and he, smiling a bit, drew his also. It was quite fun to send my father scurrying up on tables and across chairs. His eyes widened at my newfound ability. Little did he know that I have been practicing daily with the king's men—times when I was to be collecting supplies and helping Mother about the house. With Father's intelligence, he will soon work that one out, and I will be in trouble again. But no matter now. The swordplay was delightful.

But Father is good, and I was unable to pin him. At last, sweating and laughing, he called a draw. And upon wiping his brow, he nodded. "All right, lad," he said. "You win. We head home today."

And so we turned back, and sailed smooth and clear for two days. And then an hour or so ago, I was below when I heard the commotion abovedecks. I scampered up the rope ladder to see what the yelling was about. And it was then that I noticed it. The boat had come to a halt, and its sails hung listlessly, flapping in the wind.

"What hails?" I'd asked Nicholas, whose face was whiter than I have ever imagined a complexion could be.

"We can't get out, they say," he whispered. His voice was trembling, and I knew it to be serious. Nicholas thinks on himself as a man without courage, but I believe that deep down, he is a man who will face what he has to, though I am still in the dark as to who he truly is. That he has not revealed yet, and I wonder sometimes if he has killed a man. I mean to discover the truth about him before this journey is through. If he has murdered someone, it will make for a most interesting story!

I ran across the boat and climbed to the bow, where my father stood.

"Is the way blocked?" I said.

He simply stood there, just seemed to be pondering.

I looked ahead, and yes, there was nothing but ice.

"There is no way out," my father said softly. "We have sailed both sides."

"We can take tools and chip our way out, then," I suggested.

Father bit his lip. "Philip says the ice is already too thick for this remedy."

"We can haul everything across the ice," I said.

My father shook his head. "Too far."

"Then what is your plan?" I asked impatiently.

"Wait for the thaw," he said shortly, and then turned toward his cabin.

My heart stopped at these words. Surely, he hadn't meant them. Was he saying we were *trapped*? *Trapped here?*

I ran after Father, catching him as he entered his cabin. He took down a decanter of sherry, poured himself a glass, and drank deeply of it.

"Are you saying," I said slowly, "that we may be here till spring?"

He turned and looked at me. Never have I seen such seriousness in my father's eyes. "If we are lucky," he replied.

"What does that mean?" I asked.

He poured another drink, and I noticed that his hand

shook as he raised the glass to down it quickly. "I have heard it said that some springs do not warm enough for a thaw, and that this place stays cold then until the following spring."

"So what will you have us do?" I asked.

My father laughed shortly. "Pray for a hot summer," he said.

I left him then and went to the rail. Below me, the men stood, staring out at the frozen sea. All seemed lost in their dismal thoughts. Then Juet looked up. His eyes met mine, and they were filled with hatred. How could I blame him? Though Father had recently demoted him from mate over his disgruntled comments to the crew, in this he had the right to his anger.

Never had we had this happen. Never! In the past, Father has always been too careful. Other ships had faced this. Not many, but the few that had told stories of horror—of starving, death, and despair. It is one thing for me to die gallantly—shot by a savage, drowned in a storm. It is another to die slowly from starvation and cold. How impossible!

I made my way below and fell miserably into my bunk. I must have slept an hour or so, waking from a delicious dream of Isabella to the horror of our condition. If we cannot discover a way out, we will be here months. We will linger in this dark, cold place with only one another for company. I will wake to this same mind-numbing spot day after day.

I cannot let this happen to me. I cannot let it happen to the others. I must think on a solution. There has to be a way out of this horrendous situation. There must be! And I am determined to find it!

RICHARD HUDSON

*W**hat*, Richard wondered, as he came into his room and found his mother on her knees with her head under his bed, *is she doing?*

"Mama?" he said tentatively, coming up behind her.

His mother started, banging her head hard against the bottom of the bed as she quickly scooted out.

"What are you looking for?" Richard asked.

"Nothing," said Mama, wincing as she put a hand to her head, but she spoke it a little too casually. Grown-ups always thought they were fooling kids. But Richard knew better.

"You must have been looking for something," he persisted.

"I was chasing a mouse," Mama replied.

"Where is he?" Richard said, getting down on his knees. "I'll get him for you, Mama. I'm a good mouse catcher."

He scooted under the rope bed. "And then I can keep him, can't I? If I catch him for you, can I keep him for a pet?"

Richard looked around for the mouse. The floor was dusty under here, and there was the big trunk of Johnny's that took up much of the space. But there was no sign of anything scurrying about. Richard sighed. He would have liked to have had a pet mouse.

Mama bent over. "Where are you, little one?" she said. "Have you disappeared on me completely?"

"No," Richard answered. "But I don't see anything, Mama. He must have escaped."

"Then come on out from under there."

"But I like it here," Richard said. And he did.

"How could you possibly like it in the dark and dust under that bed?" Mama asked.

"Because it's quiet."

"Richard," Mama said slowly, "as long as you are there, can you pull out Johnny's trunk?"

"Why, Mama?" Richard asked curiously.

"I just want to look at something," Mama told him.

"It's locked, Mama," Richard told her.

"I have a key."

Obediently, Richard reached back and pulled the trunk toward the light, finally pushing it out from under the bed and climbing out himself. Mama took a piece of her skirt in her hand and began to clean his face. "Look at how filthy you are," she declared.

Richard yanked his head away impatiently. He looked at the trunk. "I don't know if Johnny will like you going in there. Did he give you that key?"

"No," Mama said. "It was in your father's drawer. The trunk used to be Papa's before he gave it to Johnny."

"What do you want to see?" asked Richard, as he

watched his mother insert the key into the keyhole. The lock sprang open.

"Just the logs, Richard," his mother said.

Richard shrugged. Johnny probably wouldn't care about those old logs. He was always complaining when Papa made him write in them, anyway. Papa had threatened to leave Johnny behind if he didn't agree to do them. So Johnny had, though he told Richard they were bloody boring to keep.

Mama opened the lid of the trunk. Richard peered inside. Johnny had never let him see what he kept in there. The scent of salt and sea rose into the air. Richard swallowed hard. That smell always made him think of his brother and Papa. They had been gone a very long time, five months, Mama said.

"Hey!" Richard exclaimed, reaching into the chest. "There's the marble I gave Johnny for Christmas. That was my only yellow one, and he didn't even take it with him!"

Mama smiled. "He stowed it away, Richard. Johnny probably wanted to keep it safe. If it had rolled off the boat, it would have been lost to the sea forever."

"Maybe," Richard muttered, feeling a bit appeased.

"Look at this," said Mama, holding up a tin whistle. "Oh, how I remember your brother playing this thing incessantly when he was younger. And I remember praying that it would magically disappear."

"It did, Mama, "Richard said, laughing. "It disappeared into Johnny's trunk."

"So it did," Mama agreed.

"Look, Mama, there's the little wooden boat Papa made for Johnny. I asked and asked him if I could have it, and he said he'd lost it."

"If you want one that badly, Richard," Mama said, "I'll ask Papa to make you one when he gets home."

"Really?"

Mama nodded.

"Could he make the sails nicer than those?" Richard asked, looking at the old boat.

"Oh, Richard." Mama laughed. "Those sails just look tattered because the moths have eaten them."

"Johnny should be more careful," Richard said solemnly. "I would be if Papa made me a boat to float in the pond."

"Good for you," Mama said.

Richard bent back over the trunk. "That's it, Mama," he said, "except for Johnny's logs." He was disappointed. He had believed there would be something fantastical in there, since Johnny guarded and locked the trunk.

"Hand that log to me, will you, Richard?" Mama asked.

Richard lifted up the one his mother had pointed to.

"Don't know why you want to look in them," he said, handing her the book. "They're just writing."

"But Johnny has been using them, hasn't he," Mama asked, "even when he's home?"

"Yes," Richard said, rolling his eyes, thinking of how his brother had yelled at him when Richard had tried to see what he was writing.

He moved closer to his mother, hoping she wouldn't notice. He was curious now about what was in those journals Johnny had been so bent on keeping secret, especially since now Mama wanted to look at them too. He read the first page. The writing Johnny had done there was about their last trip on the *Half Moon*.

What an exciting voyage that had been! Richard still felt disappointed that he had been too young to go on that trip. The crew had actually attacked real savages! It had sounded like a fearsome fight, but Johnny and Papa had argued long and hard about it when they returned. Johnny accused Papa of paying his charts too much attention and letting the crew go unchecked. Papa had told Johnny that his mission had been to find the Northwest Passage, not to worry about the actions of his crew. Johnny had stomped away in a huff.

Richard didn't know who was right, but he had heard people talking lately. They said Papa was obsessed with this quest, and that his obsession was going to be his downfall. Richard wasn't sure what downfall meant, but it didn't sound good.

Mama drew in her breath as she turned a page of the log. Carefully, Richard looked over her shoulder again.

Isabella—pages and pages with Isabella's name all over them. Richard rolled his eyes. What did Johnny see in girls? They were nothing but trouble, in Richard's opinion, and he thought of Alice.

Richard snorted his annoyance, and Mama looked up, shutting the book quickly.

"What's the matter?" he asked.

"You shouldn't be reading that," said Mama.

"Just boring stuff about a girl," Richard said.

Mama sighed. "A girl your brother has no right to think on."

"Why ever not?" Richard asked.

"Her father would run your brother through with a sword before he'd agree to John marrying his daughter."

"Why would Johnny marry her?" Richard said disgustedly. "And why would her father care? Wouldn't he be glad to get rid of her?"

Mama laughed. "Do you think my papa was glad to get rid of me?"

"Of course not, Mama," Richard said, scowling. "What a silly question."

"Well, you'll understand when you're older, Richard, but you can't just marry whomever you like."

"I'm not marrying at all," Richard stated. "So you won't have to worry about me getting run through with a sword. Besides, I'm going to be so good at dueling that no one would be able to best me anyway!"

Mama smiled. "I shall hope that to be true, little one."

She put the book back in the trunk, laying the whistle, boat, and marble back on top. She closed the lid and locked it, pushing the trunk back under the bed. Mama sat for a moment, looking wistful.

Richard suspected that his mother probably shouldn't have been looking through Johnny's things, even if it was just writing about a stupid girl. He could tell that now she was feeling badly about it.

"Mama," he said, sitting down next to her on the floor, "if I tell you a secret, do you promise not to tell?"

Mama nodded. "I promise."

"I hide under there sometimes when Johnny is in the room," he revealed, hoping that telling her this would make her feel better.

"You do?" Mama asked.

Richard nodded. "I can't see much," he said. "Only Johnny's feet, but I can hear him humming and brushing his hair. And once, when he was in here, he was singing a bawdy song. It was awful, but I liked it a lot. And then his voice went real high. He's not a good singer, Mama."

Mama laughed. "No, I agree he's not, Richard."

Richard propped his chin onto his hands. "He puts on a lot of lavender water lately. I hate the smell of it."

"Do you? It didn't make you want to leave your hiding spot?"

Richard scowled. Was Mama daft? "Of course not! Then Johnny would know that I was there." He sighed. "I miss Johnny."

Mama reached out her arms to him and pulled him onto her lap. He laid his head on her chest, felt it rising and falling with each breath she took.

"I miss him too, Richard," Mama said softly. "I miss him too."

ISABELLA DIGGES

October 31, 1610

    *The candle before me is but a stub as I write this entry
with a hurried hand. It is late, and I have been hours redrawing
the map I saw tonight. As I worked, my heart was thankful to
my dead mother for employing a drawing teacher for me at the
tender age of twelve. For while it is right and proper that a
young woman of property should take up the pencil and brush
as a genteel hobby, my father was against it, both for the cost
and for the fact that the tutor was Spanish and not English-
born. Yet Mother insisted. And now, due to the Spaniard's
tutelage, the drawings of the Dutch East Indies map I
have just sealed to send to my father are truly magnificent
in detail!*

    *I almost laughed when I found how easy it was to look over
Emil's shoulder as he pulled me to him and to memorize the
maps that spilled about me in that locked room.*

    When I had been too long staring and Emil grew restless,

a demure kiss and a sworn oath of love quickly put him back in my sway.

I will admit, he is not a particularly good kisser, nor very good with verses of love. He is lazy and arrogant, assured of his charm. But this matters little. For the Diggeses are back in the good graces of the king, and for that, I would lie to Emil about the cleverness of his tongue until the devil himself plucked my own from me.

For we are there, risen once again. My father is mad with the success, writing me daily, as our situation grows more and more assured. Upon receipt of the first map, he immediately took the drawings to court and insisted on an audience with the king. It took a bit of begging to the warden outside His Majesty's door and a promise of coins, which we could hardly spare. Yet that was a small matter compared with the king's reaction when he saw what my father had brought. His Majesty was astounded that I, Isabella Digges, had been able to memorize and redraw that Dutch map so accurately.

The king sent at once for the young mapmaker, Oliver Hudson, son of Henry and brother to John. Oliver Hudson bent over the map I had sent, growing increasingly excited when he became aware of new areas of which England had had no knowledge. He left with my map straightaway in order to make copies for all of our explorers so that they may have access to this valuable information. And when Oliver Hudson had taken his leave, the king beckoned my father to him. He asked my father to attend court more often, saying he had missed seeing him there. And he asked my father to accompany him to Hampton Court within a fortnight, for he wished my father to teach him the memory techniques he has taught me.

As if he could use them in the same clever manner that I

*have! But what does it matter? For with the invite came an
order for coins from the treasury! My father went immediately
and paid off the worst of our creditors and has sent me a new
dress of blue silk. Emil will be enthralled when he sees me in it,
which may allow me the leisure to memorize more than one
map a night. With two maps being conveyed to His Majesty,
perhaps the king will entertain my father's request for an
introduction to the wealthy duchess.*

*Ah, I was pleased with myself and with the tone of my
father's letter to me, for he was most grateful, as he should be.
But in the last of his paragraphs, he did question me about
John Hudson, saying that Oliver Hudson had inquired about
my health and whereabouts in a tone my father found too
familiar. He reminded me that John Hudson is beneath my
station and unsuitable for me. He asked what promises I had
made the Hudson son.*

*Oh, my anger rose then. How could my father, after my
having risked life and limb for his sake, have the audacity to
ask me about my relationship with John Hudson? Was it not
his plan in the first place for me to seek him out and spy
upon him? Was it not his worry that Captain Hudson would
not follow the plan he and the other investors had determined
upon, that made him send me as his secret envoy?*

*And can I help the fact that in spying on John Hudson I
found a boy whose temperament and desire for life matched my
own? A boy whose broad shoulders and humor make Emil look
like a half-wit when I am with him? Can I help a heart that
seems bent on keeping John Hudson close even as my mind
reasons him away?*

*Oh, these foolish thoughts irritate me no end. Can I not
just revel in my success? Can I not just toast myself for being*

the clever spy I am? Can I not plot and plan for the next day's adventures in the map room without feeling guilt over what has been said and done?

No, I will think no longer upon my father's complaints. Instead, I will concentrate on the situation I have created and the future success I plan on achieving. For I, Isabella Digges, am intent on being known forever as the greatest spy England has ever produced!

SETH SYMS

⁓◯ ◯⁓

November 1, 1610
Dearest Mama:

How quickly yer fortune can change on a boat! Today
we dropped anchor. And while I know that might sound
like good news to you, believe me, it ain't. I've certainly
waited long enough for the sound of that chain splashing
into them waters and the clunk as it hit the bottom and the
steadiness of a boat that has come to shore at last. But
unfortunately, it ain't exactly some celebratory occasion.
All the men, me included, stood out on the bow of the boat
and tried to muster some sense of happiness at the end of
trying for weeks to sail through them frozen ice and floes
we've been in, without getting ourselves crushed to death,
but we just couldn't. Dropping anchor meant only one
thing—we was trapped in this ungodly place. We'd hoped
the ice might melt just a little, enough to let us out.
But no luck.

Young John piped up, "Not to worry. We'll get out of this
fix," but he quickly shut his mouth when he saw the rest of

the crew's sour looks. Poor kid. He's trying. But I mean, really, who was he fooling?

I looked around me before they lowered the small boat to take Philip and Abacuk Prickett onshore to find some place to shelter up for the winter. There's good enough hills surrounding us, I guess. Their sides are high, even if they are snow- and ice-covered. I mean, I ain't never had to spend no winter in some desolate place on a wooden boat, but if I had to do it, I guess I would have chosen this spot. It seems safe enough to weather storms, snow, ice, or whatever else we might have to expect over the next few months. It's the "whatever" that gives me the shivers sometimes.

I went down to me bunk afterward and tried to catch a few winks, but me heart felt kind of numb. I liked keeping busy with work, as it kept me mind off our present situation. But seeing as we're now stuck for the winter in this here harbor, there ain't much to do in the way of the boat and sailing things. And so me mind kept traveling back to the thoughts that made me mouth go dry. We were trapped, trapped in this here lonely, cold place. The horror of that thought kept making me want to puke, something I ain't done in weeks. What if we run out of food and supplies? What if we run into one of them creatures they call polar bears, with teeth they say are the size of your hand? These very thoughts sent me to shivering and shaking so much that I slept little, and at last, I was called to the watch again.

I went up to find the men walking around, doing their few chores and not looking at one another much. The despair is so thick, ye could of cut it up as if it was a side of beef. I didn't say nothing, just set about doing some small repair work on a torn jib, when who should saunter by me and sit down but none other than old Robert Juet. He leans over today and whispers into me ear, real snaky-like. "And so we are here now, stuck as it is, and all because Captain Hudson did not think of our concerns first, eh, mate?"

I guess we should have turned back a while ago. And I guess the captain, seeing all that ice building up, should have known that. But I thought, *Why think on things past? What's done is done. And you've already been reprimanded for such talk.* I looked at him but didn't say nothing. I just went right on with me mending as if the guy was a ghost.

It wasn't that I wanted to anger him. He wasn't the kind of guy ye wanted angry with ye. I just didn't want to get involved with no scheme of his. I may be trapped on this boat, but I ain't gone that daft yet. No, Seth Syms is out to watch out over one person and one person alone—and that person is me. I ain't about to get caught up in something that might just get me thrown in the brig.

"Ah," Juet whispered, "not much to say, I see. Well, ye go and think on it all this winter, me lad. When the food runs out and yer hands are frostbit, maybe ye'll be able to see me point of view just a wee bit better."

I still said nothing, just hawked and spit over the side of the boat.

He patted me on the back and then rose. "Think on it, Mr. Syms. Think on it."

I did think on it. I thought that I had just better keep me

head on this one. That guy was up to no good, and I wasn't about to be a part of it. He would land in the brig and be brought up on charges when we got back. And while he was there, he'd be the last one fed, being out of favor and all. Nah, I was staying quiet, keeping me head low. I wasn't about to join forces with that dark one.

I heard a noise out on the ice and rose then to see Philip and Abacuk returning from their scouting venture. I watched as they climbed up onto the deck of our boat. Captain Hudson came from his cabin and stood on the bridge. John was with him. He looked about as unhappy as an innkeeper low on ale.

Philip Staffe yelled up to the captain that there weren't no place out there for shelter. The men around, me included, let out a collective groan. His findings meant we was stuck trying to make do on this here wooden ice raft for the while.

I saw the captain frown, knew it didn't bode well. He questioned Philip again about what he'd seen.

Philip shrugged, then told the captain that there weren't nothing but marsh and mud and stunted trees that even God couldn't build nothing with. He weren't worried or nervous. He was just accepting that this was the way it was going to be. Ye could see it in his eyes and the way he went about bringing his gear in from the shallop as if it were the most natural thing in the world. Even if he hadn't been so nice to me these days on the boat, I would have liked him then. He was just so calm-like.

"Well, there's got to be something out there to build with," the captain roared out, surprising us all.

Abacuk spoke up then. He shook his head and said that there weren't nothing there, just like the carpenter said.

Now, he didn't look as calm as old Philip. No, Abacuk's eyes were wide with this frightened look, like he was the only seal in a sea of whales.

The captain hit his hand hard against the rail of the bridge and then turned abruptly and went back to his cabin. It weren't hard to see that he was none too happy with the news just delivered. But then neither were any of us. But I did feel kind of sorry for the captain then. It couldn't be easy being the man in charge of this mess.

Only Robert Juet seemed satisfied. He turned, this big old smug look on his face. His eyes met mine. His mouth didn't turn up into no smile, but his eyes said he was laughing on the inside. It made me sick.

I went to the rail and began helping Philip haul his things back down below. John joined us there.

"Really nothing?" John asked, hoping, I guessed, that maybe Philip might say that if he tried really hard he might be able to work some kind of shelter up, but the carpenter shook his head.

"How are we going to survive?" I asked. I hadn't meant it to come out all squeaky-sounding, but I guess I was more scared than I had thought. I mean, Mama, I sure do like being a man and all, but I ain't much for the survival thing. And though I'd challenge any man to say I was a pansy, I will admit to being a mite less adventurous than the men who surrounded me there.

Philip stood and smiled kindly at me. His mouth, unlike

Juet's, matched his eyes. "We'll be fine, Nicholas," he said. "Just fine. Don't you worry."

He turned, and it was then that it hit me. He'd called me Nicholas. They all called me that, thought I was me cousin. And that little fact made me worry even more than I had. If something happened to us over this winter, if for some reason I didn't return, who was to know I'd gone in the first place? I been writing these here letters, but I ain't had no way to send them. When we was in Iceland and then Greenland, I didn't know some of them boats would take them for me, so I missed getting them off to ye. I just been saving them up for when we get back. But if we don't return, ye'll never get these letters. Oh, Mama, will ye spend the rest of yer years wondering where I'd gotten off to, not knowing that me bones lay trapped inside some wooden prison sunk in some freezing cold waters, long from the shores of England? Would Nicholas fess up? Or would he lie low like the coward he is and decide it was better to stay quiet than risk yer wrath? If I died, waiting here, trapped here, would I be mourned by anybody?

I had to turn then and leave the others. Me thoughts were just too depressing, and I could feel that sadness and fear tight in me throat. I may not have been a tough man, but no one was going to see me cry with fright. I hid all this night, wallowing in sorry thoughts, and then today, I said to meself, "What is, is, Seth," and I gave up the sadness and just became resigned.

Yer loving son, Seth

JOHN HUDSON

All day today we have worked like crazed men, pushing and pulling and hauling the *Discovery* up onto solid ice. It was a task for more men than we had on hand, but it was a task that had to be done. If we had left the boat to freeze fast in the arctic waters, the spring thaw could have easily ripped our only salvation into pieces with the ice twisting and turning as it melted, and the *Discovery* caught in its fearsome grasp. Of course, this would happen only if we *have* a spring thaw—and the alternative is something I don't even *let* myself think on these days.

Cook has already rationed everything, so that one gets only a quarter mug of ale, a bit of cheese, and a bit of hard-tack. We've saved the rest for the voyage home. Already my stomach makes so much noise that it is a wonder anyone is able to sleep next to me. But then an empty stomach makes one sleepy, I am finding. I seem to have little interest in anything, and there is not enough activity to coax us into wakefulness these days. So I sleep long, long hours.

I am so well rested that by the time we reach the sunny shores of England, I will have enough pent-up energy that I am afraid I might wear everyone out around me. Lord knows I certainly welcome trying. For that is all I have to look forward to in this cold and dreary place.

The days themselves grow darker and darker. Sometimes, it seems as if we have only an hour or so of light. It is truly depressing. When I do get home, I swear I am going to live out of doors just so I can soak up every ray of sunshine that lands on fair old England's shores. Mother will never coax me inside again, even with her admonitions and threats when she needs help with the chores. Perhaps I shall find a place of my own when we return. I am old enough, I think. And I shall do no chores at all but live with everything in total disarray. I will never churn butter or wash dishes or sweep floors or tend to pigs but shall live on sweets and visits to Issa. That I should like very much!

Now, Father gave me a most unpleasant surprise. But then I, too, have shocked him, I suppose. He called me into his cabin for a bit of a dressing-down—*again*. I had tarred a shilling to the deck and then sat back and watched man after man try to pry it up. I found it quite amusing, considering that there is little else to do now that we are trapped. But nobody else seems to have enjoyed the experience as much as I. And so I was in trouble once more. Someday, I swear, I shall have my own boat, and it shall be the merriest boat ever, with nothing but adventures and danger and good-natured souls accompanying me!

But until that time, I shall have to live with Father upbraiding me, I suppose. He told me that no one is in the mood for my pranks. As if I didn't know that! We are like a boat of dead people already. Most everyone just sits and stares, lost in whatever dark thoughts they wish to think on.

When Father finished with his lecture, which was both lengthy and boring, I asked him how he then proposed to help us all through this ordeal without a little levity.

"What ordeal?" he said to me, acting surprised. "We are positioned perfectly! Come spring, we will be able to proceed to the Orient. It will be a hard winter, no doubt. But a glorious spring, John, a glorious spring."

At first, I was sure that he was joking. But I knew that he has always had his eye on the Orient and ignored the practicalities that daily surround him—such as how low our rations are getting, the lack of shelter, and the growing anger the men feel toward him. I may love the humor of a good prank, but this was no joke my father was pulling. He was mad to think we could continue on in the spring.

"Father," I said to him then, "you cannot be serious. Once spring comes, we must head home to England."

He ignored me and bent over his maps. "I've been at it all week, John. And I think I know where I made my mistake. Come see."

He showed me the map and traced where we had sailed, and where he thought the East might now lie. As usual, it was all gibberish to me, though for once, I truly wished I could read a stupid map. Then I could perhaps offer an argument that might appeal to him. He has always said I was just too lazy to learn. He is right.

"Father," I said, trying to put all the maturity I had— and it wasn't much—into my voice. "You must not even entertain the idea that we are going on come spring.

Already our clothes are beginning to fray, our stomachs growl with hunger, our bodies grow weaker. Can you not see that?"

"Of course I see it, John," he replied. "But we are talking about a passage to the Orient, man."

I stared at him, amazed. And in looking for so long and so hard, I did see him clearly then. My father, the man I have followed faithfully since the age of seven, was a bit mad. This quest was consuming him. Before me suddenly was not a hero of the seas, but an old man crazed with an obsession.

"What makes you so overanxious to go home?" he asked me then. "I have never known you to prefer dry land under your feet to the wind in your hair."

"Food," I said bitterly, without meaning to. "Food has got me yearning for home."

My father chuckled, *actually* chuckled. "No," he said to me. "I believe it is this dream you have of the young lady from Thorton Hall. And, I might add, your dream is just that, son, a dream."

How had he known about Issa? His knowledge infuriated me. "It is no dream, Father," I informed him, all my anger at his inability to face our situation realistically and being so frustratingly hungry turning now to a different source. "We have promised ourselves to each other."

My father's face whitened at my admission, and I was glad to have shocked him some as he had me. "Sir Dudley Digges will kill you should he discover this," he said to me. "John, my son, what have you done?"

"What Issa and I wanted," I replied angrily.

"And if her father should discover this?" he asked me. "You have left her in England to face that alone?"

This did bring me up short. Father might be mad, but then who was to say I hadn't been a bit reckless myself?

"Her father will not honor such a pledge," my father said, dismissing my announcement carelessly then. "He will have her married to someone of her status before we even return. For you are but a sailor, John, and unless you plan on giving up the sea for a more lucrative job or we do discover a passage to the Orient and I am knighted, she will never be yours."

I left Father's cabin then, feeling very agitated. Would Sir Dudley give Issa away while I was at sea? Would he do it against her will? I do care for Issa and cannot imagine a life without her. Yet give up the sea? No, there is too much of the explorer in me. Father is right when he said that more have I longed for the wind in my hair than the land under my feet. So perhaps my father's and my quests are not so different after all. If only a discovery of the route east will grant me Isabella's hand, then I must link myself with my father in this quest, foolish as I know it to be.

I came upon Nicholas Syms—or whoever. He was staring out at the vast whiteness that surrounds us. There is something about him that is gentle and kind in spite of his rough speech and his having so much to do with the coarse ways of the world. And so I told him my absurd situation.

Nicholas gave a laugh and told me in no uncertain terms that there was little I could do about it one way or the other. Worrying, he said, would do me no good. He was right. I am trapped on this boat. Issa is trapped at home. If she should need to stand up to her father, then she must. Worrying about her alone in England, worrying about what we would do when the spring thaws came, it was all a waste of time. And so, gratefully, I turned my mind forcibly to more creative pursuits.

"What say you," I said to Nicholas, "to a game of cards? You know, *Nicholas*, you seem to win more frequently than most. Have you a trick? Where did you learn your skills?"

Losing Issa and bringing my father to task was now far from my mind. Discovering Nicholas's true identity—that was *much* better sport!

RICHARD HUDSON

"Mama! Mama!"

Richard shook his mother hard, watching her wake with a start. He held on to his stomach, willing it to stop tumbling about as if it meant to throw his food from last night to the floor. The sun was just beginning to rise in the early November sky. He felt truly terrible.

"What is it, Richard?" Mama said, sitting up now.

"My mouth aches, and my stomach hurts," Richard cried, tears coming to his eyes. He wiped them away quickly. He was trying to be brave, but the pain was awful.

"Your mouth aches where?" asked Mama.

Richard opened his mouth wide and pointed toward a place far in the back on the right side.

Mama sighed. "I'm afraid we'll be making a trip to the apothecary. It does look sore."

"Can he make the pain go away?" Richard mumbled.

"Hopefully. Get yourself dressed. We'll go there now."

"What is he going to do?" asked Richard, his heart beating fast. He had heard horrible stories about the apothecary.

"The tooth may have to be pulled, Richard," Mama said, looking him in the eye. "It may hurt a bit."

"A bit?" Richard shouted, then moaned and held on to his mouth. "Johnny told me it's most awful to get a tooth pulled from your head."

"It's not pulled from your head," Mama corrected soothingly. "Just from your mouth, little one."

"Johnny says the man rips it from your skull, leaving a hole so wide in your mouth that bugs can climb up into it," Richard cried. His palms grew sweaty with fright. Was there not some other way to rid himself of this pain?

Mama smiled. "And since when have you believed the stories of your brother?"

"'Tis true, Mama," Richard said angrily. "You know he had it done himself."

Mama nodded. "That he did. And your brother did prove himself to be most brave for the surgery. I know you'll be stouthearted too."

Richard stared down at the floor. Finally, he looked up at his mother. "So bugs won't enter my head and fly around bothering me like Johnny?"

"No, Richard," Mama reassured him. "And bugs didn't enter John's head that day either."

"Aye, they did," Richard said insistently, wishing his mother would stop denying it. Did she not understand the seriousness of all this? "Johnny held on to his head all that day, moaning and groaning. And the next day, when you took the bandages from him, he screamed that the bugs were driving him mad."

"And how did this crazy brother of yours finally rid his head of these bugs, pray tell me?" asked Mama.

"He begged me to take some of my coins and go to his friend Andrew Johnson and get a potion from him that would rid him of those pests," Richard said.

Mama stared at her young son. "And did you do it?"

Richard nodded. "Of course, Mama. Johnny was in terrible pain, and you were out running errands, and Papa was at court. I took all my coins and ran straight to Andrew and got the potion for John to drink. And he did drink of it, Mama, and the bugs flew from his ears, he said. And then he was better."

"And why did you not tell me of this?" Mama asked. "I heard nothing of it when I returned."

"Johnny said I mustn't worry you or Papa," Richard explained proudly. "He said you both had much on your minds, and that now that I had saved him, there was no need to cause you more concern."

Mama laughed. "Richard, my child," she said, bending down near him. "You've been fooled by your brother again, I'm afraid. Was John feeling better that night, and did he go out?"

Richard nodded, a sickeningly familiar feeling in his gut. "He said he had to go thank Andrew."

Mama laughed again. "Oh, I'm sure he did have to thank him."

"He was making it all up?" Richard choked out, his mouth throbbing again.

Mama nodded.

"And now Andrew has my coins?" asked Richard, understanding slowly dawning.

"I think the pub owner probably has your coins now," Mama said.

Hot anger rushed over Richard. He stomped his foot. "Oh, I hate him. I hope he doesn't come home. I hope he drowns out there."

Mama's face whitened. "Richard, that's bad luck! Please don't say things like that. I insist you take that back right now."

Richard kicked at the floorboards with his bare feet. His mouth pulsed with pain. "Oh, all right," he mumbled, holding on to his mouth again. "I hope he doesn't drown. I hope he comes home. And I want Papa home too. But I will get him back for this. I'll cut off his hair while he's sleeping, or put oatmeal in his shoes, or a dead rat in his pocket so when he goes off to see girls, he smells something awful."

Mama smiled. "Those are all wonderful plans. But hurry now to dress. Let's go see about that tooth of yours."

Richard nodded. He went to the door and looked back at her one more time. "No bugs though, Mama, you promise?"

Mama's face was serious now. "I promise. No bugs."

Richard went to get dressed, realizing as he did, that his mother may have promised him about the bugs, but she had said nothing more about the pain.

They made their way along the crowded streets in the early morning. The air was cold and crisp, with a hint of wetness. Richard wrapped his arms around himself as they hurried toward the apothecary. His body was cold from the sickness in his stomach and the pain in his mouth.

Mama opened the shopkeeper's door and a little bell tinkled. The apothecary came out from the back.

"You're out early this morning, Mrs. Hudson," he greeted her.

Mama pulled Richard inside and shut the door tightly. Inside the apothecary's, a fire slowly began to warm Richard's nose and fingers. His mouth was dry, and his jaw was twitching with worry. In spite of the cold, he considered running back outside.

"Richard's complaining about his mouth," Mama said, trying to pull her son around from where he had hidden behind her skirts. "Come on now, Richard," she admonished him. "John and Papa have had plenty of their teeth pulled."

"Aye," agreed the apothecary. "Most men who go to sea lose teeth. So if you are to be an explorer like your father, young man, you will probably lose a few too."

Richard poked his head out, curious now. "Why?"

The apothecary shrugged. "Don't know. Perhaps the sea air rots them. But whatever the cause, men of the sea are brave when they lose teeth. Do you want to go to sea someday?"

"Of course," Richard said, drawing nearer.

"Well then, let's have a look," said the old man, pulling on a pair of spectacles, "and enough of this hiding."

Dutifully, Richard opened his mouth, moaning a bit as he did so.

"Aye," the apothecary concluded. "The tooth will have to come out. Let's have you up in the chair then, young man."

Richard looked at the straps that lay across the arm-rests. His resolve to be brave broke. He clung to his mother.

"It has to be done, Richard," Mama said gently. She

pried his fingers from her gown and lifted him up and into the apothecary's chair. "I'll be right here with you, though. I'll hold your hand."

Richard struggled to get free. He didn't care about the pain now. He would rather live with it than be put in that chair!

"Have to strap those hands down, I'm afraid, Mrs. Hudson," the apothecary said. "Can't have him trying to interfere once I begin pulling."

His mother nodded her agreement. Richard felt the sickness again in his stomach as the old man tied his arms to the chair. When he was done, Mama took his hand and squeezed. Richard turned his head from her in anger.

"Do not cry, my little man," she whispered. "And when your father returns, I'll tell him what a stouthearted boy he has for a son. You can be brave for your father, can't you, Richard?"

Richard stopped struggling. He did want to be brave. But when the old man brought the iron pliers out, his heart beat in fright, and he tried once again to get himself free.

"Open up, then," the apothecary ordered. "And let's have done with it."

Richard squirmed even harder. He had changed his mind. He did not want to do this! He did not want to do this!

"You'll have to hold his nose, Mrs. Hudson," said the old man.

Richard thrashed about as his mother did as the apothecary said. How could she? How could she do this to him?

"Listen to me, Richard," his mother said softly in his ear. "Listen to me. I want you to close your eyes. I want you to imagine a beach of fine white sand. Imagine your papa there now with Johnny in the Orient."

"They have been gone a long time?" the apothecary asked, as the pliers touched Richard's sore tooth. He let out a scream and tried to bite the apothecary's hand, but the big pliers got in the way.

"Seven months," answered Mama.

"Then they must be there by now. That is good news, Mrs. Hudson."

"Aye," Mama said.

The apothecary began to tug. Richard's head felt like it was going to explode. He tried to scream again, but no sound came from his mouth. Tears ran down his face. The pain was hot, searing. He gasped for breath. The tugging seemed endless, and his head felt as if it was being pulled from his neck. Richard wanted to die from the hurt. Then a loud snap sounded deep in his head, and it was over.

The sudden cessation of pain was overwhelming, and Richard saw black at the corners of his eyes. He could not speak. He could not cry.

"It's out," the apothecary announced, holding up the tooth.

Richard watched him turn, drop the tooth in a waste can, and wash the blood from his hands in some dirty water in a basin by the chair. "Keep a poultice on his cheek to prevent infectious pus from entering. The hole where the tooth has been extracted will take some time to heal. And I'd consider having him bled if he doesn't feel better in a day or two."

Mama nodded, and through the shock his body felt,

Richard saw two tears trickle down her cheeks. His own body seemed unable to respond to anything.

"That'll be half a crown," the apothecary said, as he unstrapped Richard's arms.

"Money!" Mama gasped. "I . . . I . . ."

The apothecary looked at her.

"I'm sorry," Mama said, her face red. "I'm out just now, sir. Could you extend me credit until Henry returns?"

"A little late to be asking that of me," said the man coldly.

Mama nodded. "I'm sorry. But I was so concerned for my son that I forgot to mention it to you earlier."

Suddenly, Richard's stomach came to life, and he threw up all over himself.

The apothecary gave Richard a disgusted glance. "Well, Mrs. Hudson. Apparently, credit has already been extended. Now you'd best be on your way. And do not come back here again until your husband has returned, and you have real coins in your pocket to spend!"

Mama nodded. She bent over and picked Richard up, haphazardly wiping at the puke on his shirt. The sudden movement of his body sent pain waves through Richard's mouth. He moaned. Mama began to carry him awkwardly toward the door. The apothecary did not move to help her. Mama did not bother to close his shop door behind her.

"Oh, Richard," Mama whispered to him as she hurried them home, her voice beginning to sound as if it came from a very far-off place. "Heal soon. And when you are all right again, you and I shall make the most terrible of plans to repay John and Papa on their return. Truly, they will deserve it, sitting as they most assuredly are now, in the sun somewhere, eating, drinking, and celebrating their great good fortune, while here we struggle on without money in this damp and dark place."

As they moved through the streets of London, the rain came down in earnest, and Richard gave in to the pain and let blackness consume him.

ISABELLA DIGGES

November 10, 1610

Emil is fast becoming a liability. Daily, he grows more and more amorous, asking me over and over for favors I have no intention of granting him. He argues that my insistence on meeting him in the locked map room indicates my willingness. How little he knows!

And yet, I must proceed cautiously. If he even begins to suspect that the information guarded so carefully in that room where he makes his unwelcome advances to me has been couriered to the good king of England, I will hang. As the days progress, my nervousness has been growing. My head spins as I silently memorize those maps, all the while enduring the ardent embraces of Emil. My palms sweat as I redraw each remembered piece of information on letters to my father. Twice now, a servant has come upon me at work late in the night, the fire cold in the grate and my candle almost gone. Twice that same servant has looked at me askance, for what gentle lady leaves a warm bed to write greetings to her loved ones when the next day presents

*endless opportunities to accomplish the same task? While I
admit that spying is an exhilarating way to spend one's days, the
longer the spy remains in enemy territory, the more she must
swallow her fear to go and spy yet again.*

*And my father has been pressing me of late. He demands
more and more of me, even as he spends his time hunting with
the king at Hampton Court, feasting on some magnificent stag
they had cornered that day and drinking late into the night, all
the while trying to woo the wealthy duchess. For he has gotten
his introduction and was pleased as pleased could be with the
approval of our king, noting to me that the king said to him—
and I remember the words exactly— "Of my blessing on the
match, you shall have it, as long as you continue to provide
us with such valuable information."*

*By telling me this, could my father not see the enormous
amount of pressure he has laid at my door? Can he do nothing
but remind me that we are still on shaky ground at court and
still in need of coins to soothe our creditors? Can he do nothing
himself to relieve us of our monetary crisis but depend on me
alone to risk it all to save us both? For his part of the bargain,
the courtship, seems to be going less than smoothly.*

*Oh, how he did go on and on about his appearance and how
well he looked upon meeting the duchess. He wrote incessantly
about the cut of his blue velvet doublet, how it showed his eyes off
to his advantage, and how in spite of his loss of hair these past few
years, he still cut quite a figure. And yet that night at dinner, he
did admit that despite his turning upon her all of his charm, she
seemed singularly disinterested. He complained of her looks, telling
me that her face was pale and her nose a bit pointed.*

*Does he think this is what I want to hear? Does he have
no conception of how it goes for me, sitting here daily, worrying
about the coming evening with Emil, who looks at me as
frequently as a cat watches a mouse? Oh, how I loathe these*

letters now, for they irritate me no end. I have become my father's asset. He has forgotten I am his daughter, and he has chosen to ignore what I must endure here.

And if this was not enough, he informed me yesterday that he had given the duchess some of my mother's jewels as a present. My own mother's property! Jewels that should have rightly been mine!

I vow here and now that when I am through with this spying, I will make my father's life a living nightmare for what he has put me through and how little concern he has for my well-being. For today, a new concern has entered the realm of my spying world.

At dinner, as Emil gave me a look across the table, making me want to vomit into my plate of inedible Dutch food, I caught Von Dectmer looking at us both curiously. If the father should suspect us, I am doomed, for while I may be able to fool that simpleton of a son, the father is another matter altogether. I threw him a smile and laughed often at his idiotic jokes, but uneasiness is creeping into my very bones.

I would give anything now to be back spying on John Hudson, safe with him beside me, unsuspecting and easy. My thoughts turn more and more to him, for there has been no information from my father on that front. Even though I have written him twice to tell me news of the voyage, my father has remained silent on the matter.

And that, too, distresses me, though I know it should not. With the exception of the outcome of the voyage, what happens to John Hudson is not of my concern.

And yet, it is.

And so I swallow hard tonight, both the unappetizing food before me and my fears. And I smile as if all the world was right. For now I, Isabella Digges, must, out of necessity, become more than a spy. I must become the greatest of actresses!

SETH SYMS

⤳ ⤶

November 20, 1610

Dearest Mama:

There has been quite a row today! As if being stuck in this cold ain't enough, the captain is choosing to pick on the very men who might support him in this here barren land amidst these bitter moods.

I had risen early, regretting it almost as soon as me eyes opened. It's so dismal in this place that all of us, and me mainly, do pray to sleep soundly and long. A good sleep makes the time go faster, and now that we're stuck here on this boat, with nothing around but white and snow and little to eat, ain't nothing much to do but pray that the time does go by quickly and spring comes to free us from this ice trap. But this morning, I had no luck and was awake with no means to turn meself back to that dreamland. And so I got up.

It was dark as I made me way up into the freezing air abovedecks to relieve meself overboard. I almost stumbled upon them, gathered as they were so close and hidden on the deck behind them barrels we'd placed up there to give us a wee bit more space below. It was Juet and Greene and another no-good called Motter. They was whispering so secretive-like, I couldn't help it. Me curiosity got the better of me. As ye know, Mama, it's been me curse in the past, and this day weren't no different. What I heard them say made me head start to spinning.

"He ain't never had our interests at heart, and that's a fact," Motter was growling. "I could sense it the minute I stepped foot on this boat. I sailed with a lot of captains, but never one so crazy mad that he'd risk it all and get us trapped like this."

"Aye," said Juet, shaking his head. "I been with Hudson three trips now. Each time, he thinks only of the East, sailing on when any prudent captain would have turned back to protect his crew from this very thing that's happened to us."

"I say he's dead we make it through this winter," Greene added. "Nobody'd call it mutiny, ye ask me. We'd be doing all sailors a favor ridding the world of this captain, any captain that puts his own greedy ambitions above the safety of his men."

Juet agreed. "No one could blame us after this winter we'll spend."

Now, I've been known to be able to sneak in and out of a room quiet as ye please, and I knew it was no good for me to stay where I was, so I tiptoed back down the ladder then, holding me need to go until later. I swung meself back onto me bunk amidst the snores and groans of the others. Me heart was pounding hard in me chest. And I wished with everything I held sacred that I hadn't heard what I had. I didn't want to know no more. I'd seen sailors who came home having mutinied. They hung, they did! No mercy there! Now, not only was it possible I wasn't going to survive the winter, but if I did, it was just as possible I'd be hung for a mutineer if they went through with their plan. And what was I to do if that choice was presented to me? How in the bloody world was I to choose? And should I tell someone? Be a stoolie?

I am a lot of terrible things, but I ain't one to squeal on others. So where did that leave me? With an unsettled head, that's for sure. I closed me eyes and tried to forget it all and slip back into blissful unconsciousness, but it weren't to be. Me bladder was full and me thoughts were troubled, and neither would let me sleep. So I laid like that, worrying plenty, until everyone else was up and about, and then I rose too and went about the few chores we had with an aching head.

Philip asked me what was wrong.

"Head aches," I replied shortly, not wanting to risk conversation with him. He was a good man, loyal to the captain, and I didn't want to worry him none if there weren't no cause for concern. After all, Juet and the others had been talking and nothing more.

Young John came and sat with the carpenter and me. He shivered as he ate his hardtack. "Getting colder every day," he said. He was thin now, and ye could sense the cold going right through him.

He grinned, and I could see the bleeding of his teeth. This rough time was taking a toll on all of us physically.

Philip told John that my head was hurting, and John offered me a piece of hardtack from his own meager breakfast.

"I can't take that," I protested, trying to hand him back the biscuit.

But he shook his head, telling me that a big guy like me couldn't exist on so little. As for him, he was tall but thin and didn't need so much to eat.

Philip told John he'd need something soon for his teeth, and asked if they was bothering him.

John grimaced and nodded. "A bit," he admitted. "I'm more worried they'll fall out before I get home to Issa. What's she going to think about me arriving home without teeth?" He laughed. "Ah, don't know why I'm worried. If I can't look like an angel, at least I'll make a handsome devil."

I admired his bravery; I knew what it was like to have a mouth full of sores. I'd been there once before when I was about twenty. It was that time, Mama, when I had been thrown in jail two months for pickpocketing some gentleman down by the docks. Remember I came out sporting two fewer teeth? It ain't fun having a mouth full of blood and aching bones. And it's less fun if the teeth don't make it and have to be pulled. I knew what it took for him to grin at all.

There was a commotion over near the ladder, and Captain Hudson descended below. None of us stood. We was all too cold and tired. And I don't think that he expected us to do it neither. But either way, this was the beginning of the row.

He headed over toward where we sat on crates, trying

hard to warm ourselves by the cook's meager fire, there being so little wood in these here parts.

"Philip," the captain said, "I want you to go ashore today."

Philip nodded.

"We need shelter," he'd continued. "It's still November, but it's going to get harder and colder these next months. We need more space for these men."

Philip reminded him that there weren't nothing out there to build a shelter with. Them trees were too stunted, good for burning, that's all.

"There's got to be something," Captain Hudson said curtly. "Find it."

Philip looked away, and the captain left without even so much as an apology to blunt his harsh words.

John apologized for his father.

Philip shrugged and told us it didn't matter much. There weren't nothing out there, and even if there was, it'd be too cold now to work. That wood would be like stone and them nails would be frozen.

Still, he rose and put on a heavy overcoat before heading out, taking a few others with him. John and me sat for the afternoon, playing cards, throwing dice, doing small chores about the boat, telling each other every dumb joke we could think of, trying hard to keep warm and think positive thoughts.

We heard the shallop being pulled back along the ice late in the afternoon, heard it scrape against the side of the boat as some others pulled it up on board. John and I went out to see Philip and the others, more out of boredom than anything else, I suppose. When ye sit all day, in near darkness, 'cause the sun here don't shine for very long, ye search for something, anything to relieve the sameness of it all. Well, we weren't long for asking for some kind of drama.

No sooner had Philip and the others stepped out of the boat than Captain Hudson made his appearance to question him.

"Nothing, Captain," Philip had replied. "All I found was them stunted trees like I told you, good for burning is all."

The captain shouted that that wasn't the answer he wanted.

By now, the decks above were full with us all.

Philip looked at Captain Hudson, and it was the first time I ever saw the man mad. "I can't build something out of nothing, Captain Hudson. Everything's frozen fast, including the nails. It ain't possible."

The captain came down the stairs then at a clip until he stood in front of Philip. And without so much as a how-do-you-do, he struck him, roaring to Philip to go and make it possible and not to come back until a shelter was complete.

He turned on his heel then and left. Philip stared after him, an imprint of the captain's hand shining redly on his cheek. I felt goose bumps on me arms. It weren't right what the captain just did. It was foolish, truly. Philip was a loyal sailor to him. The captain shouldn't have made him so angry. John knew it too. He went to Philip and said a thing or two I couldn't hear. Philip shook him off and stepped back into the boat by himself, his eyes snapping with anger. They lowered the boat, and he pulled it across the ice to a narrow strip of water. Then he rowed away in that tiny shallop, his arms moving fast and furious.

Philip was the calmest man I know. There weren't no anger in him at all. Captain Hudson had had to push hard to find it, but find it he did. Now there wasn't just Juet and Greene and Motter. The numbers were growing.

I turned me back on them all and crawled below to me bunk. I lay here shivering the rest of the day. No good thoughts have come at all into me head, and I have to force meself to keep me eyes closed, hoping for sweet thoughtless sleep to overtake me.

Yer worried son, Seth

JOHN HUDSON

We have lost the first of our crew members. John Williams, our gunner, died from the cold today. Lord knows why he was out so long and did not come back or seek refuge below. I suppose it's because of how close the quarters are here, with twenty-two men packed tightly together, and the way everyone's tempers seem to be raging.

We found him one hundred yards from the boat. His eyes were open and staring. His skin was a sickening blue. I have seen men dead before. I have seen men die by hanging. It is not a pretty sight. And yet, John Williams was perhaps the ugliest sight of all, being frozen in place as he was, and reminding us all what might be our own unfortunate demise. I do not like thinking on this, yet here was the thought in full form. It made for a most unpleasant day.

I can only guess that he misjudged his ability to withstand the temperatures, became tired as one does when the cold begins to seep into your bones, sat down and thought he'd just rest awhile. We'd all been warned about the dangers of feeling that false sense of wanting just to sleep. We'd been told a thousand times how you must fight that feeling at all costs.

Maybe Williams was just tired of it all. I don't know. He was a bachelor—no real family waits for him back in England. Perhaps he just saw the winter stretching out in front of us and lost heart. It would be easy to do, that's for sure. Everyone's in a foul mood, me included. And it's all due to Father. Daily, he grows more unreasonable, as if some fiendish ghoul has taken over him.

After Williams died, Greene asked my father for Williams's heavy gray cloak. My father told him he could have it, though it is traditional to auction off a dead man's clothes and belongings when he dies. Usually the proceeds from the auction go to the next of kin when the ship returns to port. But Father ignored this age-old tradition and promised the cloak to Greene.

Of course, this angered the rest of the crew. No one liked thinking on the fact that he could die and his belongings be handed to someone else without recompense for his family. Even I cringed at the thought. But Father ignored the ugly mood around him.

And things worsened later. Greene went out in the afternoon with Philip to hunt. Father became so enraged with Greene for taking up with Philip that he refused him the cloak. This made no sense at all. In the first place, the men were hunting for food—a necessity, as our supplies are dwindling fast. And secondly, Philip Staffe is one of the more calming men on this voyage. I know Father was angry with him for not building us a shelter, but there was nothing for the man to work with. He did the best he could, built a lean-to with what wood he could find. It didn't help us at all, but at least he tried. And yet Father remains angry with him, and with anyone who speaks or spends time with the man. This unreasonableness of Father's worries me no end, and puts me in the uneasy role of being the responsible member of the Hudson clan. I do not like this role and want my easygoing, pleasure-seeking self back. I can only wonder if the cold has affected his mind some. Perhaps when the weather warms, he will return to normal.

The men did manage to shoot a few fowl and catch a few fish, so for tonight, the crew will eat well. I know I should eat while there is food, and yet my stomach remains queasy. I keep seeing Williams dead and remembering the sound of prying him from the ice. We had no cloth to wrap him in, there being little we can spare, and so we found a bit of open water and dropped him through unclothed. I watched with the others as he slowly sank out of sight, his eyes still staring up at us. He died cold and will remain cold, I suppose.

I am haunted most, though, by why he gave up, why he gave in to death. I would fight it with every fiber of my being. I know sleep is peaceful, and I suppose death is the same. And yet who would want peaceful forever? Surely there would be a part in all of us that would fight to the end to retain the glory and excitement of living? It scares me, thinking one could give up so easily. Will I feel that way come a few months more when perhaps we shall be hungry and colder still? And yet how could I, knowing what I can still do and see in this world? Surely the thought of all the wonderful things there are yet to experience on this Earth will keep me from falling to sleep surrounded by nothing but white and cold. And yet . . . if one is to die, I suppose the simple closing of one's eyes, the act of nodding off as if to sleep only for the night, this might not be so unpleasant a way to die, would it?

And what waits on the other side? Where is John Williams now? In heaven with the angels as the priests would have us think? Or nowhere—just floating in a cold watery grave—all thoughts and passions turned now to nothingness?

These thoughts seem to consume me tonight. I try hard to remember my mother's words to me when I expressed my horror after watching a French spy hung, drawn, and quartered. At first, I remember being fascinated. I was about nine, I think. And then, that night, the nightmares came.

Mother woke me from my screaming. She held me tight, smelling as she always does, I remember fondly now, of food cooking and fire. She asked me what I had been dreaming about, and I told her of the hanging. (She had not known then that I had gone. Oliver had snuck me there, and Mother's eyes were on fire when she heard. Oliver did take a good whipping for that one, which delighted me no end.) She hugged me tight for many minutes without saying a word. And then she spoke softly.

"John," she asked me, "do you know that dragonflies are born in water, that they swim for months in the ponds, and then eventually take flight?"

I nodded. Many was the time I had observed them in the woods.

"Can the dragonfly go back to the water and tell the others where he is? Can he return and tell them that in leaving the water, he became a flying creature, with much more freedom of movement than he had ever experienced before?"

I shook my head no.

"That, my darling son," my mother had whispered to me then, kissing the top of my head, "is what death is—an experience no one can come back and tell us about. But I believe we will be like the dragonfly when we die, soaring and swooping with more freedom than we can even imagine."

I think on her words, and try to get them to calm me. I was nine then. I am seventeen now. Can I still believe her as I did then? For the sake of having hope, of returning to London and living a good, long life, I will force myself to believe that even now, John Williams flies free and fast beyond us all. And that in having hope, I shall soon be flying free and fast over the water myself, returning to merry old England and home.

RICHARD HUDSON

I'm tired," Richard whined. He sat down heavily on the frozen road. They had walked long and hard today and already dusk was falling fast upon them.

"Get up, Richard," Mama said impatiently. "We have to get moving. If we linger too long, the road will be dangerous. There have been bandits about lately, and they are known to prey on people once darkness falls."

"I hope a bandit *does* come get me," Richard complained, but he rose to his feet and trod slowly behind his mother. "Maybe he'll have a fine steed and ride me away to a warm fire where they'll feed me roast sausages and plum pudding rather than terrible old mutton."

Mama laughed, but it was a tired laugh.

As they walked along, Richard stuck his tongue into the hole where his tooth had been. It had become a habit with him after the sore had healed. It had felt odd at first, but now he liked poking the empty space. It made him feel brave and big. He couldn't wait to show Papa and Johnny that he, too, had had a tooth pulled from his mouth.

He wondered how soon it would be until they got back. Richard knew it had been longer than normal. In the past, he and his mother had always had to shop at different vendors, asking for credit when their money ran out, but never had they had to walk as far as they did tonight, trying shop after shop, having door after door closed in their faces.

One shopkeeper had even shouted out, "Do ye truly expect me to be fool enough to bet on the fact that yer husband will actually return with a passage east and a settlement with which to pay yer bills? It's been too long, Mrs. Hudson. Accept the fact. Yer husband ain't coming back."

Richard remembered once hearing Johnny telling a girl that only half the ships that set sail for a voyage of discovery returned. But he had been bragging, and so Richard had not believed him. Now, he was not so sure.

"Mama, how long have Papa and Johnny been gone?" Richard asked.

"Ten months, little one," Mama replied.

Richard remembered that one night, right before they had left, Johnny had complained loud and at length about how much food he had to buy for the boat, keeping Richard awake long after he wanted to be asleep.

"I thought Papa took food for only eight months," Richard said.

"Yes, he did," Mama said. "But he has probably found the way to the Orient and is now there, resupplying his ship to sail home to us. You mustn't worry."

"But none of the boats coming in have brought letters from him," Richard pointed out, "and there have been a lot coming from Africa lately. Timmy Dobbins counted two just yesterday."

"I know that, Richard," Mama suddenly snapped, making her son stare up at her in surprise. "Now come along. We have to hurry. It's getting dark."

She pulled hard on Richard, dragging him over the rough road. He bit his lip to stop from crying. Why was she so angry with him for asking about Papa and Johnny? Was the shopkeeper right? Were Johnny and Papa never coming home?

"Make way! Make way!" a loud voice called.

Richard turned to see a fine carriage rolling up the street toward them. Mama pulled him to the side of the road in order to let the carriage pass. The vehicle roared by, splashing mud on Mama's cloak and Richard's breeches, then suddenly, came to an abrupt halt just past them.

A man in full livery stepped down from the coach.

"Mrs. Henry Hudson?" he asked.

Mama looked up from inspecting her mud-splattered cloak. Her face whitened.

"Yes?" she said.

"Sir Dudley Digges would like to offer you and your young son a ride home," the liveryman stated.

A ride? In a real carriage? Richard's eyes widened. "Come on, Mama," he said, tugging at her dirty skirts. "We've got a ride!" He couldn't believe their luck.

But Mama hesitated.

"Is there a problem, madam?" the servant inquired.

"Mama," Richard said, looking at her in disbelief. "Don't you want to ride? You said you were scared of bandits."

Reluctantly, Mama nodded. It was all Richard needed. He ran to the carriage. The servant opened the door, offering Richard a hand, and he climbed into the relative warmth of the coach. Mama clambered in behind him.

Richard turned to the man who had offered them a ride. Sir Dudley was rail-thin, with barely a wisp of hair. His clothes were of the finest silk, and he wore jeweled rings upon his fingers. He coughed slightly and put a handkerchief to his nose.

"I apologize, Sir Dudley, for our appearance," Mama said, taking a seat. "My young son Richard and I have been walking a great distance."

Sir Dudley inclined his head slightly to acknowledge Mama's explanation of their disheveled state, but said nothing more. The carriage moved forward with a jolt, and silence enveloped them. Richard examined the seat he was sitting on, its velvet smooth to the touch. The uncomfortable swaying back and forth of the coach told him that they were moving quickly, and he could hear the horses' hooves pounding on the dirt road. He had never ridden in a carriage before and probably never would again. It was unfair that it was too dark for him to look out at the world flying by or for his friends to see him inside!

"Do you have news of Henry, Sir Dudley?" Mama asked, her voice trembling as if she was afraid.

Richard looked curiously at the old man across from them. How did he know Papa?

Sir Dudley shook his head. "No news, Mrs. Hudson. But then no news is probably good news."

Richard sighed. All grown-ups said the same thing.

"This is a grand carriage," Richard spoke up. "Do you ride in it often? And do you have more than one?"

"Richard," Mama scolded, "please don't bother Sir Dudley with questions. I'm sure he would like his ride to be quiet and meditative."

"Not at all," Sir Dudley said, removing his handkerchief and smiling slightly for the first time. "Yes, young man, I do indeed have more than one carriage. And no, I don't ride in them often at all. I happened to ride in this one today as I was at court seeing our great King James."

King James? This man knew the king? Richard was impressed.

"Is the king as sickly, as some say he is, because he does nothing but eat and drink all the day long?" Richard asked.

"Richard!" exclaimed Mama.

Richard looked over at her in confusion. Was he in trouble? Why? He had only asked about what everyone else said about the king.

Sir Dudley laughed. "Oh yes, my young one. He does eat and drink much, and today he was in a very jolly mood. He has granted me the hand of a duchess. We are to be wed this spring."

"Congratulations to you, Sir Dudley," Mama said, but Richard could tell his mother was not being sincere. Clearly, she did not like this man.

"Yes, yes," Sir Dudley said, his smile widening. "It is a most auspicious joining. I am quite pleased."

"As is the duchess, I'm sure," Mama remarked.

Sir Dudley's smile faded for a moment. "But of course, the duchess will think this a fine match for herself," he said, raising his head until his nose pointed into the air.

Richard wanted to laugh. The man looked silly.

"And your daughter?" Mama said. "Has she learned of this happy event, sir?"

Sir Dudley shook his head. "Not yet, Mrs. Hudson. But I know she will be most pleased with the turn of events."

Mama nodded. "You must be in a hurry to reach your home and tell her the good news, then."

Sir Dudley smirked. "Isabella is not home at present, madam. She is currently in Denmark, serving as companion to the daughter of Von Dectmer."

Isabella? Richard thought. *This was Isabella's father? The man who would run Johnny through with a sword if he found out Isabella was to marry him?* Richard wanted to laugh. This man hardly looked strong enough to even *lift* a sword. Truly, Mama worried about the oddest things.

"Von Dectmer?" Mama said. "Von Dectmer of the Dutch East Indies Trading Company?"

Sir Dudley nodded. "Yes, the head of the company, actually. I believe your husband was once financed by them?"

"And almost jailed for it," said Mama irritably. "I'm surprised that your daughter went so willingly to be in their employ, as the king seems so adamantly against them."

"It is as companion only," Sir Dudley said, his lip curling a bit. "Not to explore for them, Mrs. Hudson."

Richard saw Mama's face redden.

"Your daughter is of marriageable age, Sir Dudley," Mama said, her voice smooth as honey. Richard knew that tone. Mama was angry, and about to say something that Sir Dudley would not like. "Perhaps you will be sharing in *her* wedding day in the not too distant future?"

Sir Dudley gave Mama a sharp look. His face soured. "Issa is much too young to be entertaining marriage ideas," he said, leaning forward and rapping on the front of the carriage. "And when that time comes, the king and I will provide her with a suitable husband."

The carriage came to a halt.

"One," Sir Dudley said coldly, "who will be within her station and of good standing. If you will excuse me, I forgot an earlier appointment. I will be unable to take you all the way to your home. I bid you a good night, Mrs. Hudson."

"But I was just warming up," Richard said, shocked at their unexpected expulsion from the carriage.

"Come along, Richard," Mama said, opening the door and pulling him out after her. "We mustn't bother Sir Dudley, who has more important matters to attend to."

Mama stepped carefully out into the chilly night. She lifted Richard out after her and then pulled herself up to her full height as she went to close the carriage door. She looked one last time directly at Sir Dudley.

"Your daughter is truly fortunate that she has you to look out for her," she said softly. "I do the same for my sons. Sometimes, however, Sir Dudley, they will do what they wish, without our consent. I know that was true for my Henry and me. Good night."

With that, Mama shut the door and turned to take Richard's hand. Sir Dudley's coach bolted forward and rolled quickly down the road.

"I wanted to ride all the way home in his carriage," Richard grumbled. "Why did he make us get out? Is it because he knows about Johnny?"

Mama nodded. "That, little one, is *exactly* why we were made to get out."

"Don't know why you brought it up, then," Richard complained. "And how does he know Papa?"

"He is one of the investors in Papa's voyage," Mama said.

Richard was confused. Sir Dudley was paying for Papa's trip? Johnny was in love with Sir Dudley's daughter? Sir Dudley would run Johnny through with a sword if this Isabella girl married him? It was too much for Richard to think about now. He refused to. He was too tired and too cross.

"When I'm older, I'm going to have a carriage like that, and I'm never going to walk again," Richard stated confidently.

Mama smiled. "Ah, Richard, that man may have a carriage and be wealthy, but he is unhappy and so, to me, he is nothing but a *poor* man."

"Mama." Richard sighed tiredly. "Sometimes you make no sense at all."

Mama laughed. "Come on, little one," she said. "Let's go home."

ISABELLA DIGGES

January 12, 1611

 My father denies me my request to come home, though I have written pleading my case. He has been granted the hand of the duchess, and yet he refuses me safe passage back to England! He says the king insists upon my staying, that my help to the throne is invaluable.

 They are both mad. Daily, I grow more concerned about discovery. How can they turn their backs upon the threat I face here? The longer I stay, the more precarious is my position. It is not in human nature to keep secrets, and it will not be long before word of the information at the hands of the English explorers will reach Dutch ears. And then I am doomed. For while Emil may truly believe that I worship the very ground upon which he walks, the father is not so stupid. I can feel his eyes upon me when we are in the same room, and it is no longer with interest, but with speculation. I am working hard to keep him amused and his mind occupied with the genteel conversations of women, but when I move near Emil, he is like a hawk.

Already he may have received whispered warnings about a spy in his midst.

And yet when I write my father of my concerns, I hear nothing but an insistence that I stay, many congratulations on my latest drawing, and a deep satisfaction with his place among the court. For he is favored these days.

He will marry the duchess, but not until the spring. And I am crazed thinking that he may make me stay here until then. Months more of this spying, months more of this fear, and I shall take a horse and head for home without his permission. I have thought of doing this many times already.

And yet, common sense stays my hand. For if I disappeared too quickly, it would not take much for Von Dectmer to surmise that something had occurred, and he and others would be in hot pursuit. As a woman, how far could I get on my own? And while in the past, the very idea of riding fast across moonlit meadows, pursued by agents of a foreign government, would have made my heart race with excitement, I confess I have had all the adventure I need for a lifetime these past few months. And too, I grow weary of the idiot son.

Absence, rather than helping me to forget, has increased my thoughts of John Hudson. Sometimes, I almost feel as if he was by my side, easing my tension, listening to my concerns. For he was good at that, listening, caring. Always, when Emil insists upon a kiss, it is John Hudson's lips I am kissing. This makes the whole spying business slightly less fearsome, and Emil's advances a bit more acceptable—though even my imaginings are becoming more tenuous to hold on to.

And it seems as if my father, too, has thoughts of John Hudson. For just today, he has written of an encounter he had with John's mother, telling me how he had so gallantly invited her to ride in his carriage as he saw her by the side of the road, looking tired and weary. He says the conversation was pleasant *until she was bold enough to ask after me. He turned her out when she implied that I had made promises to her son, calling her "an odious sort." He is mad with concern, reminding me that an alliance with the Hudson boy would be disastrous. How many times must he write me of this?*

I know that if the father should return with a passage east, he will be most amply rewarded. My father has even admitted that he might be knighted. But already the Discovery is ten months out, and my father has told me there is no sign of return. Is it possible that Captain Hudson ignored our instructions, has found the passage, and is even now in the East, contrary to our wishes for him to return if the passage was discovered? It would not be out of the ordinary for him to ignore the desires of those investing in him. He is a man who does what he wants. If he were not so good a captain, we would never have invested in him. And yet we did. And truth be told, it is not for the monies that I am now fretting at the long absence.

For what care I now about money? Life and keeping it has become my sole concern. The only solace in my father's letter to me is the possibility that if Captain Hudson did find his way east, a knighthood would surely be his, and John might be mine. I try to think on this and ignore the rest. But deep in my bones, there is a dread.

SETH SYMS

March 4, 1611
Dearest Mama:

Glad I am that the water around us remains frozen fast,
and whiteness is the only thing I can see. Foolish as that
may sound, it is only because I dread me first glimpse of
what I have become when the waters warm enough that I
might catch me reflection in them. I have only to look
upon me arms and hands and legs—thin as they've never
been even in me youngest of days—to know that I have lost
much of who I was when I set sail that fateful April day.
And, too, me clothes are but rags. Yet this ain't even the
worst of it.

If someone had told me a few months back that soon I'd
be longing for food more than anything else this old world
has to offer, I would have scoffed at them. But food is all I
think of—night and day, day and night. I dream of all that I
have eaten in me twenty years. I dream of every meal, trying
to recall each morsel as it slid down me throat—for not
much has slid down of late. John says I'll go mad if I keep

lying in me hammock recounting meals ye had prepared
for me, or he'll go mad just listening to me. I barked at him
today, asking him what *he* found to occupy his empty belly
and mind now. He grinned, but weakly.

That made me sad, it did. First off, I felt bad that I'd
yelled at perhaps the only friend excepting Philip I got on
this here boat. And secondly, I knew how much that grin
had cost the boy. He is suffering from the scurvy, as is
most of the crew. 'Tis an awful disease, and glad I am that
it ain't affecting me as of yet. One grows terrible weak
with it, barely able to move. John, who had been such a
monkey when we first set out, scrambling from here to
there, just a bundle of pent-up energy, has not moved
from his hammock in days.

Just this afternoon, Thomas Wydhouse went out into
the scrub around us and brought back some pieces of pine
bark. Some of the men took to chewing on those right off,
but Cook found some kind of strength somewhere and
boiled up that pine tree bark in a brew to feed to the scurvy
men. I dragged meself over there to get a mugful for John.

I had to lift him up, holding him as if he was some kind
of baby. I slipped the broth down his parted and parched
lips. He coughed as the brew slid down his throat, and I had
to slap him something silly to end the choking spell. Still,
some of the potion seems to have reached his belly, 'cause
he smiled weakly at me, asking me if this was retribution
for some of his tricks.

"That bad?" I'd asked.

He told me to try it myself if I was so curious.

I took one whiff and set the mug aside, telling him it was

a nice try, but that I wasn't having none of his wily ways convincing me to drink that poison.

John laughed a bit, but his brow grew damp. "I wouldn't wish even a drop of that for you, my friend," he said. "But still, it seems to have eased the pain a bit."

I urged him to sleep and dream deeply as he had had little rest since the scurvy came upon him.

John grinned at me then. "And if I murmur in my sleep, will you be about telling the others what I have whispered to you?"

I had to grin back at him. "But of course I would, young master. After ye tied me in me hammock as I slept and then called fire, do ye truly think ye could trust me not to tell all that ye have unwittingly revealed to me in yer deepest sleep?"

"Amazingly, yes, Nicholas," he said softly. "I believe I do trust you. I believe I could trust you even with my own life."

He closed his eyes gently then and fell asleep. I sat there, staring at the boy, me heart beating at a rapid pace. I ain't never had no one speak to me like that in a long, long time, ye being the only one willing to put up with me bad boy ways.

John began snoring softly, and I watched his eyelids twitch, as if in pain. And I wished I could have spared him that. He was a fine-looking one—dark hair falling across his brow, broad-shouldered, strong. And I knew then that he was like a brother I had never had.

There was a sudden commotion behind me. I could hear murmuring and movement. I went to rise from me stool beside John's hammock, but a heavy hand was laid on me

shoulder. I turned to find Captain Hudson behind me. The
ship had grown quiet, for the great man rarely ventured
down in the hold these past few weeks but had chosen
instead to remain sequestered in his cabin with his maps and
books. John had joined him frequently, until just a few days
ago, when he grew too weak to move. And yet this was the
first the man had come to see his son. It embittered me, it
did. Shouldn't he have been sitting here beside the boy
instead of me? Still, I wouldn't have traded his position for
mine given all the world. Time and starvation was making
him the enemy of us all. His was a terrible responsibility.

He asked me gruffly how John was doing. I told him that
he slept well now but that his pain had been great.

The man closed his eyes for a moment and took a deep
breath. I felt him sway a bit, and he gripped me shoulder
more tightly as if for support. "John has told me that you
have become good friends, Mr. Syms," he said, "and seeing
you here now with him, watching over him, I can see that
this is true."

I nodded.

He asked me if he could trust John to me as he was not
down there beside him himself, and try as he may, he had
not been able to persuade John to take room with him in
his cabin.

"Ye have asked him that?" I asked, unable to contain the
question, so great was me curiosity.

Captain Hudson looked at me askance. "But of course I
have," he said. "You do not imagine that I want my sick son
down here, away from me, do you?"

I felt me face redden. I hadn't even thought to imagine

that the captain might have had some fatherly feelings toward the boy. On the boat, they went about their business as any of the others on board.

The captain smiled a bit and told me how even on their first voyage out, John had insisted that he be treated like the others. He would visit the captain often, but he enjoyed the feeling of being a sailor, just that and nothing more.

The captain was proud of it, but he truly wished John would let him care for him now. While he realized John was almost a grown man, with a man's way of making his own decisions, tomorrow he planned to try again to convince him.

He turned and bent near me. "He will be better," he said softly to me. "He will grow stronger and we shall be on our way, eh?"

I nodded. What else was I to do?

Captain Hudson turned to look at his son one more time, telling me that this had been their worst trip together by far and that he must take him back to his mother in one piece, hale and hearty, or she'd have his hide.

"And too," he added in a whisper, "I do not think I could bear it should something happen to him."

Then he turned and made his way back to the ladder abovedecks.

When he was gone, Greene came up beside me. "Making conversation with the captain, eh, Syms?" he said with a nasty sound in his voice.

"He was just checking on his son," I said. "I was sitting here already. He has a right, and I got a right. Ye got a problem with that?"

Greene shook his head and smiled at me. "No problem,

Mr. Syms. Just remember, though, it might be in a bit that ye will be required to consider just whose 'rights' ye find more to yer liking."

"That talk sounds a bit treasonous," I said, keeping me voice calm, though inside I was shaking. Just how far had these men taken that talk?

"No, no," Greene said. "Not at all. Just something ye might want to think on."

He stood up then and took his leave. I watched him go, feeling queasy. This was such a pickle I was in, and it seemed to be getting more picklish every day. I turned back toward John and watched him move and moan a bit with the pain. And I knew then that the longer we were here, the more we risked the chance of losing it all, not only our strong bodies but worse, our reasonable heads.

I can smell something fishy going down, and it ain't real fish. No, something's brewing on this boat, and it ain't a storm, I can tell ye that. I prayed then for the ice and snow to give way to clear sailing—even if it does mean me catching a glimpse of what must be the worst I've ever looked in me life.

Yer loving son, Seth

JOHN HUDSON

Never before have I so heartily wished for a voyage to end. And I can even say it is not very *heartily* I can wish it. For now, I have taken with the scurvy and am weak and ill and have lost two teeth and have a lengthy scar upon my cheek. Lord, what a sight I must be. Not that I would know much about my looks, being unable as I am to even make my way up the ladder. Five days now, I have not moved from my hammock.

The last time I saw the white that daily surrounds us, it was quite an effort to pull myself abovedecks. But I had to see him—the savage who had come. How strange he looked in his big furs with animal hides round his legs. Three times now on my voyages with Father, I have seen natives from this land, and even so, I have still not gotten used to them. They are a different lot, murmuring in a very odd tongue. Still, we are able to communicate by waving our hands and gesturing. I sometimes have to laugh watching Father try and trade without the advantage of words. He does look absurd. It took all I had in me the other day not to imitate him as I have on past trips. But I know this time around it would only add to the men's growing tendency to ignore his commands and to not take him seriously as captain of this ship. And so I had to hide my laughter. But it was hard.

We did have high hopes that this savage could provide us with food. Father asked everyone to give him knives and hatchets. King, Prickett, and Staffe gave him theirs. I would have gone to get mine, but I was weak enough just from the climb above that to try it again would have been suicide. Father gave the man his own knife, a looking glass, and some buttons. The savage seemed most pleased and made signs that he would come again. Father gestured as if putting food in his mouth, and the native nodded as if he understood.

But when he returned the next day, he brought only deerskins. (He must have eaten the food himself—wise man that he was, for I do believe we would all have fallen upon him if he had indeed brought any food at all.) Still, the skins were something. Father offered him a hatchet for both pelts. The savage did not seem pleased. He wanted to offer only one of the skins, but in the end, he gave in to Father's bargaining. I am still not sure why Father was so insistent on getting both deerskins—they will hardly alleviate our problems with hunger. Still, the cold is pervasive, and perhaps Father intends to barter with those onboard, rationing further for the pelts. I don't know, and Father refuses to discuss it. All I do know is that the savage seemed a bit disappointed. I almost felt bad for the fellow. It is hard to bargain when languages are so different, and too, he was certainly outnumbered as we all stood about like big baboons watching the whole process.

When the trading was done, he indicated that there were many others like him to the north and south and that after a bit, he would return. This gave us hope again. If there are so many of his people about, there must be some food to keep them going. Truly one wonders how these people survive this land. But alas, he did not return. And now, even if he did, I could no longer find the strength to pull myself abovedecks to see him. Instead, I spend my days drifting in and out, barely aware of those around me, eating only when Nicholas Syms, in his kindness, brings me a bit of whatever we have—and that isn't much, lately only moss and frogs. The French must be mad to think frogs' legs a delicacy. Let them spend a month eating them daily, and they will look upon good English mutton as a treat the palette *truly* longs for.

Oh, how I wish for this sickness to pass. The weakness of it angers me to no end. How incredibly boring to be lying here, day after day, barely able to lift my head. I can but sleep and think. And think much I do. I think of the day when the illness first hit me.

It was a dark day—as are all the days here now. Greene had infuriated the crew by not doing his share of the few chores we each had about the boat. "What's the point?" he had said angrily. "Them same chores will still be there and waiting tomorrow." But we liked to keep things going, to feel some purpose in the day, and Greene pointing out so clearly that we hadn't much to do and not much point to do it, depressed most of us—myself the exception. I couldn't let him get away with lowering all our spirits.

"Greene," I said, "seems you need to get some action. How about a little friendly swordplay?"

To be honest, I was itching to take up the sword again. It had been weeks since Father and I had jousted, and I felt in need of some practice. I had heard Greene wasn't bad with the sword, and I thought it might provide a little entertainment for the crew. Father would have my hide when he found out about it, but he had gone off on his own in the shallop for an hour or so, and I felt it safe to be about some mischief. Besides, my body was crying out for some exercise. There's only so much dreaming and thinking one can do before one goes mad unless he lets off some steam. And so when Greene agreed, I picked up the sword eagerly.

The crew came up from below, gathering around us as Greene and I circled each other. They clapped and cheered, and it felt good to give them a little diversion from all this cold and darkness. My heart pounded with excitement.

Green gave the first thrust, shoving his sword out swiftly toward my side. An inexpert move, one I expected. And I moved quickly, sending him reeling toward the other side of the boat. The crew exploded with laughter. I took a slight bow, sensing even as I did, Greene coming for another attack. He was behind me, but I turned swiftly and deflected his sword. Lord, it felt good to raise a little sweat on my brow—at least, at that moment, it did.

He attacked again. I deflected. He attacked yet again, and once more, I deflected. I moved to my left. He followed. I turned and ran across the deck, jumped onto a barrel. We came to blows, he from below and me from above. I jumped from the barrel back to the deck. I felt so alive and laughed aloud as he missed again. I knew my footwork and laughter were infuriating him, but truly, this was the most fun I had had in weeks.

The crew was cheering us from the sides, some for Greene, some for me. It was exhilarating. Greene took a high swing. I lifted my sword and met his with a loud clang. I twisted his sword from his hand. It fell to the deck, the crew going wild. Greene scrambled for it, and I let him. Then he was upon me again. I took blow upon blow, each harder than the last. I danced around him. He followed. I was enjoying each and every thrust, each and every parlay, until it happened.

Swordplay is rough business, and I had worked up quite a sweat. But even I realized it was perhaps a bit more sweat than was warranted for Greene's efforts. He was a good enough swordsman, but I had been practicing with the king's soldiers. I was younger than he and in better shape. It should have been no match at all, but of a sudden, the weakness hit. My knees buckled on me and sent me sprawling to the deck. I retched. And Greene, the mean spirit that he is, ignored the sickness overcoming me, raised his sword, and with a swift blow, split my cheek open wide.

That was the last I remember. I woke, still in a sweat, my gums and teeth aching. My bones were tired beyond imagining. My cheek was throbbing from where Edward Wilson, the surgeon, had sewn the split ends back together, not too well, I might add.

"How's the swordsman doing?" Syms had said when I woke.

"Is it bad?" I'd asked, reaching unsteadily to touch my cheek.

"Let's just say it hasn't improved yer looks much," Syms said, grinning. "And ye hadn't much to start with."

"Not what the girls of London tell me," I'd said, as I'd struggled to sit.

Syms grinned again. "To tell the truth, the scar might make ye the toast of the town, that is, if ye can think of a good enough story for it. I'd leave out the part where ye fell weakly to yer knees and exposed yerself to a cowardly shipmate for the taking."

"I owe him," I'd responded angrily.

"And ye shall have yer revenge," Syms said softly, pushing me back into the bunk. "But only when ye get yer strength back, young pup. The man was hard-hearted to take ye when ye was down. We all seen it. We know what he done. He'll get his when the time comes, don't ye worry."

"My only worry," I said angrily, "is that I won't be the one to give it to him."

"Rest assured," Syms said, "he's yers for the taking. Everyone agrees."

And so I have a score to settle and a reason besides boredom to get myself up and out of this hammock.

RICHARD HUDSON

Richard was hot and wanted nothing more than to be off with his friends, playing with the slingshots they had recently made. Just the other day, his friends had watched in awe as his stone had sailed far off the dock, arching high and splashing down several hundred yards into the harbor. Why did churning butter take so awfully long?

"My arm's tired!" Richard yelled to his mother.

The shutters of their house had been flung wide open, and spring sunshine dotted the pathway in front of him. Richard could hear his mother pull bread from the oven. He breathed deeply. Between Mama's newly baked bread and the smell of warm earth, it promised to be a great day. *If only butter could churn itself*, Richard thought sourly.

"My arm's tired!" Richard shouted in again.

"I don't think it's done yet, but I'll check," Mama called back.

She came outside, wiping her hands on her apron.

"It has to be ready," Richard whined. "I've been beating this thing for hours now."

Mama lifted the heavy lid on the churn. Richard looked inside and rolled his eyes. The stupid cream was still just that, cream!

"Sorry, Richard," Mama said, "not yet."

She put the lid back on and handed the churn back to him. He made a face at the wooden bucket. "This is a girl's job, you know," he said.

"But I don't have any girls," Mama reminded him. "I only have you."

"Johnny should be doing it," Richard complained.

"Johnny's not here," said Mama.

"When Johnny comes back," Richard muttered, "I'm going to hand him over all my chores. He can churn the butter, cut up the logs, feed the chickens, weed the garden, and run errands for you. He can do it all. I've had to do it for so long now. It isn't fair."

"I'm sure John has chores enough of his own, young man," Mama said curtly. "Life at sea is not easy, Richard. You can't possibly think that your brother and father do nothing all day. I suspect they work a lot harder than you do!"

Richard was hurt by his mother's harsh words. She was so ill-tempered these days, and Richard had heard the talk of the town. Some people said Papa was gone forever. Even Richard's friends had suggested horrible things to him: that a terrible storm had drowned Papa and Johnny, that some dreadful beast no one had ever heard of had eaten them, that they were lost and would wander the seas forever, *never* finding their way home.

But Richard did not want to worry Mama more than

she was, and so he had kept his own fears to himself and pretended as if all was well. But today, he could no longer do it. He felt his face pucker up and knew he was about to cry. He turned away so Mama would not see. But it was too late.

"I'm sorry," Mama said quickly, brushing the hair back that had fallen into his eyes. "I know I am a bit out of sorts. I don't mean to snap at you. Truly, I don't. I know you are working very hard. Why, you are my best little helper. I really don't know what I'd do without you."

Richard was relieved. Mama thought he was crying about the churning. "I did carry that whole load of wood in yesterday," he reminded her, then remembered that he had broken her best pitcher when he had dropped the wood to the floor, shaking the table so hard, it sent the pitcher crashing to the ground. He drew in his breath, waiting for her angry reply. But she surprised him.

"Aye, you did."

His mother seemed suddenly agreeable. Perhaps, he thought with hope, he would be granted a reprieve. "And I have been churning this butter for a *long, long* time," he said, wondering just how far he could press the matter.

"So you have," said Mama. "You are a very hard worker, Richard. I was wrong to say otherwise."

Richard nodded, pleased. "Johnny's not such a good churner," he said.

"No," Mama agreed. "He's not. And I shall tell him and your father what a great help you have been to me this past year. Your father will be pleased."

"Maybe he'll take me with him on his next voyage, then," Richard said eagerly. "I should like nothing more,

Mama, than to sail away to places others have never seen before. I would be a great explorer. I know I would."

He had gone too far. Mama's face whitened. But instead of yelling at him, she knelt down.

"Not yet, Richard," she whispered softly to him. "Can you imagine me here all alone? I would be so lonely then, wouldn't I?"

"Oliver could come visit," Richard pointed out.

"Oliver has his own family. He has Alice to look after," Mama replied. "Perhaps you will go one day, little one, but not yet, not yet."

Richard sighed deeply and rolled his eyes. "Back to the churning then, I guess."

Mama laughed. Richard smiled at her with delight. He had not heard her laugh like that in a long time.

"Aye, back to the churning," Mama said. "But if you finish this, young man, perhaps I could see my way to giving you an hour or so with your friends. It is such a fine day."

"Really, Mama?" Richard asked, throwing his arms about her neck.

Mama hugged him back. "Really. But you must finish the churning."

"I will, Mama. I promise."

Mama stood, just as Mistress Howley stepped out next door, a basket over her arms.

"Good day, Mrs. Hudson," she called.

"Good day, Mistress Howley," replied Mama. "I hope all is well with you."

"Well enough," Mistress Howley said sharply. "Have you any news on the whereabouts of your husband?"

Mama shook her head. Richard scowled. Now Mama would be sad and depressed all over again—just when Richard had gotten her to laugh and think about letting him go free for the afternoon. Didn't the old crow know that if they had news of Papa, Mama would be telling everyone?

"Then perhaps he's reached the Orient after all," Mistress Howley said. "It has been a year. Surely if he hadn't, he'd be back by now."

Richard's mouth dropped open. Was the old woman being nice to them? She had never done that before!

"Then again," Mistress Howley added, "perhaps he's drowned, along with that other young rascal of yours." With these words, she raised her chin into the air and scurried off down the road.

"May you be cursed with the plague!" Mama shouted after her, raising her fist in the air and shaking it after the old woman.

Mistress Howley turned, a look of surprise on her face. Richard stared, amazed. Mama spit in Mistress Howley's direction, a spit Richard knew that even Johnny would have been proud of.

Richard giggled. "Mama," he said, "you mustn't speak like that to older people. You tell me so all the time."

"That woman's the devil himself," Mama muttered.

Richard crowed with delight. He couldn't believe his mother. "I like you like this, Mama. I wish you would get mad at Mistress Howley all the time. Then maybe you wouldn't yell at me when I let go a toad in her backyard."

Mama turned. "Richard, my dear," she said, "hurry up with that churning. For when you finish, you and I are going on a little junket."

"To where?" Richard said, his smile fading. He regarded his mother with suspicion. She had said she was going to let him spend time with his friends, but instead was she going to give him more chores now?

"We are going down to the Thames with several baskets," Mama told him. "There we will fill them with all manner of toads we manage to find. We will then sneak back here and let them all loose in Mistress Howley's yard. And if by chance she is still out, I might even let you slip a few into her house."

Richard's eyes widened, and he laughed out loud. "Mama, you are wicked," he cried out.

Mama grinned. "I am wicked, aren't I?" she said, turning to flounce back inside.

Richard let his arm fly up and down as fast as he could. He couldn't believe it! Mama was going to help him put toads in Mistress Howley's yard. He almost shouted with excitement. Mama hadn't been this fun in such a long time. And though he knew he wanted to see his friends, the slingshot contest could wait. Mama might be ready to pull a prank today, but Richard was sure this good mood would not last forever.

ISABELLA DIGGES

April 23, 1611

Tonight I have done what I should have done months ago.
I wrote my father and told him, in as few words as possible, the
state of my mind. I sealed the letter and sent a courier off with
it, breathing a sigh of satisfaction at having, at last, laid bare
my utter disgust at his disregard for me.

His last note to me was one of panic, for at first, the duchess
refused his proposal, even though the king himself had ordered
the match. Apparently, the duchess threw a loud and lengthy
tantrum upon learning that she had been promised without her
consent. In fact, had she not been related to the king by
marriage, she might even now be facing the gallows, as many of
her words could have been interpreted as treasonous.

My father was wild with worry, for when our creditors heard
about the duchess's refusal, they panicked and began again
demanding monies from him. Thus his insane insistence that I
send another map posthaste.

It is true that I have not sent one for weeks, nor do I

intend to, for while sitting with my young charge and practicing the harpsichord, I did overhear Von Dectmer being told in a low whisper that indeed others had "turned up." I am not a fool. I know what he is being told. I kept my eyes lowered that day, and slowly, I am disengaging myself from the son, pleading headaches when he pursues me in the evenings after dinner. I cannot be found in that map room!

But I must tread slowly. Too quick a refusal of him might anger him enough to reveal to his father what has taken place between us and where it has taken place. That would be disastrous. And while my father is unaware, for I dare not send this news to him, I have, in my head, the trump card. For I have one map still safely stored there, one that shows much of the New Land's shores below the Furious Overfall, an area all explorers are sure leads to the East, even as they fear the treacherousness of the waters there. A map of that will be worth a king's ransom!

But I will not send it. For this map will be my passage home, and it will stay dormant in my head until I myself stand before our great king and lay it at his feet. For that is what I intend to do. I have had my fill of my father receiving all the glory while I take all the risks.

And on that day, when at last I am returned to my beloved England and stand before the throne, I will elicit one favor only from my monarch—the knighting of Captain Hudson, whether he should succeed or fail. I do not think it a grand request, for the man, as I have, has risked life and limb to greaten the glories of his homeland. And though he may not have found the northern passage to the East, for who even knows if one exists, still he has gone out upon rough and unknown seas four times over, in order to try and find it. Surely, that deserves a knighthood.

But even should the king not agree, I am determined. He

shall not have his map unless Captain Hudson has his reward, and I shall have mine in the form of John Hudson. Oh, I am so pleased with this plan.

And so I reread my sniveling father's complaints that tomorrow night he is to be married. I read of his concern that the duchess and he might not be compatible. And while one part of my mind thinks, How dare he speak to me of having to endure an unpleasant relationship, for isn't that the very thing I have been doing for months now? the other part of my mind sings with triumph.

And so I wrote my father in no uncertain terms to quit his whining and get on with his marriage, reminding him that we have all done our part to regain our favor at court and our status financially. I added that while it would be satisfying to be in a loving marriage, it is not necessary. The duchess's money will more than make up for the inconvenience.

It gives me great pleasure to write him in this fashion, for it has been a long time coming. And soon I, Isabella Digges, will return safely to England, having spied upon the Dutch, and marry the man I have dreamed of all these months. And what a grand day that will be!

SETH SYMS

⤜⥤

May 1, 1611

Dearest Mama:

We've had a real, live savage on board. Lord, Mama, he sure gave me the shivers! It weren't as if he was all that different—I mean he looked the same as me, only younger, perhaps eighteen or so—it was just knowing that this here was a savage, not some good Christian English soul. I had to wonder what he was thinking behind those big brown eyes of his. It couldn't be the same thoughts that I had. But then again, maybe it was. Maybe me looks gave him the shivers too. Who knows?

But Mama, the way he was dressed! I ain't ever seen anything like it—all these animal skins covering his body. I will say, I did think twice once me eyes got used to the strange sight. The boy looked warm, I'll give him that. Made me want to go on out and try and find me some deerskins too.

Not that we haven't looked hard enough for meat. We've sent party after party out in search of food. And as time goes on, it's harder and harder. Now not only ain't we finding nothing, but those that go out is weak from lack of eating. Even if they did see something to go after, I ain't sure they got the ability to chase it and kill it or to even aim straight. Hunger does all kinds of strange things to the body, eyesight included.

Some of that anger has died out today, though. Wilson, Greene, Pierce, Thomas, Motter, Mathew, and Lodlo all went off this morning, same as always, to see if they could find some food. And Lordy be, for once these men did! They came home with fish. Now I ain't much for fish, as ye know, being a beef man meself, but I sure *loved* fish today.

The men on the hunting trip called out loud and strong as they reached the *Discovery*, and those of us with any strength left—and there ain't many of us—ran to the side to see what all the shouting was about. And there they were, those seven, holding up two fish in each hand and waving like mad toward their boat, which was filled to the brim. We all let out a cheer, in our creaky half-starved voices, and even the weak and sickly ones from below came up to see what was about.

John hobbled up next to me. He took one look out at the longboat heading toward us and said, "Something's fishy, I see!" and then under his breath, I heard him whisper, "God be praised!"

I had to chuckle at that. It seemed almost irreverent for this one to be praising God. This same young one who drove us all half-mad with his jokes and pranks, who scampered halfway up the mast and swung himself around it, giving us all a goodly scare. This one was praising God now like he was some kind of saint? Thinking on this, for a moment, I had a small fright that God might think the same and turn that longboat over in anger, losing us all those hard-won fish in the process. But no, the longboat pulled in, and we dragged it across the ice and up the side of the *Discovery*.

And then we set about to feasting! There must have been at least five hundred fish in that boat. I will say they were tiny, but I do believe I ain't ever had a meal that I enjoyed so much. Some of the men just couldn't wait, and they set on those fish once they were divided up and ate them raw. Not me. Like I said, I'm more a beef man meself. So I waited a bit until Cook got the fire going, and then I took an old nail that was lying about, stuck those little bitty fishes on there, and roasted them good. Then I went abovedecks, sat meself down with that plate of food, and leaned back against an old barrel to soak up some sun that the Lord had provided this fine day too.

John came and sat next to me. His face was drawn, and he had some difficulty keeping those fish down. But at least some of it stayed, and I think both he and I knew he would get better because of it.

"Would be a feast fit for a king if we just had some ale," he said, smiling at me, the juices from his cooked fish dripping down his chin. He wiped the juices away with what remained of his sleeve. There weren't much. It was mostly just holes.

I told him that for a half-starved man, he sure was demanding.

He laughed. "Not half-starved anymore, my friend. Now

that my belly's full, I can once more think of all the other things I'm truly half-starved for."

I rolled my eyes and told him that maybe I should have eaten his portion if it meant he was going to start talking about that Isabella again, and filling me shoes with pieces of ice.

John grinned. "Aw now, Nicholas, I know that you will welcome the return of my good sense of humor."

"Good sense," I grumbled. "Now there's a joke if I've ever heard one."

John laughed good-naturedly, stretched himself out in the sun, and lay back.

It was then that his father came and stood over us, asking if his son had gotten enough to eat, and I could now see the concern where once I had been blind to it all.

John opened one eye and grinned up at his father. He answered in the affirmative and inquired if his father was also feeling satisfied.

His father nodded and smiled, his relief at his son's obviously heightened spirits evident to me this time.

He looked out then at the vast whiteness around us, the whiteness that now, with a bit of food in me belly, didn't seem so completely foreign or unwelcoming. I even thought, just for a minute, that I might have smelled a bit of earth warming, but more than likely that was just me stomach feeling satisfied for once.

"The ice is beginning to break, I feel it," the captain said.

John agreed with him.

"We shall be on our way then, soon," the captain went on, a sigh in his voice, "and there shall be more food as we

had today. Our bad luck is changing, John. I can feel it. Soon
we shall be back at sea."

"And on our way home," John said, his eyes wide open
now and looking up sternly at his father.

I turned to look at the captain. *What made young John say
that?* I found meself wondering. Could there be any other
choice but to return to the good old shores of England?
Surely the captain wouldn't continue on, searching once
more for that passage to the Orient? We have been at sea
for over a year now. We have no provisions to speak of. Our
clothes are in tatters. But mostly, our spirits are broken. We
have to go home. We have to. I couldn't bear it if we kept
on now. I have had enough. Everyone has had enough.

"But of course, John," the captain replied to his son's
comment. "But of course."

Yet the captain's manner was distracted, and even then, I
saw him gazing once more—not at all that ice that was
surrounding us, but out toward where there was only a
glimmer of open sea. And I felt a shiver run clear down me
spine. Will I leave this boat alive? Will any of us? And most
of all, racing through me mind over and over now, is this:
Is Captain Hudson crazier than any of us have even
suspected?

Yer loving son, Seth

JOHN HUDSON

Father is in a foul mood today. He has just returned from having gone exploring in the shallop, hoping to find some natives to trade with. He did come across some savages, but it seems the natives, on seeing him approach, set fire to the few stunted trees around. Father could not get near the group, but he could see that they seemed fat and happy, something that we most definitely are not. And so I cannot even talk to him about what has happened while he was gone.

Truly, it was a good thing that he decided to take the boat and do some exploring, though at first, I thought he was mad to be leaving the ship. But while he was gone, I overheard a plot by Greene and Wilson, who planned to steal the shallop and leave us to fend for themselves.

The months on this boat have made us all crazy. Did they truly think they could survive on their own? And would they have left us without the means to fish or hunt by taking the shallop? We have turned from men who love adventure to animals intent on surviving. It is not a pretty sight.

And so Father will not see me, but has sequestered himself in his cabin, ranting and raving. I am sorry about it, for this would have been the first chance I have had to repay Greene for the mark on my cheek. Having heard his plan, my mind could only gleefully see him slapped in the brig belowdecks, where he would wallow in that cold and damp part of the ship. This would be a fair reward for his ungentlemanly swipe at me. But then again, perhaps it is for the best anyway. Should I have ratted on the crew and they had discovered my treachery, I would have been dead before I could say sorry. Being a captain's son brings a great burden. One likes to be part of the crew, and yet one knows you are not. You must watch each and every thing you say if you want to join with the others and not have them view you as a boy with privileges given him and no other.

So I kept my tongue and will continue plotting my revenge against Greene. Already my teeth have been improving, and my strength is returning. And yet I know I must look a sight, all skin and bones. Issa will be hard-pressed to welcome me back should I not have some time to fatten myself up a little and get a shave at a barber's before reaching home.

Home. I think on it every day. I think of my brother Richard and of my mother. What must they think has become of us? Already we are gone for more than a year. Do they think us dead? Richard may welcome that, so much do we fight these days. And yet, I truly love him, pest that he is. Mother would never give up hope. It is not in her character to admit defeat. In that, she is much like my father.

And I think of Oliver. Did he think me as much of a pest as I did Richard? Sometimes, I think that he must have. I certainly tried my best to follow him everywhere he went, even when he did most heartily try to discourage me. I remember myself at thirteen, gangly and awkward. Oliver was sixteen then and suddenly allowed out at night while I was not, and he was rather pompous about his newly granted freedom. He gave himself airs, as if he knew more than I did and so required more respect. He was always saying, "Wait. You'll see how merry it is."

His words infuriated me. In the past, I had always kept up with him, and suddenly, now, I found myself behind. It was not a situation I was overly fond of. And so I determined that I would follow Oliver one night and see exactly what he was up to on these outings.

And that is what I did. I slipped from the house that night and followed him. He walked through the dark streets of London with a determined step. I was frightened. Every dark shadow suddenly loomed large and carried great danger.

But at last, we reached a pub, and I saw Oliver go through the doors. I slipped inside myself, into a room full of smoke and laughter, music and conversation. I wasn't noticed. I saw Oliver across the room and darted around until I could see him, but he could not spy me. I watched him put his arm around a woman. She giggled becomingly, nodded, and placed her lips upon Oliver's.

I could do this too, I thought. It did not seem so terribly difficult. And so, swaggering a bit, I approached a woman who had just come in the door. I put my arm around her and asked for a kiss.

The ensuing pandemonium caught me completely off guard. I had put my arm around a *lord's* wife—a woman who had simply entered the tavern looking for her wayward husband. The pub went wild—the lord's wife screaming at me to leave her be and threatening to have everyone in the place arrested, the pub owner looking desperately for a way to calm the lady and get rid of me, and, unbeknownst to me, my own brother slipping quietly out the back door.

When at last, my father brought me home that night, my mother gave me a whipping and a tongue-lashing about propriety. But worst was Oliver. He was already long in bed, and when I came into the room we shared, he simply grinned at me. I could have killed him. And yet later, when I was sixteen, it was this same brother who took me out with him when finally, I was granted that freedom.

Thinking on this now, I miss Oliver something terrible. And too, I am reminded of how my brother Richard must look up to me as I did to Oliver. When I get back, I promise myself to take him more seriously, to stop playing pranks on him constantly, and to be the big brother that Oliver was, ultimately, to me. And I will take my mother aside and let her know just how truly I love her.

Lord, this darkness and cold is turning me into an introspective fellow. And so I think I will change this serious vow just a bit.

I vow to be a better brother to Richard and a more loving son to my mother, *and* I vow to drink twenty pints of ale, eat four sides of mutton, and kiss Issa for at least two hours the moment I return. There—now *those* are resolutions truly worth keeping!

RICHARD HUDSON

Mama, Oliver's coming down the street, and he's got Mr. Hondius with him!" Richard scampered into the yard, almost knocking his mother over as she carried a basket of herbs from the garden.

"Slow down, young man," Mama warned, putting down her basket and taking Richard by the shoulders. "What are you yelling?"

"Oliver's coming down the lane, and he's got Mr. Hondius with him," Richard said more slowly, his face hot from the run back.

Richard was excited, for Mama and he had not had many visitors of late. Jodocus Hondius was a great cartographer and map publisher and a good friend of Oliver's and Papa's. He was Dutch, and Richard loved hearing his funny accent.

The front gate opened, and Oliver came in, calling out for Mama. A small, sprightly child came running around the corner.

Richard took one look and scowled. How had he missed that Alice was with his brother and Mr. Hondius?

"Grandmama!" Alice shouted. "Here I am. Here I come."

Mama opened her arms, lifted the child up, and swung her high. Alice laughed with delight, shouting, "More, more, Grandmama!"

Richard fled, hiding behind the lilac bush in the yard. If Alice was here, the whole visit was ruined!

"You'll hurt yourself if you keep lifting her in that fashion, Mother," said Oliver, coming around to the back with Mr. Hondius.

Mama smiled. "Oh, Oliver, what do I care? It's so delightful the way Alice laughs when I swing her high. Hello, Jodocus."

From his hiding spot, Richard watched Mama put little Alice down and turn her cheek toward Mr. Hondius, who kissed her lightly.

"Hello, Katerine," Jodocus said, calling her by her name in Dutch. "You're looking vell."

Vell? Richard giggled at the word.

"It's all this lifting I do," she said, bending down to plant a kiss on the top of Alice's head. Richard thought he might throw up.

"Where's Ritchie?" Alice asked.

Richard scowled. He hated when Alice called him that. Why couldn't she learn his proper name and use it?

"I don't know," Mama answered. She turned to look for him. Richard moved back deeper into the lilac bushes. He wished he'd been near the gate. He could have escaped completely then.

"Richard, come out from there," Mama said, spying

him. "Why didn't you tell me Alice was with your brother and Mr. Hondius?"

"Didn't see her," Richard grumbled.

"Well now that you do, why don't you take care of her while I have a talk with Oliver and Mr. Hondius?" Mama said.

"What am I supposed to do with her?" asked Richard in exasperation.

Mama laughed. "Whatever you do with your friends."

Was Mama joking?

"We catch toads," Richard said. "We chase dogs and pull their tails. She can't do those things."

Oliver laughed. "Let him go, Mother. Alice will be happy sitting on your lap while we visit."

Richard smiled. Oliver was his hero! Why couldn't Oliver live with them? And Johnny could live with stupid old Alice!

Oliver came over, bent down, and began pulling Richard out from his hiding spot, tickling him in the process.

"Stop, Oliver," called Richard, laughing and grabbing hold of the bush. "Stop."

Oliver grinned and let his brother go. Alice came running to her father as he stood back up. "Do it to me, Papa. Do it to me."

Richard scowled as he crawled from the bushes. "You don't do those things to girls, Alice," he said to his young niece. "Girls are supposed to just sit and comb their hair."

"Is that what you think I do all day, young man?" Mama asked.

Richard rolled his eyes. "You're different. You're my mother."

Mama, Oliver, and Mr. Hondius laughed at this.

"Ach, my young friend," Jodocus said. "Someday I suspect you vill be happy if a young maiden vants to spend time vith you."

Richard looked at Mr. Hondius. Was he mad? "Don't think so," he said.

Mama shook her head. "All right, then," she said, "Alice can stay with us. But I do believe I had sent you for water when you came running here with your news. Where's the bucket?"

"I dropped it in the lane when I saw Oliver." Richard sighed. "I'll go get it."

"And come right back," Mama warned. "I have a few more chores for you today."

"There's always more chores," Richard moaned.

Again, the three grown-ups laughed. Richard didn't think they would find it so funny if they were the ones going for water, but he did as Mama bade and headed down the lane. As he plodded along, he kicked at the dirt. The dry dust rose in a cloud around him.

Halfway down the lane, he found the bucket lying on its side. He picked it up and headed toward the well. Moss grew on the sides of the damp stone structure, slimy stuff that Richard adored. He attached the bucket to the rope and lowered it into the depths of the well, hearing it give off a satisfying splash as it hit the water. He pried some of the slimy moss off the side of the stone, slipping it into his pocket. Maybe he'd put it in Alice's hair later, when she was annoying him too much. He began to pull on the rope to lift the bucket back to the surface, straining with the weight of it.

Slowly, the bucket rose until it hung just above the lip of the well. This was the tricky part. Holding tight to the rope, Richard leaned in to grab the bucket. Many had been the time when his hands had slipped and the bucket had gone crashing back down, leaving Richard to raise the heavy container once more. Slowly, slowly, Richard leaned forward. He reached out a hand. He had it! He swung the bucket toward the lip of the well and set it down, smiling to himself.

But just as he was about to unhook the bucket, something wet nudged his hand, pushing the bucket sideways. It tipped, its contents sloshing all over Richard before it fell to the road, breaking in the process.

Richard turned. Behind him stood Farmer Shipley's big fat cow, its brown eyes staring solemnly at him.

Richard howled. "You stupid cow! Look what you've done! And you've broken the bucket, too."

The cow blinked but did not move.

Furiously, Richard picked up the pieces of the bucket and stomped home. In the house, Mama sat with Oliver, Mr. Hondius, and Alice, who nestled on Mama's lap. They all turned when Richard threw open the door.

"What happened to you?" cried Mama.

Richard told them, anger smoldering inside. "I hate cows," he declared.

"Moo," said Alice.

Richard glared at her. "And I hate girls, too. I hate cows and girls."

Mama and Oliver and Mr. Hondius laughed.

"It's not funny," Richard insisted. He hated when grown-ups laughed at him.

"Come on, Richard," Oliver said. "Come sit with us

for a while, and before we leave, I will go and get the water for you."

"Truly?" Richard asked, his anger melting away at the offer from his brother.

"Aye," Oliver said.

Richard smiled, relieved that he wouldn't have to pull the bucket up again, making his arms ache the next day. Happily, he dumped the broken bucket pieces outside and then came back in.

"Were you and Mr. Hondius working together today?" Richard asked his brother eagerly, as he went to sit near him. Oliver had an exciting job, going to court often. "Is that why you're here?"

"Ja," Mr. Hondius said. "Your brother grows more assured as a cartographer every time I see his new vork. You should be proud of him, Richard."

Richard shrugged. Of course he was proud of his brother. Why wouldn't he be?

Mr. Hondius turned toward Mama. "There is vord on the street that many of the Dutch maps are now in the hands of the English navigators. My government is very vorried about how such information is leaking out. I had hoped Oliver could tell me how the English have come by such information, but ach, he knows nothing. So I return with nothing to tell my government."

Richard saw Mama glance quickly at Oliver, who had turned suddenly red. And Richard knew in that moment that Oliver did know, and that he was not being truthful with Mr. Hondius. Richard could tell that Mama knew too. Why weren't they telling Mr. Hondius if they knew who had stolen the maps?

"But tell me, Jodocus, how have you been and how is your family?" Mama said, changing the subject.

"Fine, thank you, Katerine," he said. "But more important, how fare you?"

"I'll be better when I receive word that the *Discovery* is heading up the Thames," Mama said. "Henry's been gone a very long time now," she added softly.

"Ja," the Dutch mapmaker said quietly. "I understand. And I know about the loneliness of the heart, Katerine. And so I asked Oliver if he vould take me here today to give you this."

Mr. Hondius reached into his pocket and drew out a small etching. He held out his hand, and Richard saw that it was an engraved portrait of Papa.

"Oh, Jodocus," Mama said, a catch in her voice. "When did you do this?"

"The last time I see Henry in Amsterdam," Mr. Hondius told her. "He visit me and ask that I make this for him. I think, Katerine, that he vanted to give it to you."

Mama reached for the small engraving, and Richard saw tears coming to her eyes. He wished then that he had thought to make a drawing of Papa. It might not have been as grand as Mr. Hondius's, but maybe it would have made Mama happier these past few months, as this one seemed to be doing now.

"Grandmama," Alice asked, "why are you crying?"

"Ach, Katerine," Mr. Hondius said quickly. "I did not mean to sadden you. I thought having the portrait might make the vaiting easier."

"Oh, it will, Jodocus," said Mama, reaching out to take Papa's friend's hand. "Forgive me. It's just that I miss him so much. I don't know what it is, but somehow I am frightened this trip."

Richard looked up quickly. His mother had not said this before.

"That's unlike you, Mother," Oliver said. "You've never let yourself believe that Father and John would not return."

Mama nodded. "You're right, Oliver. I have always believed. But this time, I don't know. It's just a funny feeling I have. Sometimes when I'm working, I'll turn quickly, and it's as if I see Henry standing there, looking at me like he did when we were younger. I feel as if something is turning me back toward the past rather than letting me look forward to the future."

She sighed. "This quest he has always had—the quest to find new places, new lands, new passages. All my life I have let him catch me up in his quests, but now . . ." She paused. "Suddenly I feel as if this questing is over, and my own quest is about to begin."

"A quest for vat, Katerine?" Mr. Hondius asked anxiously.

Mama suddenly laughed, making the hard knot of fear that had settled in Richard's stomach loosen a bit. "I don't know, Jodocus. It's probably just a woman's silliness."

She put the engraving to her chest. "But this I will always treasure, my friend. I thank you for bringing it to me. And Henry, when he returns, will know that you eased an old woman's worry and anxiety."

"You're not old, Mama," Richard said, rolling his eyes.

"And it is for statements such as these, Richard, that I love you so," said Mama, reaching out and pulling him to her for a hug. Richard wiggled away, scowling.

But inside, that cold knot of fear was back. Something did feel strange, and Richard was aware that as more time passed, the feeling was growing stronger. Was Mama right? Was something wrong? Were Papa and Johnny in some kind of trouble? And why were Mama and Oliver lying to Mr. Hondius, one of Papa's closest friends? What if Johnny and Papa *never* came home?

"Why are you crying, Ritchie?" Alice asked, toddling over to him and looking at him with concern.

Without thinking twice, Richard punched her hard. He heard his mother scream with distress and Oliver jump to his feet. He would be in trouble now, but he didn't care. Hitting Alice had felt good.

ISABELLA DIGGES

May 8, 1611

   My hand trembles. I can barely hold the quill. And yet, in writing what has befallen me, I feel I may be able to soothe this shaking and in so doing, devise a plan to rescue myself from these terrible circumstances.

   They have discovered it all! And I am as sure as the weak sunlight that peeks now and then between the thin bars of my cell window, that Von Dectmer had known for some time. By coming into my bedroom in the early hours of this morning, rousing me from my sleep and laying me bare for the soldiers who did accompany him to see me in my nightclothes, he did humiliate me as best he could.

   I did not go quietly. I denied it all. But Von Dectmer only laughed, asking me if he thought my charms had made him blind. Then he ordered the soldiers to take me away, and I began to scream, hoping Emil would come to my rescue. As much as I loathed the boy, I would have promised him anything then to save me. But he did not appear.

And so I kicked and thrashed as they forcibly removed me
from my bed, dragging me down the hallway and banging my
legs against the stone floor and walls of the house. They did not
even give me time to change, and now I sit here, shivering in
this cell, bruised, cold, hungry, and tired, wishing for the warmth
of a good fire, for they have left this one unlit.

For the past few hours, I have paced about, rubbing my
hands to keep warm, convincing myself that there must be a
way out of this horror. I know they will not allow me to send
correspondence off to England. I have no coins with which to
bribe my jailer to send word to my father. How long will it be
before he hears of my arrest? Will I hang before he can rescue
me? I run my finger along my neck, imagining how it will feel
to choke to death.

I have seen but one hanging in my life, and it was not a
pleasant sight. As the stool was kicked from the prisoner's feet,
and he fell and the rope tightened, his eyes popped out of his
head, and his tongue hung from his mouth. When it was over,
he was withered, his tongue black. Will I end my days like that
also? Will my eyes pop from my head as that fellow's did? Oh,
for a dagger to press to my chest and deny these Dutch their
triumph over me! But there is nothing here to kill myself with.
And so I wait.

Emil has finally come, his face white. He begged me to tell him
that his father was wrong, that my feelings for him had been true
and real. I assured him that this was so, pressing myself to him
and begging him to send word to my father and my king.
I pleaded for his aid in helping me escape, promising that we
would be together then. The fool refused, saying he was in
trouble enough, that if he were caught sending word to my
father, he would be turned out of his house. He said that he

loved me, but there was nothing to do but for me to convince his father of my innocence.

Ha! As if I could possibly do that! To my dismay, this avenue I had counted on was now blocked to me. And so when Emil did reach for me, trying to draw me into his arms, I pushed him away. In no uncertain terms and with a great deal of pleasure, I at last told him the truth. That I had used him all this time. That I had felt nothing for him. That my heart had always belonged to another. If I am to hang, I would do it with the look of his crushed hopes in my mind as I mounted the gallows.

His face turned white and then red, and he began shouting venomous slander at me, accusing me of all manner of vile things. I laughed. He was right. I had done just as he accused me. He stormed out of my cell, and I spat at him as he left.

And so I will hang. If this be my fate, I will meet it with dignity. The king shall hear how valiantly I faced the executioner. My father will hear nothing but praises for the daughter who was sent to spy for a kingdom. And John Hudson will weep at his loss of me. That is my fate.

A key has turned in my cell door, and the jailer has finally brought me some food. I am famished, and smile at him unthinkingly. He blinks with surprise. And I pause.

Perhaps I am not hung just yet.

SETH SYMS

෴ ෴

June 12, 1611

Dearest Mama:

'Tis been a sad day today. Me heart is weary with all
that has gone on, and yet I know deep down I should be
rejoicing. We are making ready to depart! Depart—how
dear that word is to me. If all goes well, I should see the
shores of England and ye within a few months. Aye, but
therein lies the rub—will we make it?

We weighed anchor early this morning. How good it
felt to raise the sails and hear them flapping about in the
wind! The ice had broken a few weeks back. I'll not forget
John waking me while it was still dark outside.

"What in God's name do ye want?" I had growled at him.
Being hungry and having not much to do during the daylight
hours, I was a bit put out at having him rouse me to hunger
pains and darkness—me being at that moment in a nice
dream, too.

"Don't you feel it, Nicholas?" he asked, his eyes gleaming

bright, as if he was burning from some inner fire.

"Feel what, young pup?" I'd replied angrily. "All I feel is me stomach aching for food and the desire to run ye through with me sword for waking me before what sun there is here has a chance to rise."

"The boat!" John had laughed. "The boat is rolling."

I lay back in me bunk for a moment, and sure enough, the lad was right. After eight long months of being grounded, I could feel the sway of a boat light on the water.

"Oh, John, me boy," I said, hopping up from me hammock, "I do believe ye might be right."

I followed him to the ladder, and we practically ran up those rungs. Neither of us was keen on waking the others just yet. If we was wrong, there'd be heck to pay for waking the entire ship. So off we went by ourselves to the top.

I followed him to the rail. I had to peer hard, me eyes not being what they used to be, but Mama, the boy was right. There was water beneath the hull. John let out this loud whoop, hugged me round the waist, and lifted me high in the air. Where the boy got that strength from could have only been from sheer joy, seeing as we was still wasting away for want of food.

"I'm off to tell Father," John said. "You want to rouse the others?"

I nodded. For once, it seemed it would be good to be the bringer of news. And I was sure no one was going to mind being wakened a bit early, seeing as we didn't want to miss the opportunity to hasten from there. And no one did. Nah, the crew was ecstatic, every one of them. We could leave and get out from this frozen hole. At last, we were heading back to good old England!

Every man found strength he didn't even know he had that week. We was a team, all working toward the same goal. Even the captain was part of it all, not like some distant man who was in charge, but more a part of a crew making fast for home. He strode about, shouting orders, and we all obeyed as if our lives depended on it. Which if ye think about it a little, they did.

And then today, at last, the water ahead was free and clear, and every inch of our boat was on that smooth surface, and we raised them sails. Oh, what a sight! Never have I been happier to see a patch of cloth than I was this morning.

We sailed away from our winter home. I wasn't on watch, but I stood on the rail anyway and saw the land I now knew as intimately as any person I've known before, slip away. And I wasn't sorry. Not one little bit. We headed out of the bay, catching a good breeze, making good time.

When we reached the mouth of the bay, Captain Hudson decided it was time to give out the rest of the rations he had remaining, the ones we had stored away anticipating the return home. Why he did that, I'll never know. Seems to me, it would have been much better to ration it slowly. See, Mama, there just weren't that much—cheese, that's all. By the time he had divided it up, we each got only three and a half pounds of the stuff.

Now, I'm not stingy. But I was hungry like the rest of them. For months we'd been eating moss and lichen, trying hard to save the last of that food, thinking that when we finally made the long trip home, we'd be eating well again. But I can tell ye, three and a half pounds of cheese ain't much to help a man's stomach for several months—there being no lichen nor moss around to grab up when yer at sea.

Cook had told me long ago we had nine rounds of cheese left, but Captain Hudson only produced five. It was just too sad watching him give out what was left. The man was weeping as he did it. He knows the food won't hold us till Greenland. And it broke me heart just ever so little to know the big man's heart was breaking too.

Some others, though, they was mad—thought the captain was holding out on them. I don't know how they figured that, seeing the man crying as he handed each of them their portion. The way I think on it, Cook just got confused in the counting. Numbers aren't his strongest quality, even if his cooking ain't bad.

Nah, these men, they're just plain angry, angry over the winter, angry over the captain getting us stuck, angry over the lack of food. I ain't too happy about this past winter neither, but what's past is past. We're on our way home, and I say we look forward and not back. But then, no one seems to be asking me opinion on the matter anyway.

Still, their sour looks and whispered words kind of dampened everyone's spirits. And then a bunch of them did something even a fool wouldn't do. In their hunger, they ate up all their rations. Now I ask ye, Mama, don't ye have to be a bit simple-minded doing something like that? Ye got months to go and nothing—not a thing—to eat. They turned on the captain then—accused him of holding back food—put the very words they'd been mumbling about all afternoon right to his face. It weren't a pretty confrontation.

So the captain went and brought out them missing rounds. He opened the barrels and showed us the cheese in them. Ye could tell right away they was spoiled—moldy to the point of making one sick. If they wanted to eat that, they was welcome to it, in me opinion, although now that we was heading back, and I didn't have that much rations left meself, I weren't about to carry their load of the work should they take ill from eating the stuff.

But they hadn't totally lost their heads. They didn't take the food. And so the captain dumped that spoiled stuff overboard, all of us watching it sink into the sea for the fishes and feeling kind of sick watching it go.

And so that was the day today. We're here overnight, and then we are off. What a strange set of moods we will carry with us home. But it is to home we're headed, and tonight as I lay in me bunk, I let meself think of that and nothing else. And John, too, must be thinking of home. He's spent the last few hours trying to find anything that might be used for a looking glass. I told him he ought to give up the search 'cause when he went to glancing in that mirror, he might scare himself silly. He grinned when I said that and told me I weren't nothing but jealous seeing as my Elizabeth would be off-limits once I got home. He said not to worry. He was sure Issa had a friend, and he winked at me. That made me snort. The boy is too much. I closed me eyes, chuckling to meself, and thought that if it weren't for that boy and his pranks, I'd have killed meself on this trip long, long ago. I was grateful to him, Mama. I surely was.

Yer loving son, Seth

JOHN HUDSON

Dear Lord, get us out of this place! I think that now daily, though sometimes I wonder if I should be more cautious and give up praying. Perhaps my simply thinking on the Lord, let alone saying his name, has brought us to this impasse. Perhaps the Lord is so shocked hearing *me* pray that he has decided to have a little fun with us.

We finally left our winter spot on June 18, seeing the ice slowly breaking ahead of the *Discovery*. It was dangerous going because of the ice floes. We had to be cautious steering around them. But what exhilaration it was to face that danger at last. A hundred times let me face the dangers of the sea rather than the tediousness of being trapped. We made it to the harbor that day, where Father divided what remained of the food for the journey home. There wasn't much, I'll admit. It was going to be a long, hard journey returning. But I was confident we could do it, even looking down at the small bit in my hands. The sails whipping about in the breeze and the boat rocking on the waves was all that I needed. We were headed home, and surely we would have some adventures along the way!

But that night, the Lord must have seen my enthusiasm and laughed, for the ice came upon us again. And when morning came, we found ourselves trapped once more.

Now I must say, I do think of myself as one who looks at the positive side of things, but even I had trouble that day finding anything good to say. With the ice surrounding us again and only fourteen days worth of food left, and now being a bit from *any* land, our spirits sank to the lowest ever. Everyone felt it, even Father. He ranted and raved about the weather and the ice.

He was distraught. I could see that. Everyone could, and that was a tenuous situation. And so I went to him in the afternoon. I opened the door to his cabin and found him slumped across the table, his head in his hands, his maps before him. He looked up when I entered and rubbed his eyes tiredly.

"What brings you here?" he asked me. "You're feeling well, I hope?" A wry smile came to his lips. "At least as well as one can when one is starving."

I nodded. "I'm fine, Father," I said to him. "But I could tell this new delay has upset you."

"Upset?" He laughed bitterly then. "Upset, John? It would be good to only be upset."

He shook his head. "No," he said to me. "I am ruined."

"How so?" I asked him. "Surely this is only a temporary delay. We'll be on our way to England soon, hungry of course, but we can do it."

Father sighed. "Aye, son. We will arrive home. But I will have nothing to show for having been gone more than a year."

He threw his arm onto the table and swept his maps to the floor. "Nothing," he repeated angrily. "Not a thing to show for all these months. No way to the Orient discovered. This trip has granted me nothing. I will be lucky to find a child who would invest in sending me out again."

"Father," I said to him as gently as I could, truly horrified that he was more concerned that we arrive with information than that we should arrive at all. "We have mapped new territory. Surely *that* they will welcome. And if they do not, Mother will be happy to see you. All she cares about is that you are alive. Isn't that enough?"

My father smiled slightly. "It should be, shouldn't it, lad?"

I nodded, thinking on how Issa right now would be enough for *me*.

"Your mother's a remarkable woman," he said. "She's given me so many good years and waited always for me so patiently, bearing our absence and the lack of credit. And I do love her with all my heart. It should be enough. It should.

"But," he added softly, "it's not."

He stared off for a moment. "It was always about the sea, John. Always about finding things no one else had yet discovered, going where no one had dreamed of going, and finding that passage. That is what it has always been about."

I couldn't stay then. It made me too sad, a feeling I hate. When I was younger, I admired my father so, always rushing to meetings to find investors or sailing off on some adventure, hearing his glorious tales on his return, his eyes shining with the light of discovery. Maybe that's what my mother still sees in him. I don't know.

I just know that he is incapable of holding on to what is good in his life, just the simple things, and that he must always, always be chasing after the one thing that may forever lie beyond his grasp.

"We'll find it next voyage, Johnny," he called after me as I left, his good humor seeming to have returned. "I know I can find it next journey."

"Aye, Father," I said, but even I could hear the disbelief in my own voice.

I left knowing myself to be wiser than my father. It is not a feeling I am comfortable with. I would not want to be captain, would not want that awesome responsibility. I only want the travel. For I do love the sea, as much, if not more, than he does. I love the way it is so capricious in its whims—stormy one moment, becalmed the next. But I do also love it just for what it is. It does not need to provide me with anything more than that.

Perhaps it is just that I am little more than a simpleton, or perhaps it is just that I am more easily satisfied with a good laugh and a pint of beer. Maybe he is, in truth, a great man for all his looking and questing and inability to settle for what is right in front of him. Or maybe he is mad. I do not know which, nor do I wish to think on it any longer. He is my father, and I love him in spite of his longings. I suppose that is all that is necessary to know now.

And yet if only my father could see his way clear to knowing that his quest was ended the day my mother came into his life, I think it would give him some comfort. But perhaps he will never have peace, and for that, I am truly sorry for him.

RICHARD HUDSON

Mama was still fuming a day later. Richard lay on the floor, hitting marbles, listening to his mother ranting and raving and banging pots together in her anger.

"Mama," he asked, wanting to cover his ears, "are you ever going to stop banging things about?"

"No," Mama shot back. "I intend to make noise for the rest of my life. And if that bothers you, I don't care."

Richard didn't get it. It seemed silly to be mad forever. He shook his head in bewilderment. "Women," he muttered.

There was a sudden silence. Richard looked up to see his mother staring at him. He wished he had kept quiet.

"And what would you know about them?" Mama asked.

"Nothing," Richard said quickly. "And that's why I said it."

"Do you have an interest in women these days, Richard?" Mama asked curiously.

"They're all right, I guess," Richard said noncommittally, irritated that he could feel himself blushing. Here he was now, thinking again about that girl he had met the other day. He and his friends had gone fishing, and on the way back across the field, this girl had stood on the path, just watching them. She had hair the color of the sun and eyes blue as the pond they had just come from. Her hair had been tied back in a red ribbon, and when she said hello directly to Richard, her voice was soft and lilting.

Richard had felt his heart thump in his chest when he looked at her, and for the first time he could remember, he had actually wanted to say hello back to a girl. But inexplicably, he suddenly could not speak. His friends had teased him unmercifully, for his face had turned red. They had punched him and pushed him as he made his way past the girl, nodding a greeting, which had been the best he could seem to do. He cringed now, thinking about it. Would she take him for a mute or a fool? He shook his head, not wanting to remember that embarrassing moment.

"Girls are all right, Richard?" Mama persisted. "Really?"

"They're odd, that's all," Richard said shortly, wishing Mama would drop the subject. "Even you're odd, and you're my mother."

"I'm odd?" Mama asked, pulling out a straight-backed chair and putting the pot into which she had been shelling beans onto her lap.

"I don't know why you got so angry with Sir Dudley," Richard said, glad for a chance to change the subject. "He was just asking you. Although I think it would be more interesting if they hung her. I've never been to a hanging. If you do know someone at the Dutch East Indies Company, Mama, maybe we could be invited to watch Sir Dudley's daughter hang."

"Nothing would satisfy me more than watching Sir Dudley's daughter hang," Mama said vehemently, once again banging the pot with the beans against the other pot with the shelled beans in it and creating a terrible racket. "And I hope it's a most painful death."

"Mama, please," Richard begged, covering his ears. He remembered her yelling at him when he was younger for banging her pots together, but he did not remember how awful a sound they had made.

"Can you imagine the pompousness of that man?" Mama said, fuming. "Coming here yesterday to beg me to go to the Netherlands and use my connections to save his daughter? Standing there with a lily-white handkerchief to his nose as if he might catch something just by being in our house? As if Oliver had not been protecting his precious Isabella for months already, keeping his mouth shut even when Jodocus, one of your father's best friends, asked if Oliver might know the identity of the spy in their midst. And I kept quiet too, because Oliver asked me to for John's sake. This whole family has already paid a price in silence for his darling daughter. And he just stood there, as if I don't have troubles of my own, not even realizing how his coming here in his carriage nearly scared me to death." Mama stopped short, her face reddening as if she was guilty of something.

"You were afraid he was here to tell you that Papa and Johnny were dead, right, Mama?" Richard said softly.

Mama blinked in surprise. "Yes," Mama whispered. "I was scared. But he had no such news, so there is still hope."

Richard stood up and came to stand beside his mother's chair. He was tired of pretending. He was tired of the fear in his stomach, giving him cramps night after night. He wanted to know the truth. He took a strand of her hair and twirled it around his fingers. "But not much, is there, Mama?" he said.

Mama sucked in her breath and looked fearfully at him.

"It's all right," Richard said. "It's been a long time. I know that. I know how to be strong, Mama. I'll be brave if they are gone."

He watched tears come to his mother's eyes. He had heard her late last night, trying to muffle her sobs. Richard had lain there, sleepless and dry-eyed, listening to Mama crying and the rats rummaging about in the garbage until daybreak. Now, he was so tired.

Were they dead? he wondered. If they were, how had they died? Had Papa had to watch Johnny die slowly, or had Johnny had to watch as Papa was swept away in a storm? Had the end been painful and long, or had it come swiftly and without much time for thinking? Had it even come at all, or were they still out there somewhere, trying desperately to come home?

"It's all right, Mama, if you cry," Richard said then, putting his arm about her. "I don't mind."

Mama cried harder. She pulled her son onto her lap. He struggled a bit, then gave up. It felt good to snuggle against Mama, even if he was too old for that sort of thing now.

"What will we do, Mama?" Richard asked, as Mama's tears fell into his hair and slipped down his cheek.

Mama shook her head. "I don't know, Richard."

"Do you think Papa and Johnny are gone?" he asked, hearing his own voice quiver.

Mama sniffled. "I don't know."

"How long do we wait?" Richard asked, finally letting the questions that had plagued him these past few nights tumble out.

"I don't know that, either," Mama said, crying harder. "I don't know how long one holds on to hope before you know there is no hope left. I don't know how long you wait until you put on a widow's black dress and agree that your husband and son have been lost at sea. I've never given it much thought. Papa has just always come home. And Richard, I am not willing to give up hope just yet."

"But we have no more credit, Mama," Richard pointed out, all his fears now spoken. A few tears slipped from his own eyes. "It's been more than a year now. What will we do?"

Mama stopped crying and kissed the top of Richard's head. "Oh, Richard. That is something you mustn't worry yourself about."

"But I do," Richard said. "Please, Mama. Do you have a plan?"

Mama sighed. "Yes, Richard. I do. Sir Dudley has promised me money if I go to the Netherlands for him."

"He has?" Richard asked, pulling away and looking up at Mama with relief.

"Little one," said Mama, "were you crying?"

"I can't help it, Mama," Richard said, the tears falling fast now, the walls he had built to contain his fear coming down as he and his mother were, at last, talking about the truth. "I miss Papa and Johnny so. And I'm scared about what we'll do without them. I know I said I'd be strong, but I guess I'm not that good at it."

"Oh, Richard," Mama said. "You're good enough, truly good enough. Johnny and your father would be very proud of you."

"Would they?" Richard asked anxiously.

She nodded. "Aye, Richard, they would be."

"But Mama," Richard said, "if you are going to go to the Netherlands, why were you so angry earlier?"

Mama sighed. "Because I hate doing anything for that horrible man. But it doesn't matter. I will go to the Netherlands and try and free his daughter. I have to do it. We need the money. I'll pack tonight and leave first thing in the morning."

"Will you be gone long?" Richard asked. He did not want to be left there alone. What if something happened to Mama?

"No, I'll go quickly. I promise," she said. "I will insist that Sir Dudley give me a carriage for the trip. I will do what I can for Isabella and come straight back here."

Mama raised his chin so that Richard had to look her full in the face. "I mean to be home when Papa and Johnny return, Richard. I am not giving up on them, little one, and neither should you! Promise me!"

Richard nodded his agreement, feeling some relief at her conviction. Mama hugged him to her then, and he snuggled closer while she rocked him back and forth. And though he knew his mates would laugh themselves silly if they saw, for once, he did not care.

ISABELLA DIGGES

June 21, 1611

*The jailer has just left me, satisfied with his payment.
With a shaking hand, I have drawn him the last map in my
head in exchange for his promise to send word to my father.*

*The man will not be my jailer for long. He will sell the
information to the highest bidder, as I have explained to him
its worth. That map will ensure his good fortune—in another
country, of course, but still, he will live out his days as a
wealthy man.*

*My stomach is ill at the waste of this information, but
my jailer says he will have an answer from my father within a
fortnight! Thank the Lord, for yesterday, I was found guilty and
sentenced to be hanged. I will never forget the look in Emil's
eyes when my fate was pronounced. I swear I shall rip that smile
of revenge from his face should I find myself reprieved from this
judgment. And so I wait for the jailer, his breath sour from
onions, to return with the answer from my father. And I pray.*

June 29, 1611

All is lost! My father has been to see the king, arriving about dawn and being made to sit in his antechamber and await his rising, the king's servants having refused to awaken him any earlier than he had requested the night before. At last, my father was admitted. He hurried to the king's side and sank to his knees, kissing his hand fervently and begging him to intercede on my behalf. But the king will have none of it.

After all I have done for him! Despite providing him with invaluable information on his strongest competition on the seas, my own king will not lift a finger to help me!

He told my father he had already known of my coming arrest! He was aware of it and yet had not seen fit to inform my father or me so we might have been forewarned and devised a way to help me escape safely!

My hanging was regrettable, the king told my father. He said that I was quite a good spy and that he was sorry to lose me. But, he reminded my father, we had known the risks when we decided to undertake the mission.

My father strongly protested the king's callousness then. But the king only smiled slightly and said that my father could not expect England to acknowledge me, now that I had been exposed. He told my father in no uncertain terms that he refuses to endanger the throne to save me. He said it was a shame, but that I, Isabella Digges, who have so willingly spied for him, was expendable for the greater good. He would not risk war with the Netherlands, not for me.

And then when my father began to lose his self-control, our good king did say that he was grateful to me for all I had accomplished, and he reminded my father that he still had his duchess and asked my father if perhaps there was anything else he wished?

My father turned on his heel and left then, knowing help from above would not be coming. And yet he tells me he is not without hope. He plans to withdraw a large sum from the duchess's monies and will send emissaries to the Netherlands to see if perhaps a goodly sized bribe might not coerce some minor official into freeing me and aiding me in escape.

And so I sit and wait, my heart sore from the lack of those who would come to my aid. I hold out little hope for my father's grand schemes. The monies will take time to have effect, and time is the one thing I do not have.

Oh, how bitterly I regret what I have done! For now, I shall hang for it!

SETH SYMS

୨୭ ଓ୭

June 22, 1611
Dearest Mama:

Me life won't ever be the same, can't even say if it'll
be a life at all, at that. And it came down to one word:
mutiny.

Now, I'd been just a bit worried, hearing Juet and them
others talking all nasty-like and complaining about the
captain. And I might have thought that maybe, just maybe,
they were dreaming up something this serious. But heck, we
were on our way home. I'd breathed a sigh of relief that day
we sailed from the ice, held me breath when we got caught
again, and let it out when the ice finally cleared for the last
time.

And yet today, there I was out on deck, freeing some
lines, when a few of them boys up and grabbed King. I was
bent over, me fingers numb as they pulled on that slippery
rope, when I heard the scuffle. Maybe it was that muffled
sound that made the hairs on the back of me neck rise. I

don't know. I just felt such a funny feeling that I had to look up. And when I did, I wished I hadn't.

They had grabbed King—Juet and Wilson and Greene. They were hustling him off to the stairs to the hold. It hadn't made its way to me brain what was happening, but I sensed it nonetheless. I backed up a bit, me heart pounding hard in me chest, like some blacksmith beating out the impurities at his forge. I hid meself behind a barrel or two and waited, wondering what was going on. It weren't long for me to know the truth.

Up from below them mutineers came, having rounded up the sick ones. I saw them bring up young John, his eyes angry and snapping like flames was in them. And then the captain must have heard something. Out he comes in his nightclothes. And Mathew was on him like a hungry bird on an insect. They took his arms and pinned them behind his back. And he was shouting at them the whole time.

"What do you think you are doing? Don't you know you could hang for this?"

"Shut him up," Juet had snapped, and someone had shoved a rag in the poor man's mouth.

I saw John then and saw the light in them eyes fade, and fear come into them instead. This was serious. No doubt about it. It was mutiny.

These men meant for this to happen. I could see no way to stop it.

Thomas spoke up then, questioning if everyone was present.

I felt a hand on me shoulder, and I was yanked up from where I'd been cowering behind them barrels.

"Found him," Greene said. "Last one."

Juet sneered at me from across the boat, asking why I was hiding, wondering if I had the jitters or something.

I hadn't anything to say to that, but I could feel the sweat breaking out across me brow. And me stomach was doing some real funny things too.

"I asked ye once and I don't believe ye answered," said Juet, swaggering across the deck. He got near me face. "Ye with us, Syms, or are ye against us?"

I glanced about me—there was seven of them in on the deed, each of them standing there, looking at me. It was Juet, Wilson, Greene, Thomas, Pierce, Motter and Mathew. Seven no-gooders with a deep mean streak, all staring at me like they meant to toss me overboard if I didn't answer in a seemly fashion—in other words: Aye.

But then I see John and Staffe, standing there, staring mutely at me. I couldn't bear to look at the two of them. And I'm feeling all this shame and this madness that I should be in this awful position in the first place. I had signed up to crew a boat. I ain't never signed up to be involved in no mutiny or the shamefulness or the awfulness of it. I wanted to be anywheres but there. I wished like anything some huge wave would rear up, or that fireballs would suddenly shoot from the sky, or some plague would hit that boat. I just didn't want to be at the center of all them men looking at me, each with their expectations shining bright in their eyes. I'd spent a goodly part of me life trying to avoid anybody expecting anything of me. And here I was, no way out.

I shrugged, feeling sick with shame even as I spoke. "I

ain't with no one," I said, the anger I felt about this whole mess spewing out. "I came here alone, and that's the way I intend to stay. Ye want to mutiny, mutiny. But leave me out of the whole thing. I ain't putting me lot in with either of ye."

John stared at me. Philip looked away. Juet sneered. Greene dropped his rough grip on me. I rubbed me arm. It was sore from his tight hold.

"As long as ye don't interfere," Greene muttered.

I managed to ask what they intended on doing with them.

Motter laughed, reminding me I'd just said I was alone on this one.

"I am," I said angrily. "I'm just wondering, that's all."

I saw hope flare into young John's eyes. Me throat felt suddenly thick.

"We'll put them in the shallop," Mathew said, holding tight to the captain, who was struggling a bit. "They'll have a go for it if they want."

I looked at the shallop, tied on to the side of our boat. No food, torn clothes, little water, and a tiny boat with one sail. Them wasn't the odds I'd have liked.

Wilson asked if I had a problem with that.

I shook my head, but me stomach felt sick.

"It's a far better deal than the one Hudson's offered us," Juet said angrily, "dragging us around harbor after harbor, getting us trapped for the winter, handing over Williams's coat like that, not dividing the food like a fair and true captain would. Ain't nobody gonna fault us for what we did when we reach England."

I doubted him on that. Captain Hudson might be a fool, searching like some madman for a way to the Orient, but the king had still commissioned him. Ain't no way I was going to agree. I liked me head too much to have me agreement repeated at some royal inquest. I said nothing.

Juet headed for the hold to go get King. He weren't gone long when there was screaming and yelling from below. I felt me heart lift. Someone was fighting back. I hoped with all I had in me that that someone was winning.

But then the deck went into action, men stumbling over themselves to go below and give Juet some aid. He finally came back up, looking a bit worse for the wear. King had taken a sword to him, but he hadn't hurt him much, just a gash in the arm—weren't anything, and I was sorry for it.

Juet instructed the crew to load up the shallop, telling Wilson to go get the men some bedding.

I saw Prickett climb up the ladder, pulling his lame leg behind him. He hobbled over to where I stood and watched silently as the mutineers began loading quilts and such into the small shallop.

I thought I was going to be ill. I wanted out of there so bad. Watching them men load that stuff up, seeing the miserable way those sick men looked, knowing they was about to be put off, me eyes turned toward John. He was staring straight ahead, all his joking ways gone from him.

I stepped forward and asked Juet to give me John for a few minutes. Juet stared at me. "Ye try anything," he hissed at me, "ye'll be in that boat along with the others, ye got that?"

I nodded. They let John loose, and he came and stood by me.

"Let's go below," I said.

John nodded, and we headed down the ladder. *A few minutes*, I thought. *Ye got the boy a few minutes.* But I sighed, following him down the rungs. A few minutes. It weren't much, was it?

Yer loving son, Seth

JOHN HUDSON

June 22, 1611

My dearest Isabella:

Can you truly believe that this is me? Writing a letter? Though I have spent many a day writing in my father's log, I have never put pen to paper for a girl. But it seems the time for laughter and pranks is at an end—at least for this voyage. I have been dealt the cruelest of jokes. The crew has turned against my father and mutinied.

Being a Hudson, I will be unable to return with them. Not that I would have gone with them had I been given the chance, for I would never leave my father. In spite of all his faults, my place is with him. And even if the mutineers had offered to take me back to England, in truth, they have become a tedious lot. I would rather be in a shallop with my mad father than with Juet or Greene. There! You see I have not truly lost my sense of humor.

And that is a positive. For my father, realizing that his dreams are now shattered, that he has been mutinied against and that it will be unlikely he will ever commandeer a ship again, will despair. But I am not without hope. The shallop has a sail, and I have the will of one who wants, against all odds, to return. I shall try with all my strength to make it, and make it we will!

I know it will not be easy. I know the sea is unpredictable in her whims. But then, so am I. I can best her! I can! We shall reach Greenland, just you see.

Nicholas is gesturing to me. I must close this letter before it is discovered. He was kind enough to obtain for me the opportunity to write this note—one for you, and one for my mother. He has promised to conceal the letters in his own trunk and to seek you out when he is home to deliver them.

I love you. There, now I've said it, and I suppose I

shall have to live with the consequences of these words when I return. So be it! Do not despair, Issa. I will be yours once more, only in a little longer time than we had anticipated. Look for me on the horizon. I will be there shortly.

Yours,

John

RICHARD HUDSON

I t wasn't easy at first, being away from home. Richard tried valiantly to hide his homesickness, but he still missed Mama and his own room terribly.

It was the nights that were the hardest, and sleeping with Alice in her room didn't make it any easier. During the day, he was too busy with the chores Anne assigned him or accompanying Oliver on his many errands to think about missing home.

But at night, he was alone in bed with Alice. And she talked! She talked and talked long into the night, asking Richard so many questions that he felt as if he would hit her again if she didn't shut up. The only thing that stopped him was remembering that afternoon he *had* punched her—how Alice wouldn't stop crying and how badly he had felt about it afterward.

Eventually, he made up answers to her questions until he could drift off into a mind-numbing sleep. This made for some interesting mornings.

"Ritchie says that all rivers are made by the tears of

little boys who live high in the mountains with little girls who ask questions all the time and drive them mad," Alice piped up one morning at breakfast.

Oliver looked over at Richard, an amused smile on his face.

"That is not true, Alice," Anne said, as she took her daughter's dishes away for washing. "Rivers are made by rain that comes from the heavens." Anne gave Richard a hard stare. "Your uncle knows that."

"He says that the birds that woke us this morning with their loud singing are all *girl* birds, for only girls can chatter as much as they do," she said proudly. "Isn't that nice, Mama? That the girl birds wake me so early?"

Oliver let out a chuckle.

Anne gave her husband a stern look and sighed. "Again, Alice, Uncle Richard is not truthful with his explanations. Yes, there are girl birds who sing and chatter with the morning light, but boy birds answer them by singing back. Boy birds could not live without girl birds."

Richard rolled his eyes when Anne said this. Then he remembered the girl in the meadow and wondered if perhaps Anne was right. He had thought a lot about her lately, recalling her face often late at night while Alice chattered on and on.

Alice pondered this fact. "Ritchie says kings only marry queens so that they may have babies and that if it wasn't for that, no man would want to live with a girl ever!"

"Richard!" Anne cried out in fury.

Oliver was laughing so hard that Richard couldn't help but grin. It had been the best answer he could come up with when Alice had asked, "Why is the king in charge of everything and not the queen?"

"Oliver!" said Anne, now turning her anger on her husband. "This is not funny! Your brother needs to understand that he cannot just make things up as he pleases!"

"I don't," Richard protested. "She just keeps asking me why this and why that over and over and over. Why is there water in the river? Why are the birds up so early? Why is the king in charge of everything? Why don't animals talk? Why are leaves green? Why? Why? Why? Why? I can hardly sleep, she asks me so many questions. And then she wakes me up and starts asking them again. By the time I answer, I don't even know what I'm saying, I'm so tired!"

"That's what four-year-olds do, Richard," Anne said. "They ask questions."

"I never asked so many stupid questions," Richard muttered.

"That's why you don't know anything," Alice piped up.

Oliver laughed harder.

"I do too," Richard protested.

"No," said Alice, sighing, "you don't. Boys don't know anything. Only girls do."

"Well, if you think boys don't know anything, then why do you ask me all those silly questions?" Richard asked haughtily.

"So you won't go to sleep before me," Alice said simply.

"Why do you care if I fall asleep first?" asked Richard, puzzled.

"Because you make this loud noise," Alice said, "like

this . . ." And she made loud snoring sounds. "It keeps me awake."

With that, she slid off her chair and went over to play with her doll.

Oliver laughed so hard, he almost fell off his chair.

Anne, too, was laughing. Only Richard found his niece's sense of humor decidedly poor.

Over time, though, Richard began to adjust to the house by the palace. He liked watching all the activity, the comings and goings at the king's residence. He liked the other boys he met on the streets when he slipped away to play, for they knew how to act like soldiers and how to play the king's guard.

And too, he liked the gossip Oliver brought back from his visits to the palace. Many a night at suppertime, his brother would tell them what he had seen and heard while attending the king.

"Sir Dudley tried to kill his wife today," Oliver said one night.

"He did?" asked Richard, wide-eyed, remembering the sour man who had given them a ride in his carriage so many months ago.

"I thought he was so pleased to be marrying her," Anne said.

"Will he hang?" Richard asked, hoping he would, and hoping Mama would not return in time to prevent him from seeing it.

Oliver shook his head. "He was just angry because the king granted the duchess full access to all her holdings. Now Sir Dudley will have to ask the duchess for money and will no longer control her fortune."

"Why did the king do that?" Richard asked. He didn't see why the king would let a girl be in charge of anyone's money.

Oliver sighed. "Because Sir Dudley is no longer of use to him, so the king is placating his own family, including the duchess, who did not want to marry Sir Dudley in the first place but was forced into it."

"And so the duchess has proven to have claws," Anne said, grinning.

Richard scowled. Why was it Oliver's wife always liked it when women got the upper hand? "How did he try to kill her?"

"He tried to strangle her, and he almost succeeded," Oliver explained. "But it seems his servant, Webster, realizing that the duchess was now in control of the money and knowing who would be paying his salary, rescued her just as her face was turning blue."

Richard remembered the cold walk home the night Sir Dudley had kicked them out of his carriage. And though he didn't understand the king's giving all the money to his wife, it pleased Richard to think that it was Sir Dudley this had been done to.

Two days later, Oliver came running into the house, calling them all at the top of his lungs.

Richard turned from the fire.

"News has been sent!" Oliver cried, grabbing Richard and swinging him into the air. "Our father has been sighted just off the coast of Ireland, Richard!"

Richard let out a cry of joy. At last, Papa and Johnny were coming home! He felt tears coming to his eyes.

"Oh, Oliver," Anne exclaimed, coming into the room, "that's wonderful."

"What's this?" Oliver said, setting Richard down. "No crying now, Richard! It's good news!"

"I know that," Richard grumbled, wiping away the tears as quickly as he could. "I have a cold."

"No, you don't," Alice said. "Mama, why does Ritchie always make things up?"

Anne laughed and pulled her daughter to her. "Be nice, Alice," she said. "It has been hard on Richard having Uncle Johnny and your grandfather gone for so long."

Richard went to protest that he was fine, that he truly had a cold, but then he stopped. What did it matter what dumb old Alice thought? Papa and Johnny were coming home! He couldn't wait for Mama to hear the news!

ISABELLA DIGGES

September 4, 1611

When the jailer turned the key in the lock and slowly opened the door, I gritted my teeth. The man had been here but an hour ago, grinning wickedly at me, hoping for more information to make him even wealthier than the map I had already granted him. I turned him coldly away. I have nothing left to give.

The die had been cast. If death was my fate, I refused to be about helping anyone but myself in my last few hours. What a surprise it was to me then when a woman entered. She pushed back the hood to her cape and did not speak, but looked me over carefully, as if I was a piece of meat.

I returned her gaze with some contempt. I had never seen this middle-aged woman before. Had she been sent by my father to outfit me for my hanging? It would have been just like him to be worried that I went to the scaffold dressed in clothing fine enough for a Digges!

But in this I was wrong, for at last, the woman spoke, telling me she was Katherine Hudson.

A jolt went through me, and I wondered what she could want. Had my father convinced her to come on the long journey to the Netherlands to convey me some message? Or had it been John doing the convincing? My heart leaped at this thought, but I quickly quelled it. What did it matter if John still cared enough to send his mother? He himself had not come! And, since I was to hang, there seemed little cause for rejoicing, even if he had been concerned. There was no future for us. There was no future for me.

She had the same brown eyes as John, the same tilt of the head, the same intensity of look. I forced a tired smile. "So we meet at last," I said. "It seems we have some acquaintances in common, Mrs. Hudson."

John's mother's eyes narrowed at my comment. She took off her cape and hung it on a peg as the jailer shut the door firmly behind her. Then she looked at me again and remarked that I was indeed a beauty.

I glared at her. Did she truly think I cared what her thoughts on my looks were at this point in my life? "Yes, beauty has gotten me this, Mrs. Hudson," I said, sweeping my hands around the damp, dark cell. "Am I not a lucky girl for it?"

Katherine Hudson smiled, telling me that she liked the defiance. That she had had a lot of defiance at my age.

"Ah well," I said, "defiant I am, and will be right to the gallows." I sat down upon my damp bedding, now feeling decidedly in poor humor. I wished for this woman, with her annoying curiosity, to be gone.

Katherine Hudson asked if I wanted to know why she was there.

I told her that surely John or my father had sent her with some good-bye message. Though I wondered aloud why it was that John had not come himself.

Katherine Hudson's smile evaporated. "He did not come because he has not returned," she snapped.

My heart came to my throat. "Not yet?" I managed to say. "But it goes on almost a year and a half now."

"Yes," she said simply.

I asked if there was no word at all, my voice cracking slightly. Katherine Hudson shook her head.

I lost all hope then. What mattered it if I hung? My father did not care. The boy I had thought on all these months was possibly gone, lost to the sea.

"You almost look like you care," John's mother said skeptically.

I nodded. I could not manage anything else.

She watched me for a moment. "Could it be possible that you love my son?" she finally asked.

I was quiet for a long time, thinking, Did I? It seemed right, at the last, to be honest. I finally answered her, telling her that I didn't know, for I had known so little of love. My father, I believed, had never felt it. My mother definitely did not know it.

I paused a moment, then said, "But if I could hazard a guess, I suppose that what I feel for your son is love."

I realized in that moment that John was the first man to like me for me.

I went on slowly, as the full force of what I had thrown away so casually hit me hard, like a stone dropped from a great height. "He is so full of energy and wildness." My voice shook, though I spoke boldly. "We're alike in that."

I forced myself to grin at her, telling her that most men were only interested in me for my looks. The casualness I gave this comment allowed me room to breathe, room to swallow and once more gain my composure.

I waited for a reaction, but Katherine Hudson gave me none. Finally, I shrugged.

Katherine Hudson began to pace about the room, saying that she still held out hope, that it was very possible that they had found the way east and were returning home even now. She said that she refused to dally here and must be on her way home soon.

Then she stopped and turned to face me. "Your father sent me."

I turned amused eyes on her. "Whatever for?" I asked, and I could not keep the bitterness from my voice. I reminded her that he had gotten what he needed from me. He'd married his duchess. His place at court was assured. He had his maps. And now I was to hang for it.

Really! Whatever more could he want? There was not much I could get for him from prison.

John's mother indicated a spot on the bed next to me. I moved over, and she sat down. "He asked me to secure your freedom for you, and it's cost him a pretty penny."

A flutter of hope rose in my chest. I squelched it quickly. My father would never waste the coins to save my life. This woman was playing some game.

I asked her angrily why she mocked me.

Katherine Hudson shook her head. "I do not," she replied. "Your father was distraught at the thought of your hanging, and as much as I dislike your father, I agreed to speak to the people my husband knew at the Dutch East Indies Company on your behalf. Henry's dear friend Jodocus Hondius obtained a pardon with your father's money and at my request, for my sake."

"Don't you mean for John's sake?" I asked, hearing the hope in my voice and cursing myself for it.

"No," Katherine Hudson said. "For my own. Your father offered me money. I needed it."

"Oh," I said, her words confirming the reality of my situation. I meant nothing to this woman; I was simply a means

to obtain some money for her family. And yet, if what she had told me was true, I was free. I shook a bit at the realization that I was not to be hung. For a moment, I thought I might weep.

John's mother continued, saying that she didn't regret what she'd done, that she may have misjudged me.

I barked a laugh to prevent the tears. "No," I said. "You probably have not."

She protested, reminding me that I had just said that I cared for her son.

I reminded her that I had spied on her son. That I had used him to garner information for my father. I told her that if I found myself caught in my own trap, it was what I deserved. I did care for John. I had hoped that when I returned home, I would find he still cared for me, too. But then, who knows what he feels for me now? A year in the Orient may have convinced him that I was just a passing fancy.

Katherine Hudson said quietly that her son was not like that.

I nodded my agreement, realizing the truth of this for the first time.

"Then you would consider him?" she asked.

I stared at her in surprise. She would want this? She would want me, Isabella Digges, the woman who had spied upon her son, to be with him? My eyes met hers, and I saw in them myself, defiant and strong-willed.

"I would," I finally said.

"Besides," I added, breaking into a wicked grin, "I'm sure my father would have a stroke over it. For that fact alone, I would risk it."

Katherine Hudson laughed. I did too, as I imagined my father's face when I told him I was to marry John Hudson. Oh, how that would delight me! He deserved as much for having put *me through these horrific days in this godforsaken country.*

"I won't have you use John just for that," she reminded me then.

I stopped laughing. She was looking at me with deadly seriousness.

She was right. The time for using John was over. It was up to me to make amends. I agreed solemnly. The Netherlands had taught me much.

Katherine Hudson stood. "Then let us make haste and return to England." She went and banged upon the door of my cell to attract the attention of the jailer.

I was still puzzled. I asked her if my father was truly distraught.

She answered me in the affirmative, telling me that there was much talk coming from court. It seems my father had made an unhappy marriage. And she believed that this may have prompted his looking deeper, and finding that he truly missed me.

"It would be the first time ever," I said bitterly.

John's mother turned and took my hand, pulling me to my feet. She told me to come home with her now, and see if this new feeling of my father's was something that was sincere or only temporary.

"I won't go back to him," I said sharply. "Not ever."

"Then you'll still have John," said Katherine Hudson. She took a deep breath. "And you'll still have me."

"You?" I said, unable to conceal a smirk. I had never, in all my years, known a woman to be kind to me.

"I think we could be friends," she said, "if you could see your way to dropping this infernal attitude of yours. I haven't hurt you, Issa."

"Yet," I muttered.

"Yet," she agreed. "Still, it seems it might work, our being

friends." She glanced around the room. "Seems a better idea than hanging."

That made me laugh. "All right, Mrs. Hudson," I declared. "Let's make our way to England, then. Let's see if indeed Sir Dudley is now willing to be a true father figure to his wayward daughter. It would be worth the ride home just to toy with him a bit, to let him think his daughter believes in him still.

"And then, too," I said softly, "perhaps when we return, John will be waiting."

Katherine Hudson put her arm around me. "You see, friend," she whispered to me, "already we are agreed."

SETH SYMS

⁊⁊ ⁊⁊

September 5, 1611

Dearest Mama:

I ain't eaten for days. And when someone offers me something, I just push it away. I am sick of everything, sick of meself, sick of life.

Twice now, I have thought of just ending it all, just pushing meself over the boat, letting meself go under. But nah, I'm too big a coward for even that. I can't stand to be with meself, yet I have no way of escaping. Oh, how I wish there were drink still aboard. I might just drown meself in it, were that possible.

It sure ain't easy living with yerself when ye've done what I've done. Me, helping John down them steps, whispering to him to hurry and write them a last letter, him making me promise to deliver the letters to them meself, and me agreeing. And then he turns to me, this mischief in his eyes, even though he knows he's probably not going to make it.

And he says to me, "Who are you?"

"What?" I says, all startled.

"I know you're not Nicholas," he said, grinning. "I've sailed with Nicholas before. So just who are you? I'd like to know before I go."

"I'm his cousin, Seth," I told him. "Ye ain't said nothing to nobody about me not being Nicholas?"

He shrugged, saying it didn't really matter who I was.

Then he goes and grins again, telling me as how I gave meself away a few times, not being too familiar with nautical terms and all.

I sure was wishing that this conversation weren't taking place. It almost made me more uncomfortable than the mutiny itself.

"So why did you come?" he asked me.

"Wish I hadn't," I muttered.

He gave a short laugh. "So do I."

That made me sweat a bit.

He asked me again why I'd come.

So I told him all about Elizabeth and how her husband had challenged me to a duel, and how I had found the fastest way to escape I could.

John laughed then, his eyes all lit up with delight. I could hardly bear it.

"Well," he said, standing, "that will make a good story for my father in the days ahead."

Then he urgently pressed them letters into me hand, asking me to hide them for him.

Fright gripped me hard at his words. I realized then that them mutineers might actually come looking for something like that to prevent them from coming to light when we returned.

He nodded toward one of them letters. "Take that one directly to Isabella when you return. She's Sir Dudley Digges's daughter."

I stared at him in surprise.

He smiled. "Seems impossible, I know," he said. "And I guess now it is. Still . . . ," he added. "You never know."

I looked away, and he came close to me. "Go see my mother," he said. "Give her the other letter. Tell her what's happened. Ask her to send someone to search us out. And . . ."

He stopped, drew a deep breath. "Tell Richard, that rascal brother of mine, that I love him, and that our room is not yet his!"

I looked at him then. Wished I hadn't of. He winked at me, as if he hadn't a care in the world, as if this was some kind of lark or something. It about broke me heart.

Of course the worst was to come.

They yelled for us then to get up there. John turned to face me, still grinning.

"Good-bye, Seth," he said.

I had to look away again. I mean, what was I supposed to say? It was downright the worst thing I had ever faced in me life. It hurt more knowing it was the boy's pain.

We climbed the stairs, and the men stood there, the anger still strong in their eyes. I wondered how they could stay angry like that, now that they was abandoning the captain and his son like this. I mean, what was the point? They'd gotten what they'd wanted. We were going home— and without Captain Hudson at the helm.

I watched them shove John overboard into the shallop.
I went to the rail, and there was our captain, staring stonily
out at the sea. He wouldn't look up, and I can't say as
I blame him. Who'd want to look on his mutineers at
the last?

Then the bad part happened. They loaded some more of
the crew on board, men who had voiced their disagree-
ment from the first and the sick ones. Me, not taking sides
all the while, that saved me I guess, 'cause I weren't chosen.
Still, it weren't easy standing there, watching them load
those men onto that boat: Michael Bute, Thomas
Wydhouse, Adam Moore, Arnold Lodlo, Sidrack Faner,
Henry King, along with the captain and John. Me heart was
pounding hard in me chest the whole time.

And then . . . Philip Staffe, he goes to lower himself, too.
Now this made me feel real bad. Here was Philip going with
them, even after the captain had treated him so terribly.

But Juet and Greene pulled him back and demanded to
know what he was doing.

Philip said he was joining the others, that he weren't no
mutineer.

But Juet didn't want to let him go. Said we might have
need of a carpenter.

"I wouldn't work for the likes of you even if me own life
depended on it," Philip declared. "So you might as well let
me join the others."

So Motter told Juet just to let him go.

Juet nodded and motioned Philip to go ahead. Philip
turned then, and he looked at me. His eyes met mine, and I
knew what they was saying—what the heck are ye doing?

He was right. What was I doing, staying here all neat and cozy while me friends were loaded into that boat? I knew I should step forward. I knew I should say that I was going too. But I didn't. I couldn't. And I hated meself for it.

So off Philip goes with the others. Then Juet and Greene bark at me to set the sails. I did, but me hands were shaking the whole time.

The sails lifted and snapped out in the breeze. I felt the boat sway beneath me feet. I went to the opposite side of the boat and puked. We were off.

They had tied the shallop to the boat, and it followed us for a good long time. I kept saying to Juet that he ought to let them go near land somewheres. He gives me this long look and says, "If yer so keen on saving them, why don't ye go join them?"

Me knees started to shake. I shut up right quick. I turned and went back to me work.

Then, at last, we reached the open sea, no ice to be seen nowheres. A goodly breeze was blowing, and Juet made his move, calling out for us to cut the line.

I went to the bow of the boat then. That shallop, it was a distance off, and I was thankful for that. If I could have seen their eyes, I might not have been able to watch. As it was, I thought it was the least I could do—to stand there and see them drift from the boat. I made meself do it.

The line was cut. The men in the shallop pulled out their oars and began rowing. We moved swiftly away from them.

John puts up his hand, waving his last. I put mine up too, and felt tears coming to me eyes like some big baby.

"Get back to work," Juet hissed at me, turning from the

shallop as it became smaller and smaller. "We got some sailing to do."

Me heart was so heavy that day. But I vowed then and there to help us get home right quick. I figured if I worked hard, and we got there fast, just maybe I could get them some help, send someone to rescue them.

As the days dragged on, the memory of John with his hand waving to me, it began to haunt me. First, it was only when I slept, when I'd crawl from me duties and fall into a troubled sleep. And then when I looked at them figures I'd whittled with Philip, the memory came back even stronger. And I knew it then. John and the captain and Philip Staffe, and what I done would haunt me the rest of me life. I'd live, but there wouldn't be much of me left to live with. I'd spend the rest of me life trying to fix what I'd done wrong.

Yer loving son, Seth

RICHARD HUDSON

Mama slowly poured the wax into the candle forms. "Hold it steady, Richard," she warned him.

Richard felt an itch on his nose. His hand wavered, and the hot wax spilled over the side, running down his hand. He yelped at the heat but, seeing Mama's angry glance, managed to steady the candle form until all the wax was in.

There was a knock on the door, and then it was thrown open. Oliver stood in the weak light from the overcast October day.

"The ship's been sighted, Mama," Oliver called. He had Alice by the hand, and his wife, Anne, was behind him.

Richard felt his heart leap in his chest. Papa and Johnny were actually home?

Mama set the wax pan down hard on the wooden table. "How far off?" she asked as she quickly wiped her hands on her apron.

"A bit," Oliver told her.

She threw her apron off. "Come on, Richard. We're going to the harbor."

Richard stared at his mother. She never left a mess in the house, not even when Papa returned. "But the wax will harden," he said, staring at the pan and then at his mother with a question in his eyes.

"Oh, Richard," Mama said with impatience. "Your father and brother are home. What matters the pan?"

Oliver stepped into the house. "Mother," he said gently, taking both her hands in his. "The boat is a ways away. It will be an hour or so before they are to the dock. Go on now. Put on a better dress for Father and brush your hair. Anne and I will clean up here."

"Thank you," Mama said to Oliver. "Richard, go put on a better pair of breeches."

Richard stared down at his pants. "What's wrong with these?"

"Stop disagreeing with me, young man," Mama snapped. "Your father's home!"

Oliver laughed. "Go do as she asks, Richard, and for once, stop arguing with her."

Richard rolled his eyes but went to his room. He stopped there for a minute, thinking about what it would be like to have Johnny home once more. He knew he could expect teasing and being bossed around and millions of pranks that would leave him furious. But in spite of all that, he felt his heart lift at the idea of seeing Johnny again.

He wondered if Johnny or Papa had changed. They had been gone for such a long time.

Richard knew he'd changed. He was taller. He could chop wood and lift the logs into the house without breaking anything. He could churn butter so quickly, even Mama could not do it faster. And now there was the girl.

Richard had seen her many times since Mama had come home from the Netherlands. He had told no one of their meetings, of the way the sunlight looked so nice in her hair, of the way she touched his fingers and made him feel all squirmy sometimes, but wiggly in a good way. He wondered if Johnny would make fun of him, if he should tell him.

Oliver seemed too old to ask about girls, and Mama was Mama. Johnny truly was the best of choices. If only he would agree to keep Richard's secret.

"Richard," Mama called, "aren't you ready yet?"

Richard changed his pants quickly. Then he noticed that his good pair had a big rip down one side. When had his best breeches gotten torn? Mama would kill him! He walked out into the room, keeping the ripped side of his pants away from his mother so she would not see.

"Why are you walking so oddly, Richard?" Mama asked.

Richard smiled as innocently as possible. "For fun," he said.

Mama shook her head, grabbing up her shawl. "Well, stop fooling around. Let's go, Oliver," she said.

"You look wonderful, Mother," Oliver said. "And you too, Richard," he added, winking while looking at the gaping hole.

Richard giggled.

Mama put the shawl about her shoulders. "I don't know what got into me, trying to hurry down there so fast," she said. "I know from past experience that it will be a while until the ship is ready to dock. It's just that they've been gone so long . . ."

"We're all anxious, Mother," Oliver said. "But there's nothing to worry about now. They're home. Shall we go?"

Mama nodded, and together they began to head toward the docks.

"Heard your husband's on his way in," Mistress Howley called from her open window.

"Yes," Mama called back to her. "Isn't it wonderful news?"

"It's only good news if he's found something," Mistress Howley snapped back.

Mama made a move toward the woman in the open window. But Oliver stopped her. "Don't let her ruin today," he whispered.

Mama grimaced but nodded. "Someday, though," she said through clenched teeth, "I will strangle that woman."

"I'll help," Richard said, grinning.

Mama laughed and pulled her youngest son to her. She hugged him as they walked. "And we'll bury the body. . . ."

"No, Mama," Richard said, delighting in the game. "You don't bury someone. They always find the buried ones. We'll tie rods to her feet and throw her in the Thames."

"You've given this some thought, Richard," Oliver said, laughing at his brother.

"Lots," Richard replied. "She's a nasty old woman."

They continued through the streets of London until at last, they reached the dock. The ship was still a bit off, but Richard could see it was making steady progress up the river. A good wind was at its back, and he knew it would not be long until he saw Papa and Johnny, waving their hellos. Richard danced along beside his mother and his brother, knowing that Mama's worrying was at an end and that stupid knot in his stomach would be gone forever. And he didn't even mind at all when Alice took his hand.

ISABELLA DIGGES

October 25, 1611

If I should die tonight in my sleep, I think I would not care. My head aches, and my eyes are almost swollen shut from crying. In the other room, I can hear Katherine weeping softly. When I finish, I shall go to her and hold her as she held me when I first arrived here seeking shelter.

What a day it has been! Nearly eight hours were spent questioning the crew of the Discovery. I sat beside Katherine in the great room in which they were being interrogated and listened to it all, holding her hand and drawing strength from her when I needed it most, as I believe she did from me. I still shiver thinking over all those men had been through.

Yet truly, they should hang for the mutiny. And that is the recommendation my father and the other investors have made. But of course we must wait until their trial to see what the judge thinks appropriate. I pray he does not feel any sympathy for them, even though the horrors they faced after they left Captain Hudson and John behind were great. I pray he will

*harden his heart, remembering how these animals put my John
and the others off, leaving them to face death.*

*It is true, though, that the real mutineers are not the ones
who finally put into port in London. It seems that Greene and
Juet were the leaders, and they are now dead. Perhaps that is for
the best, for had they lived, I believe I would have run them
through with a sword myself.*

*As the remaining men tell it, Greene took over as captain as
soon as they were out of sight of the shallop. After a month of
travel and much arguing over navigation between Juet and
Bylot, they reached Digges Cape, named after my father. Here
they discovered about fifty natives who gave them food and
showed them how to catch birds. These natives took them to
their camp, where they ate and danced with the heathens.*

*This very picture made me ill, but I did remind myself that
for over a year these men had subsisted on little more than moss
and fish. I suppose had I been fed such a scanty diet for so long
a time, I might overlook native ways and break bread with
them also.*

*But Greene, it seems, was quite in love with the savages,
thinking them a pleasant bunch. The next day, he again set out
to dine with them, only to find himself and the others with him
viciously attacked by these same natives. Thomas, Wilson,
Greene, and Pierce were grievously wounded by arrows but
managed to get back to the ship. Motter swam unharmed out
to the ship, as the boat prepared to make haste and depart.*

*But the crew were not prepared for such a quick departure,
and the natives continued to shoot their arrows, finally killing
Greene and Motter and injuring Prickett. Prickett survived, but
Wilson and Thomas died later that day onboard ship from their
injuries. Pierce died two days later from the attack on land.*

*Now there were only nine men left. This boded well for the
remaining food, and yet they ran completely out. The men told*

of how they ate seagulls and then, finally, birds' bones fried in candle grease. It was enough to make me seriously ill, hearing how they had to go on, hoping against hope they were headed in the right direction. And I thought of John out there, without even the Discovery to shelter him.

The others reached Ireland on September 6. Not long before they sighted land, Juet died from hunger. The mutineers were gone, and there were now but eight of them left.

When at last, they arrived at Bantry Bay, one Irishman who came to testify said they looked more dead than alive. The fishermen were actually afraid of even approaching the boat, so sickly did the men seem. But eventually, they did. And these eight have come home to tell their horrid tale.

When I got home this afternoon, I sequestered myself in the library and fixed myself a large glass of sherry. I drank it quickly but could not shake the image of these men starving or of John left to perish in that small boat. Finally, I buried my face in my hands and wept with all the bitterness in my body.

My father came into the room a few minutes later. "You were fond of him?" he choked out upon seeing my misery. "How could you be, Isabella? He is but a sailor."

I raised my head and met his gaze with all the hate I had within me. The anger I felt was so intense, it almost made my heart stop. "He was better to me than anyone has ever been," I managed to say.

My father winced and held out his hand to me. I pushed it away and stood.

"I rue the day I ever let you talk me into this scheme of yours," I spat out. "I have lost the boy I loved. I almost lost my life. The only good that has come of it all is that you are now saddled with a woman who despises you and to whom you will be beholden for the rest of your life."

And then I turned and left the room. He was a father to me no longer.

I came here, and Katherine took me in, holding me as I wept. And now I will go to her. We are all that is left of the love John had. But together, we might find a way to keep that love alive.

SETH SYMS

⸙ ⸙

June 1, 1612

Dearest Mama:

I'd been there several times before. And I can't tell ye
how long I must have stood there today, looking at that
house. It's a nice house, not too fancy, mind ye, but kept
up real good. I seen the missus first and what must have
been John's little brother. I felt real sick seeing him then,
'cause he looks just like a small form of John.

Anyways, the first time I went, they was making their
way to church and was dressed all in black, looking
deadly serious. I couldn't approach them then. I didn't
have the courage yet. And too, the boy—well, it was like
he was stone or something, and I knew he weren't
handling everything real well. I had no desire to poke me
nose about then.

And so I waited—until now, long after the trial.

Lord, Mama, there was a lot of people at the trial,
weren't there? Seems like everyone was so curious as to

what had happened on that boat. I was so glad me part went quick and easy. And at least I told the truth, unlike them others with their lies, mainly about how the captain had actually been hoarding food.

If only that had been true. But as ye know, it weren't. Ye know we sailed those last months with nothing to eat. When we arrived in Ireland, I could barely stand up, and me mouth was sporting five fewer teeth. I was a sight for the devil.

Not that time has improved on me condition much. I know I got food in me belly. And ye just keep thanking the Lord something terrible that I'm alive. Ye've wept and wept and told me to forgive you for not being a better mother, for not keeping me from harm's way. But Mama, it ain't your fault. When ye read these letters, then ye'll see. Truly, Mama, there is no forgiving to do. The fault is me own. I have only meself to condemn.

I see him every day now, young John, standing there proud as proud can be on that shallop as I was standing there safe on the *Discovery*. I am not a good man. I went looking for an escape for meself and found only me bad boy self left. How can I possibly live with what I done?

Mama, ye did the best ye could, taking care of me so well when I got back. But sometimes I would just up and leave and go and stand before that house. Them last two letters of John's and me own true written confessions, well, they was burning a hole in me coat, but I wasn't ready yet to give them up. So I just stood there and watched.

I'm a free man, supposedly. But letting me off for

hanging, that weren't the answer, and I knew that. Maybe for them others, it was all right—they hadn't been the instigators. They hadn't betrayed their friend. I had.

It wasn't an end that I could live with. So I went again today and stood outside their house. I'd been there but a minute when I seen her. I knew it had to be her. She was too beautiful and sad not to be. I watched her approach the house and knock, and John's mother open the door.

At first, I started shaking and turned away. The shame went through me all over again. Until at last, I realized I could no longer just keep running. I had to do this last thing—finish it all. I had to pull whatever measly courage I had left and face this horror. And so I turned back and walked toward the house fast enough so that I ain't got the time to change me mind.

The women turned. I see the hardness come into Katherine Hudson's eyes, and I knew then that she must recognize me from the trial. I hesitated, but only for a moment, 'cause I realized deep in me heart that if this woman went on hating me, that's exactly what I deserved. And she couldn't hate me more than I hated meself. It just ain't possible.

So I continued on, closer.

Katherine Hudson spoke up, asking me if I'd come to apologize for having abandoned her son and husband.

Miss Isabella looked at me then, realizing who I must be. Her eyes hardened too. But I was past caring.

I blurted out me name and showed them the letters John had given me to deliver.

The letters took them both by surprise.

"Why would my son ask *you* to deliver letters to me?" Katherine Hudson asked.

I paused and turned my head toward Miss Isabella, seeing for the first time the green in her eyes and the black of her hair. It took me breath away for a minute, but only a minute, 'cause then I thought on John again. "I was his friend," I managed to choke out.

Isabella reminded me bitterly that I was a friend who abandoned him.

I nodded. "Yes, a friend who abandoned him." I repeated, finally saying them awful words.

I continued talking, wanting to give them some small hope, telling them that maybe the captain and John could still make it.

Katherine Hudson laughed then and stated firmly that John and her husband were dead. Believe it or not, Mama, those investors have refused to send a search party for them, though Katherine Hudson has been begging them for weeks to help.

"John and Henry could not survive another winter. Isn't that right?" she asked me.

I knew what she wanted, and it scared me something awful. I had been there. I knew what it was like, how little food there was, how cold it got, how despair could overwhelm even someone as brave and crazy as her son. I had to stop being the coward I was. I had to tell her what she wanted to hear from me and only me—the truth.

I nodded my head. "Yes, Mrs. Hudson," I said. "That would be right."

I expected her to break down and cry. I had steeled

meself for it. But no, she looks me straight in the eye.

"Thank you for telling me the truth, Mr. Syms," she stated. "You're braver than you think."

She got me on that one. And for the first time since I'd been back, I could feel the tears coming to me eyes. Her words were some kind of answer for me at last—even if it were too late, me decision having been made. I hoped she was right.

I handed them the letters. They took them eagerly, no longer caring that I was even there.

I bowed low. Then I turned and left, John's memory dogging me footsteps now like a piece of something sticky stuck to me shoe. I took one last look at London, the town I loved so much, and I began walking.

It didn't take long for me to find this spot, Mama. The rock is high, and the tree tall. I pulled an old rope from me pocket and threw it up and over a branch on that old tree. I tugged. The limb will be strong, strong enough, I figure.

And so, I have done with me final act. I have put all me letters in me pocket, where hopefully ye will find them, dear Mama. Read them and think of me—as I will think of ye at the end. Now ye will know the truth—what kind of son I truly am. Before I climb up on this rock and put this rope around me neck, I will write this last: Mama, I'm sorry. Sometimes I wish I'd have never gone on that boat, but heck, me sorry personality would have come to the fore some other way, I suppose. 'Cause at the end, Mama, I know this one true thing: Ye can spend yer life searching and searching, questing and questing for something, but there ain't nothing out there that is more real or more true than yer very own self. At the end, that's all there ever is, all we've ever got left—just yer own self—and what ye done with that sorry self of yers in this here life. I ain't proud of mine.

Yer loving son, Seth

RICHARD HUDSON

Who would have guessed," Isabella said, laughing, "John, writing a letter. He hated recording those logs bad enough."

Richard scowled. Johnny's girl was pretty enough to look at, but he didn't like the way she laughed all the time when things really weren't that funny. Johnny and Papa were still gone. Those men in the boat had mutinied, and he had spent these last months listening to them talking about leaving Papa and Johnny behind and trying to be brave and good about it. But he was tired of trying so hard. Johnny and Papa would take a long time in getting back, and Mama's face was all pinched with the worry of it. She had been so quiet and distant since that trial, not even caring if they ate their meals or did any chores. And she would not let Richard wander from the house, not even for a minute. Isabella's laugh just made it worse. For some reason he could not understand, Richard felt like crying all the time.

"Come here, Richard," Mama said. "Johnny sent us a letter too. Would you like to hear it?"

Mama suddenly looked really tired, as if she had magically turned old as she slept last night. Richard understood that Johnny and Papa were in a dangerous place, but they had sent letters. And wasn't getting word from them a good thing?

Mama pulled a chair closer to the window and the light. Richard went and leaned against her. He didn't know if he wanted to hear it or not. He had this funny feeling that he might be hearing something he didn't want to. But how could he not listen to what Johnny had written? Maybe in listening to the letter, he would hear Johnny's voice, playful and teasing. Then he might not miss Johnny so very badly.

Mama began:

Dear Mama and Richard:

These may be the last and final thoughts I have that are committed to paper. I pray that Syms is the friend I trust him to be, and that he has found you both and relayed this last letter of love.

He has bought me this time. It was his idea I write, and for that I am grateful.

Mama, know that I have honored and loved you always as mother, and, as the years have passed, as friend. No one could have offered me a more comforting childhood nor better guidance, nor more loving moments.

Here Mama paused. Richard slipped his hand into hers and held it tight. Mama looked at him sadly and squeezed his hand back. These were awful nice things Johnny had written about Mama. She took a deep breath and went on:

Richard, though I did tease you unmercifully, I do love you dearly. You are a brave young man. Be strong now for Mama. She will need you to help her and to be the head of the house. I know you will take care of her and remember me with fondness.

Of course he would take care of Mama! And how else would he remember Johnny? He was his brother! Why was Johnny writing so seriously? Richard could not sense the clown of a brother in these words at all. Embarrassingly, he suddenly felt near tears again. Mama pulled him closer. "Would you prefer not to hear the rest?" she asked.

Richard shook his head but couldn't say anything more. Mama continued:

I regret not having had my time to enjoy the benefits of family, hearth, and home. And yet I was lucky to find one girl who pleased me greatly.

By now, if Syms has stayed true, you know who this girl is. I pray that you will find it in your heart to give comfort to Issa. Perhaps together you will find your sorrows easier to bear.

Richard looked over to where Isabella sat. Her head was bent over her own letter, and he could now see the seriousness on her face. Perhaps he had misjudged her. Johnny had liked her well enough to write about her, and so for Richard, that would be enough. He determined to be nice to her, even if she did laugh at the oddest of times.

Mama had paused again. Richard turned toward her. "What is it, Mama?" he asked.

"Nothing," she said, biting her lip.

"It's all right," Richard said. "I'm here."

"And so you are, little man," Mama said. "So you are."

She read on:

I want you to know that Father loves you. We have not spent a good deal of time together on this trip. I guess that is about to change. But when I was with him, he spoke of you fondly. I believe, Mama, that you were the foundation that let his dreams take flight. And though those dreams may not now be realized, he could not have pursued them without your support. As much as he needed to continue his quest for new territory, so too did he need to have a safe haven to return to. Be comforted that you were a wife needed and well loved.

Mama was now crying, setting the letter aside as if she could not go on. Richard picked it up and read for her.

I will try to bring both myself and Father home. But I will tell you, Mama, the one person who has always demanded the truth from me, what I know to be true. We will not make it.

Richard stared at the words. He looked up at his mother. Could this be right? Was there now no hope? All along, even at the trial, the men who had mutinied had indicated that it might be some time, but that Johnny and Papa could eventually come home. And Richard knew they had left them a boat. True, it was a small boat and would take a bit to sail all the way back to England. But Papa and Johnny were the best sailors ever, weren't they?

Richard felt the knot in his stomach again. His mother's eyes met his. He wished she wouldn't look at him like that, for in her eyes, he finally saw the truth. They weren't ever coming back!

Tears came now. They would not stop. Mama put her arms about him, and he cried against her.

"It's all right, Richard," Mama said, crying too. "It's all right."

"You mean they will make it?" Richard asked, straightening up, hope rising within him at her words.

Mama shook her head sadly. "No, little man. I only mean that together we will make it through this."

Richard choked back a sob.

Mama looked back down at the letter, and in a strangled voice finished what Johnny had written. "Listen, Richard," she said. "Listen to what Johnny tells us."

I do love you both. With all my heart, I thank you for the years, and the love you have afforded me. Think of me not with sorrow, but with a smile for the way I most preferred life to be.

Love,

John

Mama took a ragged breath and pulled Richard to her, laying his head on her shoulder. "So come, Richard," she whispered in his ear, crying a little as she said it. "We must both be strong now. For we must do as John asks and remember him with a smile."

Richard turned his head on his mother's shoulder and looked out the window, tears running down his cheeks. The sun was beating down on the Earth in all its glory. *How*, he wondered, *could the world go on when Johnny and Papa were never coming back?* Were they dead? Or would they live where they had been left, surviving in some wild place with only savages as friends?

Richard watched a cart rumble by and two men walk down the lane, chatting and laughing. How could the world behave so normally, when Mama's and his world was nothing but normal now? How would anything ever be right again?

A dragonfly flew in the window and landed suddenly on Richard's hand, which lay on Mama's shoulder. He blinked back tears in surprise. The creature rested there, poised lightly, head twitching. It was a beautiful dragonfly, its body glistening green, its wings pure and transparent. It beat its wings softly against Richard's hand, as if to comfort him. He felt a sudden lightening of his sorrow.

Then, without so much as the slightest of movements, the dragonfly lifted from his hand, flew out the window, and was gone. Richard watched it until he could see it no longer. He sniffled and wiped his nose on Mama's shoulder. Then he pulled away from her. His brother had told him to be brave, and so brave he would be.

"I will be here for you, Mama, as Johnny wished," Richard said, wiping his eyes. "But when I am older, I intend to captain a great boat and to find the way east for Papa, and when I get to the place where they left Papa and Johnny, I will search them out and bring them home.

"I swear this, Mama," he concluded, with a determination he had never felt before.

Mama's eyes filled again. "Oh, Richard," she said, and began to laugh.

Richard looked at her, puzzled. She was acting like

Isabella, laughing for no reason. "What is so funny?" he asked.

Mama shook her head as tears streamed down her cheeks. "You *are* your father's child, little man. Just as his quest is finished, now I must watch yours begin."

She reached out her arms again, and Richard let her pull him to her, laying his head once more on her shoulder. But he sighed as he did so. For truly, if he were to be in charge of this house, he would have to teach his mother to stop saying such silly things.

AUTHOR'S NOTE

Because we live at the end of a very long driveway, it was necessary for me to take our two girls out to the end of the road every day to catch the school bus. There we would sit in the car in the early morning quiet, just waiting. And so I came up with what I thought was a brilliant idea. Why not learn as we sat there?

I began to read to them from the series *What your (First, Second, Third, Fourth,* etc.*) Grader Needs to Know.* In spite of their glazed and sleepy eyes, I justified what I was doing by assuming they were picking up important facts, in spite of their seeming indifference. I was wrong.

The truth was, I loved it, and they hated it! I was getting more from reading those books than they were. For it was during one of these mornings that I discovered the fact that Henry Hudson's crew had mutinied during his last voyage and abandoned him, along with his seventeen-year-old son, in a small boat after an entire winter without food. How terrible for any human being! But how much more horrible for a boy of seventeen! I wondered what it would have been like for him, his life just beginning, his possibilities just opening up, his whole life in front of him, to see it all coming to such an abrupt and tragic halt. And so I wrote *Quest*.

The following are true: the service at St. Ethelburga's before the trip, Henry Hudson's obstinate search for the way east, the dates and routes they followed, the ill-advised display of maps by Captain Hudson, the captain's anger at carpenter Philip Staffe, the plotting by Juet and Greene and Motter, the death of John Williams, the giving of John Williams's coat to Greene, the visit from the Native American and the trading, the burning of the woods when Captain Hudson approached other Native Americans he had seen, the lack of food at the end, the mutiny, and the final return and trial of those who ultimately made it back. Ship logs recorded at that time have marked these events. The personality of each character, though, was entirely of my own making. (Because spellings of the crewmembers' names vary greatly in accounts of this voyage, I have elected to take the names as they appeared in the book *Beyond the Sea of Ice: The Voyages of Henry Hudson* by Joan Elizabeth Goodman.)

John did have two brothers, Oliver and Richard, and a young niece, Alice. His mother's name was Katherine. I made Oliver a cartographer, as this was an extremely important job back in those days. Maps were incredibly valuable, as they contained all the information a country had about the known world.

There was a burning urgency on behalf of all the great European powers of that time to be the country to find the fastest way east and to map out the world in its entirety. It was believed that the country to accomplish these tasks first would be the country that would reign supreme. And so the race was on.

And a nasty race it became. Explorers were employed by many investors, each hoping to strike it rich when their man discovered the elusive passage and came back with those spices the European countries were so crazy to have. Kings forbade their countrymen from exploring for any other country. And though James Dits is of my making, it is true that Henry Hudson's own sovereign threatened him with imprisonment after he explored for the Dutch East Indies Company. And it was also true that most explorers' wives were left begging for food or asking for credit when their husband's ship did not return by the expected date.

Spies were everywhere—uncovering which explorer had signed what contract, what that explorer had discovered on his most recent trip, and above all else, purloining those valuable maps with their precious information. And while Isabella was also my creation, who would ever have suspected a woman of such machinations? For women, especially one of Isabella's standing, were considered little more than ornamentation.

With Henry lost, Katherine was left destitute. She returned again and again to the investors, demanding compensation for her husband's death and a ship to be sent to rescue him and their son. In the beginning, she got nowhere with her requests.

Finally, in 1622, under the protection of the Dutch East Indies Company, Katherine sailed to India to purchase indigo. That trip made her a wealthy woman. In the last two years of her life, she was received at court at least twice. Katherine Hudson died in 1624.

Young Richard fulfilled his promise to captain a boat of his own. He went on to work for the Dutch East Indies Company in India and was incredibly successful. Although he did not find the passage east, as none existed, he was one of the first Europeans ever allowed to conduct trade with Japan. Richard died in India in 1644.

Three years after Henry and John were put off in the New World, the investors were finally convinced by Katherine Hudson's persistent requests to send out a ship to search for them. No trace of Henry or John was ever found.